W9-CTI-859

Praise for the novels of
Joseph A. West

"Old-fashioned storytelling raised to the level of homegrown art, told in an American language that is almost gone."
—Loren D. Estleman, four-time Spur Award–winning author of *Black Powder, White Smoke*

"Original, imaginative."
—Max Evans, Spur Award–winning author of *The Rounders*

"Wildly comic and darkly compelling."
—Robert Olen Butler, Pulitzer Prize–winning author of *A Good Scent from a Strange Mountain*

"[A] rollicking big windy."   —Elmer Kelton

"Take a pair of pugnacious cowboys who never saw trouble they didn't like, mix them with a fiendish villain and his diabolical filibusters, and the result is comic delight. Joseph West [has] an encyclopedic knowledge of the West. He keeps the body count sufficient to satisfy gluttons, frosts his cake with bawds, throws a few wolfers, a boxer, and a patent medicine huckster into the pot, rings in all the Western legends worth recounting, and seasons the stew with smiles. . . . Western fiction will never be the same." —Richard S. Wheeler, Spur Award–winning author of *Sierra*

GUNSMOKE™
THE LAST
DOG SOLDIER

Joseph A. West

Foreword by
James Arness

A SIGNET BOOK

SIGNET
Published by New American Library, a division of
Penguin Group (USA) Inc., 375 Hudson Street,
New York, New York 10014, USA
Penguin Group (Canada), 10 Alcorn Avenue, Toronto,
Ontario M4V 3B2, Canada (a division of Pearson Penguin Canada Inc.)
Penguin Books Ltd., 80 Strand, London WC2R 0RL, England
Penguin Ireland, 25 St. Stephen's Green, Dublin 2,
Ireland (a division of Penguin Books Ltd.)
Penguin Group (Australia), 250 Camberwell Road, Camberwell, Victoria 3124,
Australia (a division of Pearson Australia Group Pty. Ltd.)
Penguin Books India Pvt. Ltd., 11 Community Centre, Panchsheel Park,
New Delhi - 110 017, India
Penguin Group (NZ), cnr Airborne and Rosedale Roads, Albany,
Auckland 1310, New Zealand (a division of Pearson New Zealand Ltd.)
Penguin Books (South Africa) (Pty.) Ltd., 24 Sturdee Avenue,
Rosebank, Johannesburg 2196, South Africa

Penguin Books Ltd., Registered Offices:
80 Strand, London WC2R 0RL, England

First published by Signet, an imprint of New American Library,
a division of Penguin Group (USA) Inc.

First Printing, May 2005
10   9   8   7   6   5   4   3   2   1

Trade & copyright © 2005 CBS Inc. All Rights Reserved.

 REGISTERED TRADEMARK—MARCA REGISTRADA

Printed in the United States of America

Foreword

These days I still receive many letters, e-mails, and cards from people thanking me for making a show that affected their lives. The show also affected the lives of all the actors on the show. We became like one big family and sometimes we acted like a family, having disagreements just like everyone has with their siblings. We did, however, respect each other's privacy too.

You know, my longtime set double, Ben Bates, was a lot like me both in personality and stature. My wife and his had a hard time telling us apart when we were at a distance. A little known fact is that we both had a real-life limp, though his was just on the other side from mine. Until we pointed that out, no one noticed. We spent a lot of time together over the years and sometimes it was spooky for me to look up and see myself coming down the street. I think we even started looking more alike as the years went on.

We have remained friends after all these years. Along the way Ben sure saved me from some rough

scenes. I remember one scene we were filming up in
Utah at about 9000 feet. He had to run through knee-
level snow chasing a bad guy. Each time Ben would
get through the entire scene, the director yelled that
we had to do it all again. I think it took him two
days to recover. Another time, a scene was designed
for me to ride into town and have the horse rear
up—I was to slide off the saddle and run for cover
while being shot at. After the take, everyone kept
saying what a great stunt I did and I don't think Ben
or I ever told anyone it was him instead of me.

I recall a time prior to Ben joining the *Gunsmoke*
family—we were shooting up on the Rogue River in
Oregon. I was being chased by the bad guys because
I had a saddlebag full of money that they wanted to
take away from me. In the scene, I rode up to the
edge of cliff, and in order to get away, I had to jump
eighty or ninety feet into the river. Needless to say,
that required my stunt guy. It was getting late in the
afternoon, and as the shadows were creeping up the
canyon wall, the director kept yelling for him to
climb higher and higher. After the fact, we measured
and found out that he had jumped 120 feet and only
missed the cliff rocks by about two feet. I think it
scared both of us then, and we were glad we didn't
realize how far and how dangerous it was at the
time.

In another scene sometime later, the stunt double
had to swim the rapids and then climb up on the
bank over a large group of rocks. The crew was in a
hurry and told him not to bother with a wet suit.

But he insisted on using the wet suit and so they waited. When he crawled up on the bank, a startled rattlesnake suddenly attacked him. The only thing that saved him was that the snake's fangs could not penetrate his wet suit. He and all the rest of us were really glad he had insisted on that suit. Maybe these scenes were the reason this guy wasn't my double for long

We had a regular group of extras that played the townspeople. Usually they were not in any danger. One time, however, we were shooting a scene in which we had a herd of stampeding cattle. We found out really quickly that a herd of cattle do pretty much whatever they want. The extras, my stunt double, and at least one cameraman had to scramble to get out of their way. Fortunately no one was injured in that scene. You can be sure that we were more careful with all of our cattle scenes in the future.

We were really lucky that in all twenty years of filming, no one was ever seriously hurt. I guess we can thank our directors and producers for keeping us all safe.

You know that everyone claims that the success of *Gunsmoke* was Matt Dillon, Doc, Kitty, Festus, Quint, and Newley. The truth is that this show would never have made it without all the stuntmen, the extras, the character actors, the cameramen, the scriptwriters, the grips, and everyone else who worked on the show. We would have been lost without our directors and producers. Most days it seemed like the main characters were the last ones on the set and the first ones to leave. I always tried to make sure that everyone working on the set knew that we appreciated all their hard work and dedication to making the show a success. We truly would not have been the long-running success we were without all of them.

—James Arness
"Marshal Matt Dillon"

chapter 1

A Grim Discovery

Streaks of winter snow still clung to the Kansas plains and a long wind sighed cold off the distant Rockies as a solitary horseman rode north toward the big bend country of the Pawnee River.

Around the rider, the land lay flat, the grass browned by cold, and when he crossed Sand Creek, his mount's hooves crunched through a thin sheet of ice. So far, the tall lawman had ridden through and around hundreds of McKenna cattle and had identified a half dozen different Texas brands.

Matt Dillon had no idea how Abbey McKenna and her brother, Abe, had acquired their herd, but judging by what he was seeing, he doubted they had come by them honestly.

From what he knew of the McKenna punchers, they were a shabby, work-shy bunch, shifty-eyed border trash recruited from saloons and brothels, not the kind to build a herd by the strength of their backs and the sweat of their brows.

The creaking chuck wagon that had come up the trail with the cattle was held together with biscuit-tin patches and baling wire. And when Abbey visited Dodge the plain cotton dress she wore was darned and threadbare, her shoes down at heel, a sharp contrast to the fashionable belles from across the tracks in their buttoned boots and rustling silks and satins.

Frowning in thought, Matt reined in his bay.

From where had the ragtag McKennas gotten the two thousand longhorns they'd driven through Dodge and then up to the Pawnee three weeks before? And how had they managed to buy old, cantankerous Andy Reid's thousand-acre spread?

Abe McKenna had put out the word around town that Andy had sold out cheap because he wanted to go east and live with his ailing sister in Boston.

But Matt had never heard Andy mention that he had a sister and the reclusive old retired miner, wary of strangers, was not the kind to welcome the tattered McKennas and their two-by-twice outfit with open arms.

Matt shook his head. He had plenty of questions and no answers.

The big lawman pulled the fleece collar of his sheepskin coat up around his ears, his breath smoking in the cold air. The plains rolled away on all sides, not perfectly flat but undulating slightly, like swells on a green ocean, here and there bands of snow hugging the sheltered slopes of the rises like the white crests of waves.

In the distance Matt watched a small herd of antelope trot toward the Pawnee, seeking water. This early in March, the river was no longer frozen, though ice laced both banks, slow to melt in a truculent wind still cruel with the lingering memory of an unusually hard winter.

Dodge City had been under siege since the late fall, snow crowding in from the plains surrounding the town on all sides. The Arkansas had frozen solid and some of the cottonwoods lining the riverbanks had split in two from the severe frosts with a sound like the crack of a rifle shot.

In late December, it seemed to Matt like the town was shrinking in on itself, as though the saloons, dance halls, stores and houses were huddling closer to one another for warmth. The wind, whispering thin and sharp edged as a newly honed razor, sought out every chink and break in the warped pine boards and probed everywhere with icy fingers, defying the efforts of the cherry red stoves to keep even the smallest room warm.

Bundled up to the eyes, the citizens of Dodge had stepped warily along slippery boardwalks, now and then casting their gaze skyward, hoping to see an end to the gray clouds of winter and a release from the iron grip of the cold.

Now Matt rode under the vast dome of a pale blue

sky that stretched from horizon to horizon, the air around him sharp, each breath he took filling his lungs like shattered shards of frosted glass.

Andy Reid's cabin lay a couple of miles to the northwest. Although Matt had a city marshal's star pinned to his shirt under his coat, he had no authority here on the plains. But he swung the bay in the direction of the cabin.

Whether he was out of his jurisdiction or no, it was time to pay the McKennas a visit. The big lawman followed the bank of a narrow stream running due south off the Pawnee, here and there riding wide of lone cottonwoods and the even more rare willows. This was wide-open, level country, where a far-seeing man could scan the land around him in all directions to the horizon.

Yet Matt didn't notice Andy Reid's burro until he topped a shallow rise crowned with buffalo grass, and almost rode right into the little animal.

The burro stood, stiff-legged, at the base of the rise, its head hanging, the morning's hoar frost a silver sheen on its back and flanks, a frayed rope still tied around its neck, the broken end trailing on the ground. Like Andy himself, the burro was impossibly ancient. For nigh on twenty years it had carried the old man's pans, picks and shovels from the desert country of New Mexico and Arizona to the Black Hills of the Dakota Territory with a hundred stops in between.

After he'd moved to Kansas three years before, Andy had done nothing with his land. He used his thousand acres as a barrier between himself and neighbors he didn't like and strangers he liked even less. On his infrequent visits to Dodge for supplies and a jug, he'd paid in gold from his poke, a cantankerous and touchy old-timer who talked to no one and studiously minded his own business.

Matt reined up the bay and the burro lifted its head, looking at him with interest and no sign of fear.

Despite its age and the stiffness in its joints, the old animal made the usual display of good breeding and fine manners common to all burros as Matt swung out of the saddle.

The big lawman took off a glove and scratched the burro's head. "What are you doing so far from home, boy?" he said. He loosed the rope from the little animal's neck. "I'd say you're a ways from the barn."

By way of reply, the burro rubbed its forehead against Matt's leg, blowing softly through its nose. The marshal smiled and patted the donkey's shoulder—and his hand came away stained with blood.

Matt kneeled beside the burro and checked the wound. It looked like the tiny animal had been burned by a bullet some time before. But the wound had reopened recently, maybe when the burro rolled or pushed its way through thick brush.

"Who did this to you, boy, huh?" Matt asked. "Who shot at you?"

The big lawman rose to his feet and looked around. At first he saw nothing out of the ordinary, just the open prairie and, to the north, the bare branches of scattered cottonwoods and willows growing along the Pawnee.

But then, as his eyes scanned the land more closely, he noticed a patch of recently disturbed ground farther along the base of the rise, almost hidden by a struggling yucca.

Matt stepped to the yucca and kneeled beside it, studying the torn-up earth. Deprived of its deep roots, the grass here had withered and died on the clods of turf, turning a dry, rusty brown. The disturbed area was roughly rectangular in shape and it looked like something had been buried here, laid away shallow and quick in the iron-hard winter ground.

The big marshal carefully lifted away clods of turf. After a few minutes of digging, about three inches under the surface, he uncovered a bearded white face.

It was Andy Reid's face.

Matt dug deeper, clawing at the frozen earth with his bare hands. Clod by clod, he slowly exposed the rest of Andy's body, perfectly preserved in the frost of the topmost layer of prairie. Matt brushed away dirt from the old man's chest and found two bullet holes, no more than an inch apart, on either side of the prospector's middle shirt button.

The marshal continued to kneel for long moments, his head bent, thinking this thing through.

Andy Reid had been murdered by someone who knew how to handle a gun and was lightning fast.

When a man is shot, the impact and shock of the bullet will make him jerk away or stumble and a second wound is often inches apart from the first. But somebody had put two bullets into the old man very quickly, so quickly they'd hit close together— and that took a trained, accurate gun hand.

Matt covered up the body and rose to his feet, still trying to piece the situation together.

For certain, Andy had been killed by a gunman who knew his business. Of the rest, Matt was less sure. Out here on the prairie, Andy would have ridden a horse and left his burro behind. Later, the burro could have broken loose from where it was tied at the old man's cabin and run away. Somebody had taken a shot at it and the bullet had burned along the burro's shoulder. But that hadn't slowed the little animal, and it had instinctively found Andy's grave.

Matt had no way of knowing when the old prospector had been killed or how long the burro had been here. But the animal looked gaunt and wasted, with its ribs showing, so it had been feeding for a long time on the thin graze of the winter grass.

Matt hunched his wide shoulders, deep in thought, his eyes on the ground at his feet.

This had not been a random act of robbery. A thief would have shot the old man and left him lie where he fell. He would have ransacked the cabin, found Andy's poke and hightailed it. A robber certainly wouldn't have taken the time to bury the old prospector.

It was no robbery then. That left Abbey and Abe McKenna as the only people who stood to profit from Andy Reid's death.

It could be that the McKennas had offered the old man a ridiculously low price for his cabin and land, and when he refused, probably angrily ordering them off his property, they had killed him.

It was a wild guess, but Matt was sure he was on the right track.

He had seen Abe McKenna in town, a handsome young man made less so by a weak chin and small, petulant mouth. Like most men at that time and place, Abe carried a Colt, but Matt's honed instinct had quickly pegged him a sure-thing artist, a back-shooter and not any kind of straight-up gunfighter.

Andy had been shot, but not by Abe McKenna. He had been murdered by a man who used a gun so well and fast he had no doubt killed many times before.

Even at that wild, lawless time in the West, highly skilled gun hands like John Wesley Hardin, Ben Thompson and the man who had killed Andy Reid were a rare breed and, when encountered, best left alone.

But Matt Dillon was not one to take a step back for anyone and he'd do what had to be done to find the killer of a testy but harmless old man.

The cold wind rustled among the winter-dry blue-stem grass and high above the prairie the brightening sky was the color of pond ice. The sun was shining, but gave no warmth, and Matt felt a sudden chill.

The arrival of the McKennas with their mixed herd and the death of Andy Reid nagged at him as if he had a bad toothache.

He sensed a warning carried on the wind that big trouble was coming. He was unsure of its direction or what face it would wear or what words it would use, but he was certain of one thing—however it came, from wherever it came, trouble knew his name.

And it would soon come calling . . . on Marshal Matt Dillon.

chapter 2

A Darkness at Noon

Matt rode north to the Pawnee and among the cottonwoods found what he'd been searching for, a thick, lightning-blasted trunk already stripped of its bark, looking like the white thigh bone of a fallen giant.

The marshal dabbed a loop on the trunk and dragged it back to Andy Reid's shallow grave. He swung out of the saddle and it took all of his great strength to push the trunk upright, balanced by its own weight and thickness.

When he got back to Dodge, Matt planned to speak to Percy Crump and ask the undertaker to see that old man Reid was buried decent.

Out there on the featureless prairie, the trunk would be seen from a far distance and lead Crump and his men to the spot where Andy lay.

It was a small gesture on Matt's part, a decent

thing, and at the time he gave it little thought. But compassion is one of the yardsticks by which a man is measured, and in this, the marshal was not found wanting.

The burro steadfastly refused to leave the old man's grave. The little animal stiffened its legs and planted its hooves when Matt tried to pull it away and no matter how he hauled, tugged and coaxed, the burro obstinately stayed put.

Finally Matt gave up the struggle. The burro had chosen its own fate and was determined to see it through to the end. He rubbed the little animal's forehead one last time, then swung into the saddle and resumed his ride toward the McKenna cabin.

Twice he rode through small bunches of longhorns, again spotting several different brands, and he startled another, larger group in a draw close to the bank of the Pawnee. He counted four brands that time.

It was still half an hour shy of noon when the marshal fetched up to the old Reid place. It wasn't much as ranches go, a low log-built cabin with a sod roof, a pole corral holding half a dozen horses and a couple of cows, a small, windowless bunkhouse and beyond that a chicken coop. The McKenna wagon, harness hanging from its raised tongue, was parked a ways from the cabin, close to a sandy dry wash.

Several men sat around outside the cabin, sharing a jug, and one, a lantern-jawed youngster with a shock of yellow hair, snapped up his head as the marshal rode into view. The man rose slowly to his feet, his eyes suddenly irritated and belligerent, fixed on the marshal as he reined up at the hitching rail.

The man was obviously on the prod, a fact that Matt noted and accepted, being no stranger to the kind of trouble a youngster with a chip on his shoulder could cause.

The cabin door swung open on its rawhide hinges and a couple of other men stepped out, followed by Abbey McKenna and her brother.

As he watched Abbey close the door behind her, Matt had to admit that the girl was pretty and she looked to be prospering mightily since he last saw her. Abbey's blue gingham dress was brand-new and she wore high-button shoes of the latest fashion on her little feet. The girl's thick mass of wavy auburn hair was pulled back from her face with a red ribbon, and the lecherous wind, pressing her dress close against her legs and body, revealed her generous and shapely curves to everyone who cared to notice.

Abbey gave Matt a dazzling smile, her teeth very white in a slightly tanned face. "Why, Marshal Dillon," she said, "what a pleasant surprise."

Matt touched the brim of his hat, deciding to play his cards close to his chest. "Passing through. But I thought I'd stop by and see how you folks are settling in here."

The towhead, dressed in denim overalls and a battered straw hat, stepped toward the marshal, his eyes ugly. "Well, you've seen us, so now ride on. We don't cotton to lawmen around here."

The man was a couple of inches shorter than Matt's

six foot seven, but he looked to be thirty pounds heavier, most of it in his massive shoulders and arms. Matt sat his horse, ignoring the interruption. "I must admit, this isn't really a social call, Miss Abbey. I've got some routine matters to discuss with you and your brother." Matt's smile was slight and stayed well away from his eyes. "That is, if you can spare me the time."

The girl opened her mouth to speak, but the big towhead stepped beside Matt's bay, his huge fists clenched. "Mister, maybe you don't hear too good," he said, his voice loud, hard-edged with anger. "You ain't discussing anything around here. I told you to ride on."

Alarmed, Abbey took a single step toward Matt, but her brother stopped her, grinning, his long-lashed eyes eager and cruel.

Matt raised his nose, testing the air. "I smell coffee," he said. "And something else. A pig maybe." He nodded. "Yup, judging by the stink, it's a pig all right and real close."

A couple of the loungers outside the cabin laughed and the towhead flushed as his anger flared hotter. Confident of his strength, the man cursed viciously and reached up to drag Matt out of the saddle. For a moment the lawman sat immobile; then his right foot suddenly slid out of the stirrup and the toe of his boot slammed upward with terrific force between the towhead's legs.

The man screamed and staggered back a few steps on rubbery legs. His face white with shock and agony, he grabbed his battered crotch, doubled over and then collapsed in a heap on the ground, moaning.

"Like I said"—Matt smiled as though nothing had happened—"that coffee smells mighty good."

Abe scowled and gave his sister a slight push toward the marshal and she said: "Please to step down, Mr. Dillon." She waved a hand at the groaning, drooling towhead. "I'm sorry about Dan. He doesn't cotton to strangers."

Matt nodded. "He's about as friendly as a mule on a sawdust diet—that's for sure."

The big marshal swung out of the saddle and one of the McKenna punchers took his horse. Matt followed Abbey to the cabin and stopped as the door swung open.

A compact man of medium height stepped outside and Matt stiffened in recognition, seeing a face from the past. Quickly overcoming his surprise, the marshal said: "Howdy, Roman. It's been a lot of years."

Roman Pollock nodded. "Time passes, Matt. And it do seem like the older a man gets, the faster it goes."

Pollock was dressed in a black shirt and pants, with wide canvas suspenders over his shoulders. His eyes were as black as his shirt, but they glittered hard, like obsidian knife blades, and his black hair was cropped close to his skull. In the fashion of the times he wore a sweeping dragoon mustache, fringing a mouth that was small and thin-lipped and slow to smile.

Matt's eyes moved to Pollock's matched, ivory-handled Colts, the holsters worn low on his thighs from crossed cartridge belts, an affectation many Texas gunmen were beginning to adopt.

The big marshal's nod indicated the man's entire outfit. "You've come far, Roman. You're prospering, seems like."

The gunman shrugged. "Far enough, prospering enough." He jerked his chin toward Matt. "Back in the old days, I would never have pegged you to become a lawman."

"Me neither," Matt said. "But a man gets older and maybe a little wiser and chooses sides." He shrugged. "I've chosen mine."

Pollock's smile was faint and fleeting. "You still as fast?"

"Fast enough."

"I could never figure which of us was the fastest, Matt," Pollock said. "Maybe one day I'll find out."

Matt tried to step around it. "Those days are behind me, Roman. Now my job is to uphold the law."

But the gunman wouldn't let it go. "You recollect Walt Tinney, tall, lanky feller used to ride with us? Talking man."

The marshal nodded. "I remember."

"Was he fast?"

"Fastest I ever saw. He was quick on the draw, almighty sudden."

"He was all of that." Pollock's smile was as cold as the snow that had drifted against the cabin wall.

"We had a disagreement him and me, and I killed him in the Silver Dollar Saloon in Cheyenne. That was three months ago."

Matt looked into the gunman's eyes and saw only darkness. That, and something else: a strange black fire that could warn of a kindling insanity.

"Sorry to hear that," Matt said. "By times, Walt was all right. Talked too much maybe." He pointed to the cabin door. "Now, Roman, will you give me the road?"

"Sure," Pollock said, "I'll step aside, Matt. But only this once and for old time's sake." He nodded to the white-faced, moaning towhead. "By the way, that one's name is Dan Finley. He's a Nebraska farmboy and he's nothing."

Matt looked down at Finley, who was sitting up, his face ashen, big hands still clutching at his crotch. "Son, better crawl down to the creek and ice them things real good," he said. "Take the swelling out of them."

The big marshal stepped into the cabin and immediately noticed that there was a fresh bouquet of store-bought flowers lying on the table. A middle-aged man sat at that same table, following Abbey McKenna's every move with adoring, puppy-dog eyes.

That man was Sam Noonan, Kitty Russell's bartender at the Long Branch.

Sam smiled and waved at the marshal. "Saw the ruckus outside from the window, Matt. It's time that boy was taken down a peg or two. He's a bad one, especially when he's drinking."

Matt couldn't contain his surprise. "Sam, what are you doing here?"

Abe McKenna answered for the bartender. "Mr. Noonan is walking out with my sister. Any law against that?"

Abbey sat beside Sam and put her arm around his waist. "Just before you arrived, Sam was talking all kinds of pretties. He's even asked me to become his wife."

"Then I interrupted something," Matt said carefully, showing nothing.

He studied Abbey more closely. She looked to be about twenty, old enough to already be a married woman with a passel of younkers around these parts. When she smiled, which was often, her face seemed very young, touchingly innocent and vulnerable. No doubt this was the face she showed to Sam Noonan.

But in repose, as her features were now, tough lines formed arcs at the corners of her mouth and there was a calculating steeliness in her eyes, suggesting that in the past she'd seen and done much, not all of it seemly. She appeared to be a woman who had been raised hard and had led a life that had brought her little by way of comfort or affection.

In contrast to her brother, who was almost too pretty and feminine soft to be a man, Abbey McKenna gave off an aura of strength and determination. Her square little chin was set and she looked like she knew exactly where she was going—and no obstacle in her path would stop her from getting there.

Maybe, Matt thought, one such obstacle had been Andy Reid.

His sense of unease growing, Matt recalled that Abbey and her brother had come up the trail with a dozen riders. Including Roman Pollock, Matt could account for six of them. Where were the rest?

But he had no more time to ponder that question because Abbey set a cup of coffee in front of him and asked: "A piece of pie, Marshal?"

Deciding to disguise his true feelings behind a facade of sociability, Matt smiled and asked: "What kind?"

Abbey gave him a sweet smile. "Why, the best kind of course, dried apple and raisin."

"Sounds just fine to me."

When Abbey left to get the pie, Sam turned to Matt and grinned. "She's a wonderful girl, isn't she?"

The big marshal nodded, tight-faced, saying nothing, keeping his true feelings to himself, at least for now.

Abe McKenna sat at the table, his eyes shrouded. Finally he smiled, making light of what he was about to say. "What kind of routine matters did you want to discuss with us that brought you all the way from Dodge, Marshal?"

Matt tested his coffee and then set down the cup. "I rode out to take a look at your herd."

Abe stiffened. "Our herd? What's our herd to you?"

"Nothing, really. Well, except the fact that maybe a hundred people in Dodge saw you drive two thousand longhorns through town. Folks told me the cows were wearing half a dozen different brands." Matt shrugged. "Odd things like that interest a lawman."

Abe's anger flared, his small, full-lipped mouth hardening. "Are you implying something, Marshal?"

Matt shook his head, his face unreadable. "I'm implying nothing. I'm sure you've got bills of sale for all those cattle."

"That's none of your damned—"

"Your pie, Marshal," Abbey interrupted, her eyes slanting a warning to her red-faced brother. She set a plate in front of Matt and looked down at the big marshal. "Of course we have bills of sale," the girl said sweetly. "But I can't put my hands on them right now since we still haven't unpacked our belongings from the chuck wagon."

Matt picked up his fork and raised it over his wedge of pie. "I understand. Of course, I don't reckon the bill of sale you got from Andy Reid is in the wagon."

Abbey's smile brightened. "Why, no, in fact I have it right here."

The girl crossed the hard-packed earth floor of the cabin to a rough pine dresser, opened a drawer and pulled out a sheet of paper. She slid the paper in front of Matt.

"As you can see, Marshal, Mr. Reid sold us his entire property, one thousand acres of grassland and all buildings appertaining thereto for five hundred dollars." She pointed to the bottom of the document. "And he signed it right there."

Matt quickly scanned the paper. The copperplate writing laying out the terms of the agreement had been done by a fair hand, and another, shakier and less certain had signed in block letters: A. REID.

The marshal had still to taste his pie, which lay forgotten in front of him. He looked long at the bill of sale then said: "Five hundred dollars doesn't seem like much for a cabin and a thousand acres of well-watered grazing land."

"Mr. Reid was so anxious to leave he sold cheap," Abbey said. "His sister is keeping poorly and he wanted to be with her. He's probably in Boston by now."

Matt shook his head. "No, he's not. Andy Reid is dead. I found his grave not two miles from this cabin. He'd been shot twice." The marshal's hand moved to the center of his chest. "Here and here."

The girl's hand flew to her throat and her eyes widened in shock. "Oh, that's just awful. Poor Mr. Reid, he was so excited about leaving for Boston. I . . . I . . . just can't believe he's dead."

Matt was studying Abe's reaction, but the man's face was expressionless. "Andy rode out of here on a gray horse," he said. "Somebody must have seen him coming and killed and robbed him on the trail."

"Maybe," Matt said. "Maybe it was that or something else."

Sam, who had been silent, his eyes constantly on

Abbey, now leaned across the table and frowned his annoyance. "Matt, you surely don't think Abbey and Abe had anything to do with Andy's death." He waved a hand around the cabin. "These are all good, hardworking people here."

Matt turned his head and nodded in the direction of Roman Pollock, who had just stepped inside. "And what do you think about him, Sam?"

Something that could have been fear flickered across Sam's face. "I don't think anything about Roman. He comes and goes as he pleases."

Matt placed his fork beside his uneaten pie and rose to his feet. His glance took in Abbey, her brother and Pollock. "Somebody murdered Andy Reid and I aim to find his killer. That's something you all should know."

Abbey's eyelashes fluttered. "And we'll help you any way we can, Marshal. All you need do is ask."

Matt stepped to the door, and Pollock pushed it open, his black eyes heavy-lidded with menace. "Remember what I told you, Matt. I stepped aside for you once. I don't plan on doing it again."

The big marshal nodded. "I'll bear that in mind, Roman."

"See you do."

Matt walked outside and one of the McKenna punchers brought him his horse. He swung into the saddle just as Abbey appeared at the cabin door. "Marshal," she said, "you didn't touch your pie."

Matt laid a forefinger against his hat brim. "Maybe some other time," he said.

The marshal swung his horse south and spurred the bay into a lope. After a couple of minutes he looked behind him at the cabin. Everyone had gone inside but Roman Pollock.

The gunman stood immobile in the yard, watching him, his thumbs tucked into his gun belts.

"That man is trouble and he knows my name," Matt said aloud.

And again he felt the gnawing, icy chill of the wind.

chapter 3

Indian Trouble

When Matt Dillon walked into the marshal's office in Dodge, his deputy Festus Haggen was asleep in his chair, his booted feet on the desk. Festus' mouth was open and he was snoring softly.

Matt hung up his hat and gun belt, crossed to the stove, poured a cup of coffee and slammed the pot down with a noisy clang.

"Wha' the . . ." The deputy's eyes flew open and he saw Matt grinning at him. Festus sprang to his feet, trying to cover his embarrassment. "I was jest takin' a little nap, Matthew." He scratched his hairy jaw. "Patrollin' the lace-curtain side o' town all night takes a lot out of a man, you know."

Matt nodded, his grin dwindling to an amused smile. "I'm sure it does."

The deputy was surprised by Matt's easy agreement, saw his opportunity and eagerly seized on it. "No one ever said the life of a deputy marshal was easy, especially on account of how little we get paid an' all."

Festus' meager salary was a long-standing sore point with the deputy, and Matt literally stepped around it by walking past him to his desk, where he sank into his chair, slow and tired.

"Did I miss anything while I was gone?" he asked.

Festus shook his head. "Not a dang thing, Matthew. If'n you ask me, the town's lost its snap."

Matt nodded, testing his coffee. "Be that way until the herds arrive."

"By the by, Iron Hawk is in one of the cells."

"Again?"

"Again." Festus smiled. "I picked him up off the street this time. Matthew, how a drunken Indian who swamps out a saloon can call himself Iron Hawk is beyond me. Seems like a highfalutin name for a man whose favorite drink is his next one."

Matt blew on his coffee. "We don't know his story. He's Cheyenne and maybe he deserved his name once." Matt shrugged. "Who can tell? Maybe he did."

"Want me to let him go when he's sobered some?" Festus asked.

Matt nodded. "I sure don't want him here. He gets to puking and stinks up the place and I have to clean it up."

"You mean, I have to clean it up," Festus said, his eyes accusing, making sure Matt was aware of his martyrdom.

The deputy poured a cup of coffee and sat opposite the big marshal. "Want to tell me what happened up there on the Pawnee?"

"There's a fair piece to tell," Matt said.

Festus, his face eager, said: "Well, have at it, Matthew."

In as few words as possible, Matt told how he'd found Andy Reid's body and of his subsequent visit to the cabin and his suspicion that the McKennas had murdered the old man.

"Abbey McKenna said she had bills of sale on the cattle, but didn't have them right to hand," Matt finished. "But she showed me Andy's signature on a paper selling her the ranch."

Festus jerked back in his chair, his face registering his surprise.

"Signature? You mean writin' out his whole name like you do?"

Matt nodded. "Yeah, Andy signed the bill of sale with his name."

"Then he didn't write that signature, Matthew," Festus said, shaking his head. "Like me, ol' Andy wasn't much of a hand for writin' readin' or readin' writin'. He always made his mark on a paper."

Matt leaned forward in his chair. "Festus, are you sure about that?"

"Sure, I'm sure. You can bet the baby's milk money on it. One time I was with Andy over to Mr. Bodkin's bank when he changed up some gold nuggets for folding money. Mr. Bodkin gave Andy a paper to sign and the old man made his mark"—Festus

quickly traced an **X** in the air with his forefinger—
"like that, same as I always do."

Festus drained his coffee cup. "Matthew, now I've
studied on it some, I'd say Andy's murder is a case
for the United States marshal."

Matt shook his head at his deputy. "Not unless I
can find evidence against the McKennas that will
hold up in court. As of now, Andy Reid was killed
by person or persons unknown. That happens all the
time around these parts and the U.S. marshal won't
get involved in an investigation unless I can give him
some hard facts. The thing is, I can't press a murder
charge against the McKennas unless I can get my
hands on that forged bill of sale."

"How you gonna do that, Matthew?"

"I don't know. Get them away from the cabin I
guess, then grab the paper."

"Tall order," Festus said, his wary eyes revealing
his doubt. "From what you told me, there's always
McKenna hands skulkin' around the place, to say
nothing of that Roman Pollock feller."

Matt nodded, his face thoughtful. "Roman is a
problem."

"How come you know him, Matthew?" Festus
asked. "I mean, if'n it ain't pryin' or nothin'."

"We go back maybe nine, ten years," Matt said.
"There was a dozen of us then, young, feeling our
oats, riding the border country, ready for anything."

"You were an outlaw, Matthew?" Festus asked, his
suddenly slack jaw revealing his shock.

Matt shook his head and smiled. "Not exactly. We

ran some cattle into Mexico now and again, but mostly we chased after the senoritas and had us a real good time. I guess you could say we were just wild youngsters, and Roman Pollock was the wildest of us all. When I first met him, he'd been running with John Wesley and the Clements brothers and that hard DeWitt County crowd. By then he'd already killed three men and I reckon he's added to his score since."

"I guess Roman Pollock is one of them slick, out-of-Texas gunfighters, the kind folks around town love to talk about all the time."

Matt nodded. "He's slick with a gun all right, but Roman never said where he was from or who his folks were. He did mention one time that he was raised by lobo wolves in a hanging valley up in the Chiricahua Mountains, and maybe he was."

The big marshal rose, eased a crick out of his back and poured himself another cup of coffee. "It was a long time ago, Festus, and a man changes. I changed and so did most of the others. Unfortunately, it seems that Roman Pollock never did."

Matt returned to his desk and sat. "I saw something in his eyes today, Festus, something I didn't like. Roman always had a killer's eyes. You looked into them and it felt like you were trying to stare down a coiled rattlesnake. But there was something else in them this morning. I don't know, some kind of madness maybe."

"You mean he's plumb loco?"

"Like I said, Festus, it could be that he is."

"Being good with a gun and loco at the same time is a mighty dangerous combination, Matthew," Festus said, concern showing in his face. "You step careful around that Roman Pollock feller."

"I plan to," Matt said, "unless he backs me into a corner, and that's a bridge I'll cross when I come to it."

The marshal snapped his fingers. "Oh, I almost forgot—Sam Noonan was at the McKenna cabin."

Festus jerked back in his chair in surprise. "Sam? What was a good, upright man like Sam Noonan doin' among that crowd, Matthew?"

"He's walking out with Abbey McKenna."

"But Sam is twice, maybe three times, that little gal's age."

"Doesn't seem to make no never mind to either of them. Sam has asked her to marry him."

Festus gulped down his shock. "Does Miss Kitty know? She sets store by Sam Noonan. Maybe she could talk him out of gettin' himself involved with that kind of trash."

Matt laid his cup on the desk. "Trash or no, seems to me Sam is already involved and liking it just fine."

Matt rose and glanced at the railroad clock on the office wall. It was almost four and outside the day was already shading into evening; the cobalt blue sky was streaked with narrow bands of jade, scarlet and gold.

"Better let the Indian out, Festus," Matt said. "He should have sobered up by this time."

The big marshal buckled on his gun and settled

his hat on his head. A few moments later Festus appeared from the cells at the back of the office with Iron Hawk.

The Cheyenne was not much above middle height with wide shoulders and long, muscular arms. He was dressed in filthy buckskins and a pair of down-at-heel Army boots on his feet, and his unbound hair hung over his shoulders in matted black tangles. The man's face was wide and hard boned, the color of new bronze, but swollen and puffy and his black eyes were dead, seeing nothing, interested in nothing.

Staggering a little, Iron Hawk stepped beside Matt. He touched his tongue to his upper lip and stretched out his hand, palm uppermost. "Money. For whiskey," he mumbled.

Before Matt could reply, Festus shoved the Indian away from the marshal. "Here, that won't do," he said. "We have no money." He grabbed the man by an arm, opened the door and pushed him outside. "Go swamp out the Alhambra, Iron Hawk," he said. "They pay your wages in rotgut." Festus' right eyebrow crawled up his forehead like a hairy caterpillar. "Or don't you recollect that since this mornin'?"

The deputy stood on the boardwalk and watched the Indian fade into the gathering darkness. When Festus stepped back inside he shook his head at Matt. "You can't be civil to a drunken Injun like that, Matthew. He'll take advantage of your good nature an' pester you day an' night for whiskey money."

"How old do you figure he is?" Matt asked, changing the subject.

"Who, Iron Hawk?"

Matt nodded.

"I dunno. If you asked me to set right down on a notion, I'd say he's a couple of years shy of thirty. No more'n that."

"He's a young man," Matt said. "It's a real shame."

"It's a real shame for all of them, young, old and not borned yet, Matthew," Festus said, with more than usual perception.

"Yes, I guess it is," Matt agreed. "Like the buffalo, what the Cheyenne once had is gone and it's never coming back." He shook his head. "Pity. It was a fine, free way to live." The big marshal stood silent for a few moments, then sighed. "Well, I'm walking over to the Long Branch, Festus. It's time I had a talk with Kitty about Sam."

When Matt stepped into the saloon the day bartender was polishing glasses behind the bar and Kitty Russell stood close by, her head bent over an open ledger.

As always, the sight of Kitty made Matt's breath catch in his throat. She wore a dress of red silk, her beautiful shoulders bare, the dress cut low enough to reveal the firm swell of her breasts. He hair was bound up with black ribbons and another of the same color circled her slender throat. The woman didn't look up when Matt walked inside. She was busily frowning over the ledger, her long lashes fanning over high rose-colored cheekbones.

"Get you something, Marshal?" the bartender asked.

Matt shook his head as Kitty looked up and saw him. A warm, affectionate woman, she smiled a welcome, rushed to the big marshal, threw her arms around his neck and stood on tiptoe to kiss him.

After their lips parted, it took Matt a few moments to catch his breath and when he did he said: "Mayor Kelley would probably tell me kissing a pretty woman is not allowed when I'm on duty. But that's one order I'd be happy to ignore."

Kitty's smile slipped a little and annoyance flared in her eyes. "If Jim Kelley ever tells you that, send him to me. I'll soon set him straight."

Matt laughed. "Kitty, I bet you would." The laughter quickly fled from Matt's face, to be replaced by a frown. "I've got something to tell you, Kitty."

The woman nodded. "I'm guessing it's about Sam and that Abbey McKenna girl."

Matt was shocked. "How did you know?"

"Matt, it's not much of a secret. The whole town knows Sam is walking out with a girl half his age." Kitty shook her head. "Sam is crazy about her. He says he wants to marry her."

Matt nodded. "Heard that from Abbey this morning."

Now Kitty was surprised and her eyebrows arched as her beautiful eyes widened. "You were out there?"

"Sure, I checked on the McKenna herd. Their cattle are running maybe six or seven different brands."

Matt's eyes were suddenly bleak. "Found old Andy Reid too. He'd been murdered."

Kitty's face registered her horror. "Matt, you don't think—"

"I think," Matt interrupted, "that the only people who had anything to gain from Andy's death were Abbey McKenna and her brother. That's what I think."

A crease appeared between Kitty's eyes, signaling her annoyance. "Matt, that's a very hard thing to say when Sam is head over heels in love with the girl."

Matt shrugged. "Kitty, there's no accounting for love. It's like the morning dew, as apt to fall on a cow patty as a cactus rose."

Kitty touched the front of Matt's vest. "If what you say is true, is there anything you want me to do?"

"Yes, you can try to talk Sam out of marrying Abbey McKenna." The lawman's thin smile didn't reach his eyes. "But I doubt he'll listen."

Kitty nodded. "If you find proof that ties Abbey McKenna to Andy Reid's murder, Sam will listen. But just be sure, Matt. Be very sure, because you'll hurt Sam terribly."

"When the time comes, I'll be sure," the marshal said. "I won't make a move until I can find evidence that will stand up in court."

Kitty's face showed sudden concern as though she'd just remembered something. "Matt, I don't know if you've met him or not, but there's a man named Roman Pollock working for the McKennas. Watch out for him. He's been here at the Long

Branch a couple of times and there's something strange about him. He . . . he scares me."

"Roman is a man to be scared of, Kitty. He's a funeral maker from way back."

"Do you know him?" Kitty asked in surprise.

"I knew him, once. And he knows me." Matt's expression was grim, his mouth tight. "Roman Pollock knows my name."

After he left the Long Branch, Matt sought out Festus and found his deputy as he stepped out of the lobby of the Cattleman's Hotel. Festus said he'd just successfully concluded an investigation into the theft of three pairs of lady's bloomers off a washline across the tracks and the two lawmen headed back to the marshal's office.

"First tell me how you solved the great missing bloomer mystery, Festus," Matt said. "Then I want to ask you a question."

The deputy scratched his hairy throat and said: "Well, it weren't real difficult police work, Matthew. Miz Shaw, the lady that's the rightful owner of the bloomers, saw the thief and she gave me a pretty accurate description. She recollected that he was a little, bald, pale feller who favored his right leg some. I'd seen a corset drummer in town who looked a lot like that and walked with a limp, so I went to his hotel room."

Matt was only vaguely interested. "Was it him?" he asked.

"Damn right it was. I caught him red-handed, Matthew. His door wasn't locked, so I charged right inside, and guess what?"

The marshal smiled and shook his head. "That's something I really don't want to guess at. But I'm sure you're dying to tell me."

Festus grinned, his eyes alight as he warmed to his story. "The little feller was all rouged up and he was prancin' an' dancin' in front of the mirror, nekkid as a scalded hog—'cept for the fact that he was wearin' a pair of them bloomers. Right nice ones too, with lace all around the bottom of the legs."

Matt laughed. "What did you do then?"

"Do then? Why I made him take off the women's fixins and dress hisself. Then I marched him over to Miz Shaw's house by the scruff of his neck and made him give back them unmentionables."

Matt's eyes moved to the door that led to the cells. "You arrest him?"

Festus shook his head. "Nah. That drummer feller gave me a story that will keep me in whiskey for a week. Maybe a month." The deputy shrugged. "I marched him back to his hotel, kicked his butt an' let him go."

"Well, that's one way to enforce the law," Matt said. He hesitated, then added: "I'm sure Mayor Kelley would say that a kick in the butt instead of jail time saves the town money."

Festus let that pass without comment and asked: "What was it you was plannin' on askin' me, Matthew?"

"Festus, any of those Rangers you used to ride with still active?"

"Most of 'em, I reckon," Festus answered. "Why do you want to know?"

"I want to send a wire to Texas and ask if they have any information on Abbey and Abe McKenna."

The deputy scratched his chin thoughtfully. "Captain Lee McNelly makes his home in Brownsville, Matthew. He keeps right poorly on account of the consumption, but if anybody in the Rangers knows about the McKennas, it'll be him. There ain't much happenin' in Texas that escapes Captain McNelly's notice."

Matt nodded, frowning in thought. "Seems to me I've heard the name before."

"Could be. McNelly stopped the cattle rustlin' along the border, and he was the Ranger who put an end to the Sutton-Taylor feud that was killin' all them folks down to DeWitt County where John Wesley an' your man Roman Pollock was runnin' wild."

"Sounds like the Ranger I need," Matt said.

"He's a good man all right. Matthew, tell Barney Danches to send your wire to the telegraph office in Brownsville and mark it to the attention of Captain L. H. McNelly. He'll get it."

An hour later Festus left to patrol the respectable part of town across the tracks, one of Mayor Kelley's efforts to please potential voters.

Matt was sitting bent over at his desk, trying to catch up on his paperwork, when the deputy slammed open the door and rushed inside, his eyes wild.

"Matthew!" he yelled breathlessly. "Iron Hawk is makin' big trouble over to the Alhambra. You'd better come."

chapter 4

Once a Warrior

When Matt stepped inside the Alhambra saloon, he took in what was happening at a glance.

Abe McKenna and a couple of his riders were sitting at a table, Roman Pollock lounging against the bar, his black eyes alert and watchful, missing nothing.

McKenna, grinning, was bent over, holding a glass of whiskey just above the floor. "Come get it, Injun," he yelled. "Come get it."

Across the room, Iron Hawk was on his hands and knees, a three-hundred-pound saloon girl who called herself Big Bertha straddling his back. Somebody had strapped a pair of large-roweled Texas spurs around the woman's thick ankles and she was kicking her legs, gouging the Cheyenne's thighs and hips unmercifully.

"Yeehah!" one of the McKenna hands yelled. "Ride the wild Injun, Bertha. Ride him over here."

Iron Hawk began to crawl toward McKenna's table, the grinning Bertha spurring him on, the man's hungry eyes fixed on the whiskey.

But when the Indian finally reached the table, Abe McKenna quickly snatched the glass away.

"Whiskey," Iron Hawk begged, bending his neck as he tried to look up at McKenna. "Give me whiskey."

Bertha viciously slammed her spurs into the man again before getting off him. McKenna laughed. "I ain't going to give good whiskey to no drunken Indian." The man slid a wicked-looking bowie knife from his belt. "But I tell you what I am gonna do, I'm gonna get me a Cheyenne scalp. Here's one for Custer."

McKenna, who looked to be mean drunk, pulled Iron Hawk to him and locked the Indian in a stranglehold with his left arm. In his right hand McKenna held the knife and he shoved the blade against the Cheyenne's hairline, drawing a thin streak of blood.

"That's enough, McKenna," Matt shouted. "Drop the knife and let that man be."

Surprised, McKenna looked up and his petulant mouth twisted into a smile. "Aw, I'm only having a little fun, Marshal. I'm just gonna scalp me an Injun."

The knife bit deeper with a sawing motion, and Matt drew, his hand a blur of motion. "Drop the knife, McKenna," he said, his voice low, flat and hard. "Now! Or I'll blow you right out of that chair."

McKenna hesitated. His angry glare sought the

marshal's eyes, but instantly his face paled, not liking what he read there. The man dropped the knife and it clattered to the floor. McKenna turned to Pollock, his voice a petulant whine. "Roman, you gonna let a hick lawman get away with this?"

The gunman shrugged. "This isn't my play, Abe. Maybe you should brace him your ownself."

McKenna thought about it—for the single second it took him to decide that he didn't like the odds. "Aw, the hell with you, Dillon," he said, his eyes ugly. "You may be wearing a star but underneath you're nothing but a damn squaw man."

Matt ignored McKenna as though he was a thing not worthy of notice. He holstered his gun and hauled Iron Hawk to his feet. The Cheyenne was hopelessly drunk and he staggered against the bar. Pollock reached out, grabbed the Indian and pushed him toward Matt and Festus.

"Here," he said. "Take him. He stinks up the place anyhow."

The big marshal held Iron Hawk by the neck of his filthy buckskins and shoved him toward the door of the saloon. Pollock's voice stopped him.

"You were fast, Matt, very fast and smooth." The gunman's grin was malicious. "But even so, you were way slower than Walt Tinney."

"Roman," Matt said, his own smile cold, "I wasn't even half trying."

The gunman's grin cut and run and was replaced by a scowl. "Maybe so, but you showed me nothing."

The big marshal ignored Pollock's comment and pushed Iron Hawk through the saloon door. A couple of minutes later he turned the key on the man's cell.

"Iron Hawk, you puke all over my cell again and I'll scalp you my ownself," Matt said.

But he was talking to no one. The Cheyenne was already passed out on the floor.

Matt rose early the next morning and sent a wire to Captain McNelly. When he returned to his office, Festus was already there and had coffee boiling.

"Mornin', Matthew," the deputy said cheerfully. "How's ol' Iron Hawk?"

"Sleeping, last time I looked," Matt answered.

"He almost lost his hair last night, sure enough."

Matt nodded. "I'd say he came mighty close."

"I don't understand that Abe McKenna." Festus said, scratching his hairy jaw. "Matthew, what gets into a man, makes him all-fired mean like that?"

Matt shrugged. "I don't know, Festus. I reckon any coward can be mean when he thinks he's safe."

Festus poured coffee and the two lawmen sat and, in a ritual of long standing, discussed their routine tasks for the coming days.

Mayor Kelley was again on a rampage about stray dogs within the city limits and wanted them shot on sight. The owner of the Alamo Saloon had made a complaint about vagrants sleeping outside his door, and a peeping Tom was bothering the widow Thompson across the tracks. The Santa Fe Railroad angrily wanted to know why the water tower in Dodge City was in such a state of disrepair and a female goldbrick artist out of Denver called Shiloh Jones was said to be working the town saloons under an assumed name.

"I'll go check on the water tower, Matthew," Festus said. "But why the Santy Fe Railroad figures it's the city's responsibility is beyond me."

"While you're at it, talk some pretties to the widow Thompson," Matt said. "Reassure her some, Festus. I don't want her making any more complaints to the mayor."

"I'll do that, Matthew, and—"

The office door swung open, stopping Festus in midsentence. An old man stood in the doorway holding a flat brown paper parcel in both hands.

The man looked to be in his seventies, dressed in a threadbare black frockcoat and pants and a striped, collarless shirt. He wore a flat-brimmed, low-crowned hat and his thin white hair hung over his shoulders. His face was brown, wrinkled from sun and remembered laughter, and his faded black eyes were nevertheless still proud, bold and direct.

"What can I do for you?" Matt asked, setting down his coffee cup on the desk in front of him.

"My name is Black Buffalo," the old man said. "I have walked from Fort Dodge to come to this place and talk with my son."

"Well, well, well, you must be ol' Iron Hawk's pa," Festus said.

The old man nodded.

"What you got there in your poke, pops?" Festus asked.

Black Buffalo carefully, almost reverently, opened the parcel. He showed the two lawmen a folded cloth made from red fabric and tanned skins. "This is the sash of a Cheyenne Dog Soldier. It was once my son's sash and he wore it in many battles with great honor."

"Pops, you sure we're talkin' about the same Iron Hawk?" Festus asked, his left eyebrow crawling up his forehead.

The old man's face was unreadable. "He is my son."

Matt rose to his feet. "You ready to see your boy?"

The old man nodded in reply.

"This way," Matt said.

The marshal opened the door to the cells and Festus and Black Buffalo followed. Matt stepped to the bars of Iron Hawk's cell. The Indian was sitting on the cot, his head in his hands, apparently nursing a wicked hangover.

"Iron Hawk," Matt said. "Your pa's here to see you." The marshal turned to the old man. "Speak English, Black Buffalo, so I understand what you're saying to him."

The old man's smile was bleak. "For what I have to say, one tongue is as good as another."

Iron Hawk lifted his head, the young Cheyenne's bloodshot eyes trying to focus on the three men standing on the other side of the bars.

After a few moments his eyes settled on his father.

"What do you do here, *mahahkese*?" Iron Hawk waved an arm angrily. *"Taanaastse!"*

Black Buffalo turned to Matt. "He asks why this old man is here and then, without waiting to hear my words, he has told me to leave."

The old Cheyenne held the parcel close to his chest. "Iron Hawk, you will hear my words, even though you wish to close your ears to them."

The young Cheyenne shook his head violently and buried his face in his hands.

"Hear this, Iron Hawk," Black Buffalo said. "Once there was a time when you were armed to the teeth with revolvers and a mighty bow of Osage wood. You rode tall on a spotted war pony taken in battle from the Nez Percé and you were proud, haughty and defiant as befits a *Hotamitaneo*, a Dog Soldier, a mighty warrior come to grant favors, not to beg them.

"Once you knew how to die, but not to be led captive. But now the white man's whiskey leads you captive and your warrior pride has blown away like smoke in the wind and all that's left for you now is to die the death of a cur."

"Taanaastse!" Iron Hawk hissed through his teeth, his black eyes blazing. *"Taanaastse!"*

Black Buffalo nodded. "I will leave, my son, but first this." The old man held up the scarlet sash for Iron Hawk to see. "Once on your chest hung a whistle made from the bone of a bird, a mark of respect among the warriors, and you were one of only four Cheyenne allowed to wear this sash, a sacred thing

our people call the dog rope. On your head you wore
a war bonnet made of four hundred magpie feathers
and among them the plumes of the owl and the
eagle.

"Five times in battle you staked yourself to the
earth, driving a pin through the red sash I hold in
my hands, signaling to all that you would never re-
treat while an armed enemy still held his ground.

"Once you were respected by the warriors, admired by the young women and your counsel was
heeded by the elders. You were my son, and I was
proud to be your father. Now you are respected and
admired by no one. Your counsel is not heard among
the Cheyenne, and when I think of you, I feel only
shame." Black Buffalo reached through the bars and
threw the sash at his son.

"Take that," he said. "Pah! It is a dishonored thing
and I will carry it no more."

The old man turned on his heel and walked back
into the office, Festus following close behind him.

Matt glanced at Iron Hawk. The Cheyenne still sat
bent over on the cot, but he had picked up the sash
and had buried his face in its soft cloth. Matt felt a
sudden pang of sympathy. If what Black Buffalo had
said was correct, this man had once been a Dog Soldier, the bravest and proudest of all the Cheyenne
warriors, the supreme fighting man among other
fighting men.

Now he was just another filthy, defeated, drunken
Indian, stripped of his dignity—a willing, broken-

down nag for a two-dollar whore, ready to run in a mad race for whiskey.

"Iron Hawk," Matt began, but when he could not find the words, he fell silent.

Without taking the sash from his face, the Cheyenne whispered: *"Taanaastse."*

Matt nodded and stepped back into the office.

Festus and Black Buffalo were gone and Matt sat at his desk, alone with his thoughts.

Matt Dillon was a hard man, bred tough for a hard land, but witnessing the destruction of another human being was a terrible thing and the big marshal felt oddly depressed, an emptiness in his belly that was almost an ache.

Matt sat, staring into nothing for several minutes. Then he heard the shot.

chapter 5

A Death in Dodge

Matt sprang to his feet. Listening. There was no second shot.

Feet pounded on the boardwalk outside the office and Festus rushed inside. "You better come see this, Matthew. Ol' Black Buffalo just up an' shot hisself."

Matt followed Festus onto the boardwalk. Diagonally across Front Street an excited crowd had gathered at the entrance to an alley between the Dodge House Hotel and the New York Hat Shop.

Matt walked across the street, shouldered gaping people aside and stepped into the alley.

Black Buffalo lay flat on his back, his eyes open, looking at a sky he could no longer see. A Colt was still clutched in his hand and there was a small bloody hole in his right temple.

Matt kneeled beside the old man and closed his eyes.

He rose to his feet, and said over his shoulder, "Somebody get Percy Crump. He's got a burying to do."

A big red-haired man elbowed his way through the crowd, his eyes ugly, scarlet veined with anger. "Dillon, you ain't burying that dirty Indian in town. He ain't gonna lie next to decent white folks."

His own anger flaring in him, Matt turned. The huge redhead was Ephraim Stanley, a bouncer at the Alamo, a belligerent troublemaker whose ready fists had earned himself a reputation as the town bully.

"This is none of your concern, Stanley," Matt said. "Now step aside."

"I'll be damned if I will," Stanley said, his face blackening. "What I say goes—that Injun isn't gonna be buried in Dodge. Put a rope on his feet and drag him out on the prairie someplace. Let the coyotes have at him."

Percy Crump, with the accustomed, eager punctuality of the undertaker, stepped into the alley and walked up to Matt. "Where is the body of the late departed, Marshal?"

"Right behind me," Matt answered, his eyes cold on Stanley.

"Crump!" the big redhead yelled. "You leave that damn Injun be." The man grinned and looked around him at the crowd, encouraging others to support him. "We ain't burying no filthy redskin in Dodge, and Marshal Matt Dillon be damned."

A few voices murmured their approval, but most were silent, waiting to see what would happen next.

It was not long in coming.

Matt slowly shook his head. "Stanley," he said, "I've had about all of you I'm going to take. Are you through talking?"

The big man took an aggressive step toward the marshal, his big, hairy fists clenched. "Hell no, I've still got plenty to say, and when I speak, you best make damn sure you're listening."

"Well, that's a real pity," Matt said, and he threw a crashing right to Stanley's jaw.

The redhead rocked back on his heels and his eyes glazed. He staggered a few steps and fell flat on his back. The man lay there dazed, but only for a moment. Grinning in triumph, he clambered to his feet, his fists coming up.

"I've been looking forward a long time to tearing down your meat house, Mr. high-and-mighty Matt Dillon," he said, shaking his head to clear the cobwebs. "When I get through with you, they'll have to pick you up with a sponge."

The man threw a straight left to Matt's jaw, but the marshal sidestepped and swung a roundhouse right that landed on Stanley's ear, splitting it wide open, a sudden rush of scarlet splashing over the shoulder of the redhead's coat.

Stanley roared his rage and stepped forward, getting a hard left and right to the face for his pains. The big bouncer lowered his head and charged, swinging.

A wild right caught Matt in the ribs and staggered him and Stanley came in low again, trying to grapple. Matt took a step back and brought his knee up hard into the man's face, smashing his nose and lips.

Stanley fell on all fours and shook his head, blood and saliva flying from him.

Matt stepped back and let the man get to his feet. He saw a worried look in Stanley's eyes. The man was a bully and Matt realized at heart Stanley was a talker, not a fighter.

Wary now, Stanley circled Matt. He feinted with a left, then swung a powerful right to Matt's jaw. The marshal caught the blow flat-footed and it knocked him on his back.

Stanley came closer, his right boot stomping for Matt's head. The marshal saw it coming and rolled away, then jumped to his feet. Matt's head was reeling and he found it hard to focus on the big redhead.

A jubilant grin split Stanley's battered face and he charged again, his fists swinging, trying to pound Matt back into the dirt.

For a few minutes, both men fought hard; then Stanley gathered himself and connected with his Sunday punch, another crashing right to Matt's jaw. The redhead slowed, then stepped back to give the marshal room to fall.

But Matt was still on his feet and Stanley's expression changed from triumph to one of absolute horror. Matt had taken his best shot but was still standing. One of the big lawman's eyes was almost swollen shut and a trickle of blood ran from a split lip down his chin. But he stood immoveable as a rock, tall, grim and terrible, and Matt knew by Stanley's stricken face that the man realized he'd made a bad mistake.

The redhead had no time to think about it, because Matt's right shot out hard and straight, pulping Stanley's lips against his teeth. Spitting blood, the redhead stumbled back a single step. His fists were up and ready but he made no move to close with the marshal.

Matt read the man's expression, and saw despair and fear. At that moment Stanley, the town bully who many times had unmercifully beaten lesser men and drunks to a pulp with his fists, must have known he was not going to win this fight.

Stanley had never before in his life come up against a man like Matt Dillon, an experienced fist-fighter who could take his best punch but still stay on his feet and hit back. Hard.

Stanley rushed again, but the fight was going out of him. Matt landed a right and left as the man came inside. The redhead stumbled forward, his arms wide, trying for a clinch. Matt took a single step to his rear, then swung a right uppercut that smashed into the redhead's chin, snapping back the man's head. Stanley, badly overbalanced, fell on his belly, then rolled on his side and Matt again waited for the man to climb to his feet.

But Stanley had had his fill of Matt Dillon and now he wanted no part of him. The redhead raised an arm, feebly fending Matt off, and gasped: "I'm beat. I've had enough."

Matt grabbed Stanley by the collar of his coat and hauled him upright. He jammed the man's hat on his head and asked, his voice hard and merciless: "Do you have a horse?"

Stanley nodded and answered through smashed lips, "I got a horse."

"Then climb on its back and ride," Matt said. "You're through in Dodge. If I see you in town again, I'll take up this fight where it left off."

Like a blind man, Stanley stumbled through the jeering crowd, and Matt turned to Percy Crump. "Tend to the old Cheyenne, Percy," he said. "Bury him decent."

The undertaker nodded, something showing in his eyes that was akin to admiration, tinged with an odd glint of fear. He stepped to the old man and bent to his melancholy task.

Matt pushed through the crowd and walked across the street. He stopped at the horse trough near the marshal's office, bent over and splashed water on his face. The water was ice cold and it stung, but it felt good.

"I'm glad I saw that, Matthew. I bet ol' Ephraim feels like he was beat with a *bois d'arc* fence post."

Matt turned, water dripping from his chin, and looked into Festus' hairy, grinning face. "You could have stopped it, you know," he said. "Buffaloed him, maybe."

Festus stiffened in shock. "Stop it? While you was having such a good time hanging ol' Ephraim's hide on the barbed wire? Why would I do that?"

Matt stood and pointed to his tender left eye, which he could feel was swollen almost shut. "Because of this, maybe."

The deputy shrugged. "Matthew, folks will be talkin' about that fight for years to come. Seems to me, a black eye is worth it."

"Uh-huh, maybe so, Festus," Matt said. "The only thing is, it ain't your eye."

The marshal walked back to his office, stepped inside and eased slowly into his chair, his entire body aching. His head was still ringing from the blows he'd taken and blood tasted like smoke in his mouth.

A few minutes' rest and then he'd have to talk to Iron Hawk.

The Cheyenne was standing close to the bars when Matt stepped to his cell. If the Indian noticed the marshal's bruised and battered face, he didn't let it show.

"Iron Hawk," Matt said, "there's no easy way to tell you this, so I'll say it straight out—your father is dead."

Iron Hawk's expression didn't change. "How did this thing happen?"

"He killed himself." Matt hesitated for a heartbeat, then added: "With a Colt's revolver."

"Then it is over for him," Iron Hawk said. The Indian was silent for a few moments, thinking about what he was going to say, then added: "When he was young, Black Buffalo was a mighty warrior and a great hunter. My mother and his other wives never wanted for meat." The Cheyenne's face showed his terrible hurt. "The shame I brought to his lodge was too much for him to bear."

Matt cast around in his mind for the right words, could not find them and managed only: "I guess Black Buffalo was a fine man."

The marshal unlocked the cell door. "I had your father taken to Percy Crump's funeral parlor. You can make your farewells there."

Iron Hawk stepped from the cell and Matt noticed that his sash was neatly folded over his left arm. The marshal ushered the Cheyenne into the office, dug into his pocket and came up with a silver dollar.

"Here, take this," he said. "It will help you ease the pain."

"Money to buy whiskey, you mean?" Iron Hawk asked.

Matt shrugged, feeling a strange flush of embarrassment. "To buy whatever you need."

The Cheyenne looked down his hatchet beak of a nose at the coin in Matt's hand. In that instant, the marshal caught a glimpse of what this man had once been. Iron Hawk's black eyes glittered hard in a face that had suddenly taken on a proud, haughty expression, like that of a great warrior come to grant favors, not ask for them.

"I want to thank you for saving me last night when the whiskey was on me," Iron Hawk said. "I was drunk as a pig, but I remember."

"I was only doing my job, Iron Hawk," Matt said, the coin lying ignored in his extended palm.

"I remember the ones who were there," the Chey-

enne said as though he hadn't heard. "I remember
them, all of them, and I know their names."

Iron Hawk cast a last, contemptuous glance at the
dollar in Matt's hand, then turned on his heel and
walked out of the office.

Matt shoved the dollar back in his pocket and sat
back in his chair. His swollen eye and his jaw hurt,
but he did not feel the pain.

Instead he thought of the look on Iron Hawk's
face—and all at once he felt sorry for Abe McKenna
and his whole miserable bunch.

chapter 6

Death in Dark Canyon

As night fell, Matt stepped out of his office and looked up and down Front Street.

A cold, biting wind from the west was rustling around Dodge and somewhere an open door banged, then banged again. Gaslamps had been lit in the saloons, their windows glowing rectangles of amber, and the alleys were deep in angled shadow.

Across the tracks lay the other Front Street, this one not lined with saloons, dance halls and stores but by neat, white-painted frame and gingerbread houses, the homes of the town's respectable element. Behind the houses fronting the street, there were others, just as affluent, but scattered here and there, as though they'd decided to wander off into the prairie and had lost their way.

Coyotes were calling out on the plains, but the town itself was quiet, still trying to shake off the winter doldrums, more than ready to welcome the spring sun after months of snow, cold and the dark, bitter nights that seemed to stretch into eternity.

But the herds were already on the way from Texas. Very soon now, Dodge would bestir herself, paint her face and let down her hair.

The cattle and the cowboys were still a long ways off, making eight miles a day if everything was going right, a lot less if everything was going wrong, and it usually did.

Matt, remembering how it was, did not envy the punchers.

Herding thousands of longhorns up the trail was brutally hard work. It was months of making do, doing without, forking a half-broke bronc for eighteen hours a day in a saddle that flayed the hide, drinking alkali water that gave a man bad blood and weeping, open sores that ran yellow. Many a night a puncher would warm himself over a smoking cow chip fire during a torrential rainstorm and he'd eat clouds of dust for breakfast when the land around him was dry. After a few weeks of wearing the same clothes day after day, he'd spread his ragged duds over an anthill to get rid of the lice and stand there naked as a jaybird but for his hat, refusing to dwell on what lay behind, dreaming only of what waited up ahead at trail's end—Dodge City, the glittering, gleaming Babylon of the plains.

Cowboying was something a man did when he couldn't do anything else. He signed up for thirty a month to drive a herd through a thousand miles of dust, heat, river crossings and stampedes, and if he was lucky, very lucky, he might even make it alive to the railhead.

Such a life put a big strain on a man and many would make the drive but once, maybe twice, and vow never again to attempt such foolishness.

Now, while Dodge held her breath, the herds were again on their way and with them the cowboys and soon the town would be wakened from her long winter sleep by the kiss of shabby, down-at-heel princes forking fifty-dollar saddles thrown across the backs of ten-dollar mustangs.

Matt smiled to himself, glad the time was near. For all the problems they caused, the cowboys brought life back to his town. Their visit was as fleeting as the little cloud shadow that runs across the prairie grass and loses itself in the sunset—but while it lasted, Dodge was reborn and her spirit renewed.

The marshal took one more look up and down the street and was about to step back into the office when a tiny calico cat padded along the boardwalk toward him. Matt knew this cat. He'd had a run-in or three with the animal before, and now, as always, it was hunting trouble.

The calico walked on a direct path toward Matt, then stopped when it found its road blocked. The little animal looked up at the tall marshal, its lime green eyes on fire.

"I'm not stepping aside for you, cat, not this time,"

Matt said, looking down at the creature. The calico stayed right where it was, its remorseless stare stubborn and belligerent, ragged ears pricked forward.

"Well, walk around me then, damn it," Matt said.

The cat ignored him, its tail straight up, twitching, glowing eyes fixed on his face.

"I'm not moving," Matt said again. "And remember, I'm a lot bigger than you."

The calico continued to stare, its slender tail twitching faster.

It was a Mexican standoff and it promised to be a lengthy one and Matt knew it. Finally he shook his head, sighed deeply, and took a single step backward. The cat didn't move. Matt took another, backing himself all the way to the office door.

The calico glanced at him coolly, raised a disdainful nose in the air and slowly walked past him on silent feet before fading into the darkness.

Matt watched the cat go, wondering as he'd done several times before what the heck the animal had against lawmen that compelled it to continually challenge him.

Finally he concluded that there was just no accounting for felines and turned and stepped back into the office. He'd just settled into his chair when the door opened and Hank Miller walked quickly inside.

The livery stable owner was pale to the gills and looked badly frightened. Sensing bad trouble, Matt asked: "What happened, Hank?"

The man's words stumbled out in a rush. "It's that

crazy, drunken Injun, Matt. He stole a hoss and my rifle and lit out."

"Iron Hawk?"

Miller's badly frayed nerves snapped. "You know any other crazy, drunken Injun?"

Matt rose, tried to get Miller to calm down and asked for the whole story.

"I done told you the whole story," the man said. "I was taking a nap in my office when I woke up and felt the muzzle of my own rifle pressed against my forehead.

"That Injun is standing there, crazy camped out in his eyes, and he asks me for shells for the gun. I found a box of .44.40s and gave them to him. Then he ties me up and steals a hoss."

"Whose horse?" Matt asked, suddenly fearing for Buck.

"Mayor Kelley's hoss."

Matt shook his head. "The mayor sets store by that zebra dun. He isn't going to be happy."

"And maybe that's why you should take out after that Injun," Miller said, impatience edging his voice. "I swear I'm lucky I'm still wearing my hair."

A few minutes later, Matt rode north out of Dodge, the collar of his sheepskin turned up against the night cold. He knew he was chasing after phantoms, but the mayor would expect him to make the effort.

The moon was almost full and it splashed the plains with a pale silver light, the troughs between the shallow rises deep in shadow. The direction of the wind had not shifted, blowing steady and hard from the west, iced by the snow-covered peaks of the distant Sangre de Christo Mountains.

This was long-riding country, and Matt was well aware that Iron Hawk could be miles away by now. Miller had told him he'd listened to the hoofbeats of the mayor's dun and they seemed to be heading north. But the Cheyenne could have looped to the south—or taken any other direction, come to that.

Hunting a man out here in the dark was like looking for a needle in a haystack, but Matt was determined to go through the motions. To say Mayor Kelley would expect it was an understatement—there would be a dozen different kinds of hell to pay if Matt didn't make at least a token effort.

The big marshal crossed Duck Creek and headed due north toward the Saw Log. Beyond Saw Log Creek lay Horse Thief Canyon, as likely a hiding place as any other in a wilderness devoid of sheltering mountains and forests.

Shortly after midnight Matt fetched up to the canyon. He sat his bay, his Winchester across the saddle horn and steadied the place, his ears tuned to the night sounds. Moonlight touched the sandstone walls of the canyon, but the interior was a tunnel of darkness, mysterious and possibly fraught with danger. From somewhere deep inside, as regular as the tick of a watch, a steady drip of water fell with a plopping sound, and Matt guessed it was snowmelt from the walls dropping into a swampy, ground-level puddle.

The air was fresh and clear, and above him the sky was a vast, arched vault, the stars looking like the hand of God had scattered a million diamonds across black velvet.

The marshal's bay stomped a foot and tossed his head, fretting against this inaction, his bit chiming like a bell.

Still Matt waited.

Within the canyon there was no sound but the constant *plop, plop, plop* of the water. Out on the grassland, the coyotes were talking and a barn owl flew past on silent wings, then slanted into the interior of the canyon, like a gray ghost, and was soon lost in the darkness.

It was time.

Matt swung out of the saddle and, his rifle across his chest, stepped toward the canyon entrance. A slight smile played around his lips, as he thought that, wild-goose chase or no, at least Mayor Kelley could not accuse him of a lack of effort.

Stepping with care, the big marshal entered the canyon, his eyes straining to penetrate the gloom. There was no sound but the soft, regular splash of the dripping water and the restless rustle of the wind among the branches of the stunted cedars on top of the canyon walls.

He stopped, listening. A small creature scuttled through the grass near Matt's feet, then headed away from him toward the canyon wall. As his eyes grew accustomed to the gloom, he looked up and could make out where the walls ended and the sky began, twin columns of deep darkness that stopped abruptly and gave way to the stars.

On cat feet, Matt stepped deeper into the canyon, the sodden ground beneath him soft and spongy from spring snowmelt.

Cut off by the high rocky walls, the moon cast only a shadowy, uncertain light, but it was enough for Matt to make out a mortar-shaped bowl carved into the canyon floor ahead of him. The depression had been formed by rainwater plunging from the wall above. Over the centuries hard rock fragments carried by the tumbling water had acted like a pestle to gouge and shape the soft sandstone.

But what interested the marshal was not the bowl. It was the body of a man lying in a few inches of water at the bottom of the depression. He was on his back, one knee drawn up, his arms thrown wide.

Matt, his eyes constantly scanning the walls around him, stepped to the body and kneeled beside it. The marshal slipped a hand into his coat and found a match in his vest pocket. He thumbed the match alight and the sudden orange glow flared on the ashen face of the dead man.

The man's face was contorted in death, his eyes wide open, the horror of his own dying still frozen on his fleshy, heavy-jawed features.

Before the match burned down to his fingers and he tossed it aside, Matt recognized the dead man.

He was Justin Herrick, a wealthy Boston cattle

buyer who for the past several years had made the journey to Dodge early in the spring.

Herrick liked to choose his beef from among the first of the arriving herds, closing his deals before the rest of the buyers got into town and competition drove up prices.

As Matt recalled, the man had a weakness for poker, whiskey and women, and always traveled with a considerable amount of cash in his wallet, often as much as ten thousand dollars.

The brief light of the match was enough to tell the marshal how Herrick had died. The man had been shot twice in the middle of the chest, the bullet wounds so close, Matt could have covered them both with his hand.

Carefully, Matt searched Herrick's body. The buyer's wallet was gone, so was his watch, and someone had cut off the little finger of his left hand, presumably to get at a ring he wore.

There was no way of immediately telling if Herrick had been shot here or murdered somewhere else and his body dumped in the canyon.

Matt rolled over the man's stiffening body and found no bloodstains on the rock underneath. Nodding, his face set and grim, Matt concluded that Herrick must have bled out a fair piece from here before his body was concealed in the canyon, a place few people visited.

Herrick looked to have been dead for several days. Had the man been casually murdered on the trail, then robbed?

Matt stood, deep in thought, looking down at the corpse.

As he had after finding Andy Reid, Matt doubted that some nameless outlaw had killed and robbed Herrick. Like an iron nail would attract a magnet, Abbey and Abe McKenna drew his suspicion. Had they lured Herrick out to the Pawnee with the promise of selling him their herd and then murdered the buyer? Or had Herrick, a notorious ladies' man, seen Abbey in town, fallen for the girl's voluptuous charms and visited the ranch willingly?

Either way, the man was dead, no doubt shot by the same skilled gunman who had killed Andy.

A cold feeling in his belly, Matt told himself that the gunman could only be Roman Pollock.

Herrick had been casually murdered for no other reason than to rob him of the money he carried. He'd been killed coldly and efficiently by people without a shred of conscience . . . people like Abbey and Abe McKenna.

The marshal retraced his steps, walked to his horse and swung into the saddle.

He had just found more work for Percy Crump, and was also faced with a daunting task he'd rather avoid.

He'd have to tell Mayor Kelly that he couldn't find his horse.

chapter 7

Stage Robbery

"You mean to tell me that there's a wild Cheyenne Dog Soldier on my horse, playing hob out there on the plains?"

Matt looked into Mayor James H. Kelley's hard Irish face and realized the man was working himself up to go on a tear.

"He's on your horse, Mayor. That's true enough," Matt said. "But he isn't playing hob—at least not yet he isn't."

Kelley fished in his pocket and found a cigar. He sat on the edge of Matt's desk, thumbed a match alight and, like an angry dragon, bellowed through a cloud of smoke: "Matt, I set store by that dun. He's the best horse I ever owned and I want him back."

The big marshal nodded. "Don't worry, Mayor. I'll find him."

"Damn right you will." Kelley stabbed his cigar at

Matt. "Call out the Army if you have to, but find him and find him soon. Jesus, Mary and Joseph and all the saints in Heaven, when I think of that Indian running wild out there it makes me blood run cold. There's no telling what a savage like that will get up to, killing and scalping and raising all kinds of hell."

Matt shrugged. "Mayor, if he's still out on the plains, I'll find him."

"If he's still on the plains? Where else would he be?"

"Iron Hawk could have headed south for the Indian Territory or north, even as we speak, riding hard for the Black Hills." Unable to resist a dig, Matt added: "Like you said, Mayor, he's got a good horse under him and he can cover a lot of ground."

"Iron Hawk, is it?" Kelley snapped, angrily chewing on his cigar. "Well, Matt, you find Iron Hawk. You find him and capture him and bring him back with my horse, you understand? If you don't, Dodge City will be looking for a new city marshal."

Before Matt could reply, Kelley stomped out of the office and slammed the door behind him.

The marshal rose from his desk just as the door banged open again. Kelley stuck his head inside and yelled: "And another thing, do something about the curs roaming the streets! I swear, there are more stray dogs in this town than there are people."

The door crashed shut again, and Matt waited until he was sure Kelley was gone before he stepped outside onto the boardwalk.

Kelley had been so incensed about his horse, Matt

hadn't discussed the murders of Andy Reid and Justin Herrick. He doubted that the mayor would be too concerned. Kelley's world, like his ambition, was bounded by the city limits of Dodge, and the tough little Irishman paid little heed to what happened out on the prairie.

Matt was about to step over to the Long Branch when he stopped in midstride. The Lee-Reynolds stage thundered onto Front Street, six wild-eyed, heavily lathered mustangs in the traces. The stage bounced and jangled to a ragged halt, throwing up a cloud of dust, the billow that had been chasing behind the rear wheels immediately catching up, obscuring stage and horses behind an even thicker, swirling yellow veil.

Matt was alarmed. Jim Buck, the top driver for the Lee-Reynolds Company, would never use up his horses that way.

The marshal stepped quickly to the stage where a crowd was already gathering.

Buck was bent over the ribbons, obviously in pain, and beside him the shotgun guard lay sprawled in death. The stage door creaked open. A woman stuck out her head and yelled, "Help, somebody! We have a wounded man inside."

"See to that man," Matt called out to the onlookers. "And one of you go get Doc Adams."

Effortlessly, the tall marshal climbed up onto the box. Matt shook Buck's shoulder and the driver turned stunned bloodshot eyes to him. "Jim," he asked, "what happened?"

"Seven men," Buck gasped, blood staining the right arm of his fringed buckskin coat, running scarlet over his hand. "About ten this morning they stopped us at Coon Creek and just started shooting."

The driver jerked a thumb over his shoulder. "Took the strongbox, Matt. Twenty thousand in gold and paper money belonging to the Cattleman's Bank and Trust of Larned."

Buck turned to the dead guard. "His name is Bob Taggart and he was as game as they come. Bob was not a man to be stampeded by anyone but he never stood a chance. When the robbers demanded the box, I'll remember to my dying day what he said. He yelled, 'Never! And be damned to ye' and raised up his shotgun to make his fight. That's when they killed him, maybe four or five of them firing at him at the same time. After that, there was more shooting. I think there's a man dead inside and another wounded."

"Recognize any of them, Jim?" Matt asked.

The driver shook his head. "Never seen any of them before in my life. I couldn't see their faces anyhow, on account of they were wearing burlap sacks over their heads with eyeholes cut in them."

Matt turned to the crowd gathered at the wheel of the stage. "Some of you men help me get Jim down from here."

Jim Buck was well liked and highly respected in Dodge and willing hands helped take the driver man off the box while others carried him into the stage depot.

Matt stepped to the stage door. The wounded man had already been taken into the depot and another was inside, dead as he was ever going to be, his body jammed into a corner by the window.

The dead man had been shot several times, the deadliest wound right in the middle of forehead. Matt had never seen the man before, but judging by the eastern cut of his suit and his plug hat, he was a drummer of some kind.

The marshal searched through the dead man's pockets, looking for some kind of identification. He found a wallet containing fifty dollars and a letter in a woman's hand addressed to John J. Barkley, c/o The Bon Ton Hotel, Wichita. The letter was from Mrs. Hilda Barkley and gave a return address in Philadelphia. Matt shoved the wallet into his pocket. At least he could write the woman and tell her how her husband died, and send her the fifty dollars. She would probably need it.

There was nothing else to be done, and Percy Crump was already standing nearby, a tape measure in his hands. The man, Matt decided, could smell death like a vulture.

The marshal stepped into the depot, and the manager, a bearded, red-faced man named Happy Jack Taylor, no longer seemed so happy. When he caught sight of Matt he tilted his head toward a door at the back of the office. "In there."

Matt nodded, rapped on the door and stepped inside.

Doc Adams was just knotting the bandage around

Buck's arm as Matt entered. "He'll live," Doc said, "though he won't be driving a stage for a while. I took a chunk of lead out of his arm and another out of his shoulder."

· Matt nodded to a groaning man lying on a rough pine table in the middle of the room. "What about him, Doc?"

Doc Adams shook his head. "He's gut shot, Matt. He won't make it until nightfall."

"Know him?"

The doctor shrugged. "No, I don't. Cattle buyer maybe, or a gambler. The woman riding in the stage says she saw him flash a thick wad of bills. I searched his pockets, but he doesn't have the money anymore."

"You seen Festus around, Doc?" Matt asked.

Doc Adams made a wry face. "Last I saw him he was over to the Long Branch, no doubt cadging drinks from Kitty."

"Thanks," Matt said. He turned to step to the door but Doc's voice stopped him.

"Where are you going, Matt?"

"After those stage robbers."

Doc's stricken face revealed his shock. "Matt, that's not a job for a town marshal. You're not being paid to go chasing after stage robbers. Leave it for the government to handle. They can send a U.S. marshal down here."

Matt shook his head. "Doc, the stage was robbed about an hour ago, so those outlaws couldn't have gone far. Maybe I can still track them."

"Damn it all, man," Doc exploded, "there's seven of them. Let it go."

"I can't, Doc. I may only be a town marshal, but I reckon it's my job."

"You'll get your fool head blown off out there— that's what's going to happen." Doc's suddenly irritated expression framed his question even before he asked it: "Why, Matt? For God's sake why?"

Matt's smile was slight, without humor. "I don't quite know, Doc. Maybe it's because Bob Taggart was as game as they come and maybe because a woman named Hilda Barkley will soon be grieving for a dead husband." Matt opened the door and looked back over his shoulder. "Maybe those are the reasons."

As he shook his head, Doc Adams suddenly looked old and tired. "Matt, avenging the dead is an exercise in futility, about as useless as building a dam to catch the water you see in a mirage. The dead are gone and they're beyond caring."

Matt nodded. "Maybe so, Doc, but I still care, so I reckon I've got to do it."

Ten minutes later, Matt and Festus rode out of Dodge, then swung due west in the direction of Coon Creek.

The day was cold, though the sun was bright in a cloudless blue sky. Around the two riders the flat grassland still showed the brown scars of winter, but the thin covering of sheet ice had cleared from the streams running off the creeks, and at the heart of

the yucca, tiny white buds were already struggling
to bloom.

To the north glittered the Santa Fe's iron road,
where later in the spring the bawling cattle cars
would roll toward the markets in the East. A line of
thin telegraph poles marched in step with the rails,
growing progressively smaller in the distance until
rails and poles became one and vanished into the
horizon.

Matt's bay and Festus' enduring, long-legged mule
ate up ground in this flat, long-riding country, and
when the scattered cottonwoods and willows lining
Coon Creek came into view, the two lawmen reined
in their mounts and shucked their rifles.

"Don't see nothin' moving around the creek, Matthew," Festus said. He turned in the saddle and faced the
big marshal. "You reckon we're way too late an'
they've lit out already?"

Matt nodded. "Uh-huh. But maybe we'll come on
some tracks."

Festus sat in silence for a few moments, then spoke
his thoughts aloud. "I knowed Bob Taggart from way
back when we was both in the Rangers," he said.
"And Jim Buck was right—that ol' boy was born
game an' he had no backup in him." The deputy
shook his head, his eyes bleak. "Who do you reckon
done that robbery, Matthew?"

Matt shook his head. "Festus, I don't rightly know,
but I have a gut feeling that Abbey McKenna and
her brother are somehow mixed up in it. Seems like

a lot of bad things have been happening since they moved here and this might be another of them."

Festus scratched his unshaven jaw. "An' your gut is tellin' you that they murdered the cattle buyer feller?"

"That I have no doubt about," Matt said. "But proving it was the McKennas could be a mighty tough row to hoe."

Kneeing his bay forward warily, Matt fetched up to the bend of the creek, every nerve in his body tense and ready.

Cottonwoods lined both banks and a few forlorn willows trailed their branches into the water. At some time in the past, a settler family heading west had reached this far and made it no farther. All that remained of their wagon—a few charred wooden boards and a couple of rusted iron wheel rims—was wedged between a pair of tall trees. The yellow bones of oxen were strewn over the grass and close by were the mounds of four hastily dug graves without markers.

Of the faceless, nameless pioneers who'd been killed by Indians here, there was no record. But after a score of years and the slow-turning seasons of snow, sun, wind and rain, the merciful green earth had claimed their bodies and finally made them one with itself.

Matt swung out of the saddle, and he and Festus, Winchesters in hand, scouted the area. There were tracks of a dozen or so horses and a few scattered cigarette butts. Festus picked up a jug and smelled the neck. "Whiskey," he grinned. He tilted the jug to his lips and his expression changed to one of disgust. "An' it's empty," he said.

It looked to Matt like the outlaws had robbed the stage, then assembled here to share the loot. His notion was confirmed when he discovered that the tracks headed off singly in all directions, except for two riders who had moved northeast in the direction of White Woman Creek.

This last puzzled the marshal. Did it mean that two of the robbers had decided to call it quits? Had there been a falling out among thieves?

That pair, Matt decided, might be worth talking to.

Matt called out to Festus to mount up and he swung into the saddle of the bay.

"Where are we headed, Matthew?" Festus asked.

Matt pointed in the direction of the tracks. "That way," he said. "And keep your rifle handy, Festus. I've got a feeling you're going to need it."

chapter 8

Warpath!

The outlaws had at least a couple of hours' start on the lawmen, and Matt spurred his bay into a distance-eating lope.

There was no trail but for the tracks of the riders ahead of them. Matt and Festus rode through gently rolling country, the crests of some of the rises eight feet above the level, crowned with short buffalo grass. A few stunted ash and oak trees grew along some of the streambanks running off the creeks, but most were lined with the more hardy plum bush and willow.

The shadows cast on the grass by the two lawmen grew longer as they neared the White Woman, and the wind had picked up, whipping the tall bluestem into a tossing, heaving sea as dark green as reef water.

Matt smelled snow in the air and the sky was beginning to cloud over, shading from blue to a sullen, ominous gray. It was too late in the season for the shrieking blizzards of winter, when the temperature would plunge suddenly to forty below and a man could lose his way and freeze to death walking between cabin and barn. But snowstorms menaced the plains well into the early spring and the gathering clouds gave warning that the threat had not passed.

A few scattered flurries were already being tossed about by the wind as Matt and Festus rode on at a steady lope, now and then bending low from the saddle, intent on following the faint tracks scarring the grass.

At a depression between two shallow rises, the riders had pulled up to survey the land around them. Perhaps wary of the increasing cloud and the threatening snow, their tracks abruptly swung away to the north, heading directly toward a sharp bend of the White Woman, where sheltering trees and thick underbrush would cut the worst of the wind.

Matt and Festus followed the tracks north, and when they were still half a mile shy of the creek, the lawmen reined in their mounts and studied the area.

At first, Matt saw nothing move but the skeletal wave of the bare cottonwood branches in the rising breeze. He dug into his saddlebags, found his field glasses and scanned the creek more closely.

Nothing. No sign of the riders.

"Ain't nobody at the creek, Matthew," Festus said, echoing the big marshal's thoughts. "It's maybe so that they've moved on."

Matt nodded, disappointment tugging at him. "It sure looks that way."

"Wait!" Festus whispered urgently, grabbing Matt's arm. "Did you see somethin' move behind that lightin'-struck tree close to the bank?"

"A deer maybe," Matt said. "Could be a deer." He raised the glasses to his eyes again. There was a flicker of movement among the cottonwoods; then an unsaddled horse stepped out of the trees and lowered its head to graze on the grass at its feet.

Festus readied his rifle. "Damn it all, Matthew— would you believe it? Them boys are camped!"

Matt's face was set, his mouth a straight, grim line. "I guess they didn't expect anybody to come after them." He jutted his chin toward the creek. "How do you reckon we should play this, Festus? It's only a matter of time before they spot us out here on the flat. I say we just charge hell for leather right into the camp and hit them before they even know we're there."

The deputy grinned his enthusiasm. "Good enough plan, Matthew. But let's wait a spell. I reckon this snow is fallin' thicker by the minute and pretty soon it will give us cover until we're right on top of them."

Matt saw the logic in Festus' suggestion and nodded. "Just so long as we don't freeze to death in the meantime."

The sky had darkened into a dull iron gray and the snow was beginning to fall faster, with fat, fluttering flakes cartwheeling in the wind. After a few minutes the snowfall began to draw a shifting, tumbling white veil across the creek and Matt could barely make out the branches of the cottonwoods.

"Ready?" Matt asked. "I reckon it's time."

Festus nodded. "Me too. I ain't sittin' on my gun hand, Matthew."

"Then let's go!"

Matt set the spurs to his bay and, startled, the big horse leapt forward. The marshal charged toward the creek through the billowing curtain of snow, Festus galloping close behind him.

Matt hit the cottonwoods at a fast clip, and behind him, he heard Festus holler a rebel yell. His rifle ready, the marshal rode among the trees, his head turning this way and that, hunting a target.

There was none. This was a place of the dead.

The two outlaws lay sprawled facedown in a grassy clearing near the bank of the creek. Both were dead. And both had been scalped.

Cursing under his breath, Matt reined up his horse and swung out of the saddle. He stepped to one of the outlaws and turned the man on his back. Matt did not immediately recognize the dead man, a thin-faced Mexican with a handlebar mustache and heavy black eyebrows. The man had been shot several times in the chest, and his lips were still drawn back from his teeth in a defiant death snarl.

But Matt knew the second outlaw.

Like the Mexican, this man had been shot two or three times. He was Dan Finley, the Nebraska farm-boy who had accosted Matt at the McKenna ranch.

But now the kid's shaggy mane of yellow hair was gone, replaced by an obscene scarlet cap of blood and bone.

Festus stepped beside Matt. "Know either of them, Matthew?"

Matt nodded. "I've seen the Mexican before, but I can't recollect where." He nodded toward the second dead man. "The one over there goes by the name of Dan Finley and he rode for the McKennas."

Festus stepped to Finley and looked down at the blood-splashed body. "Hell, Matthew, by the look of him he's just an overgrown boy right off'n the farm."

His face bleak, Matt nodded. "That's all he was, Festus. Just a Nebraska farmboy who chose the wrong side and didn't much cotton to strangers."

A quick search of both men revealed that each was carrying two hundred dollars, presumably their meager share of the proceeds from the stage robbery. The snow was falling heavier and Matt and Festus led their mounts into the comparative shelter of the cottonwoods.

There was no doubt in Matt's mind about who had killed the two outlaws—Iron Hawk had begun to take his revenge on Abe McKenna and his riders.

Why the Cheyenne had followed these two, he could not guess. Then his memory tugged at him and he suddenly recalled where he might have seen the Mexican before. The vaquero could have been one of the McKenna men in the saloon the night Abe tried to scalp Iron Hawk.

Matt stepped over to the man's body. He stood deep in thought for a few moments, studying the vaquero's face, then nodded to himself. Although the features were ugly and distorted in death, it was the same man—he was certain of that.

Drunk as he was, Iron Hawk had seen the Mexican that night . . . and he had remembered him.

The outlaws had started a fire before they were killed, and a full coffeepot still sat on the cold coals. Nearby a frying pan held some slices of bacon.

Matt gathered up a handful of dry grass and some kindling from under the cottonwoods and within a couple of minutes had the fire going again.

He set the coffeepot to boiling, then unsaddled his bay and let the horse roll. Festus did the same for his mule; then the lawmen led their mounts to a sheltered spot under the trees and staked them out on some grass that was still free of snow.

Festus kneeled by the fire, shivered, and drew the collar of his ragged mackinaw closer around his neck. "Where do we go from here, Matthew?" he asked.

"First we have some coffee and a bite to eat," Matt answered. "Then we'll take the bodies back to the McKennas. It's fitting that Abbey and Abe should bury their own dead."

The deputy scratched his hairy jaw as he always did when he was thinking, then asked: "You gonna brace 'em about the stage robbery, Matthew? Arrest them maybe?"

"If I catch them red-handed with the loot," Matt

answered. "But somehow I think that isn't going to happen."

The marshal pushed the coffeepot deeper into the fire, then looked around him. He found what he was looking for: a tiny pile of drifting snow at the base of the tree close to where he sat. He grabbed a handful and held the snow to his eye, which was still discolored and swollen from his fight with Ephraim Stanley.

"Botherin' you some, Matthew?" Festus asked.

"Some," Matt admitted.

Festus clucked like a mother hen. "Snow's no good. What you need is a nice, raw beefsteak."

"You got one of them right handy, Festus?" Matt asked, an annoyed frown gathering between his eyebrows.

Festus shook his head. "Not right to hand, Matthew."

"Then I guess the snow will have to do, won't it?"

As if he hadn't heard, not in the least put out by Matt's frown, the deputy said: "Now, in a pinch, you can use a bear steak, and buffalo is pretty good. But, at least to my mind, nothin' works like a beefsteak to get rid of your partic'lar misery."

The snow in Matt's fist had melted and he dried his hand on his coat. "When I get back to Dodge I'll bear that in mind, Festus."

Festus looked pleased. "Glad to be of help, Matthew. Beefsteak, remember. Accept no substitute."

"Got it. Beefsteak," Matt said. He grabbed the

coffeepot, yelled and jerked his hand away. It was almost red-hot from the fire.

"Now, Matthew," Festus said, "for a right bad burn like you just got, a man can use snow. But I always figgered sweet butter works a sight better an' . . ."

chapter 9

Roman Pollock's Warning

After Matt and Festus ate the bacon and drank the last of the coffee, they rounded up the outlaws' horses and draped the two dead men facedown over their saddles.

"Be well after nightfall afore we fetch up to the McKenna place, Matthew," Festus said, glancing up at the darkening sky.

"I reckon," the marshal answered. "I guess if they're asleep we'll just have to wake them up and tell them they've got burying to do."

The snowfall had been brief and the night was clearing. The moon was busily elbowing aside the last clouds as it began its long climb into the heavens when Matt and Festus rode out of the cottonwoods, trailing the horses of the dead outlaws.

Two or three inches of snow lay on the plains, glittering in the moonlight, and the breath of the lawmen smoked in the frigid air. The night was very quiet, the only sound the faint crump of the horses' hooves on the snow and the creak of saddle leather.

Matt checked his watch. It was almost seven. He expected they'd reach the McKenna place on the Pawnee by midnight—if the spooked horses carrying the dead men did not give them too much trouble.

There was no trail, but the moon shining on the snow lit the way ahead and they made good time. It had just gone nine when Matt and Festus splashed across the shallows at Duck Creek north of Dodge and swung toward the Pawnee.

Two hours later they began to encounter McKenna cattle, or at least what Abbey and Abe claimed were McKenna cattle.

The Kansas plains were a land for the strong, and as Matt rode, he admitted to himself that Abbey McKenna was strong. Right now, the deaths of Andy Reid and Justin Herrick and the robbery of the Lee-Reynolds stage were raw scars. But they would heal with time. As Abbey prospered, as she was bound to do, she could point to her herds and her land and tell the law how she had found a wilderness and turned it into a paradise.

Who would then suspect such a woman of murder and robbery or lay any kind of blame at her door?

Matt nodded. Abbey had it all figured out and she seemed unstoppable. Unless . . .

Iron Hawk was hell-bent on revenge for the humiliation he'd received at the hands of Abe McKenna and perhaps he blamed the young man, in part at least, for contributing to his father's suicide.

Iron Hawk had been just another drunken, defeated Indian hanging around Dodge, but he'd proved by how easily he'd killed the McKenna riders that he was once again a Cheyenne Dog Soldier, a first-rate fighting man—and an unforgiving and dangerous enemy.

And there was the wire Matt had sent to Texas. He had as yet received no answer from Captain McNelly, but word might still come and maybe he would discover something he could use against the McKennas.

"Thin, Matthew, mighty thin."

"Huh?" Matt asked in surprise. Had Festus been reading his mind?

"I mean us tryin' to pin the stage robbery on the McKennas," Festus said. "I've just been studyin' on it some, and it came to me that all Abbey and Abe have to do is deny it and say these two"—he jerked a thumb over his shoulder at the dead man—"lit out an' done it on their own."

Matt nodded, relieved that his deputy had not added mind reading to his other talents. "I'm sure that will be the way of it, Festus. Maybe I can't prove anything as yet, but I want them to know that I've drawn the line and aim to see them both behind bars."

Festus whistled between his teeth. "Tall order, Matthew. An' Sam Noonan would take sich a thing hard."

"Sam will have to look out for himself, Festus. He's a friend, but I won't let friendship get in the way of my enforcing the law." Matt turned in the saddle and smiled at his deputy. "And if that sounds a bit pompous, it's not meant to be."

Festus shrugged. "I take your meanin', Matthew. But still, I sure do fear for Sam."

"Me too," Matt said, his unhappy eyes fixed on the moon-streaked distance ahead. And again, quietly: "Me too."

The McKenna cabin was dark when Matt and Festus stopped outside and dropped the reins of the outlaws' horses.

"Hello the cabin!" Festus hollered.

A few silent moments passed. Then a shadowy figure emerged from the corner of the cabin. "You two just sit there and make no fancy moves," a man's voice said. "Me, I got a heap o' faith in this here scattergun."

Matt's smile was thin. "Evening, Roman. Still don't sleep, huh?"

"Could say the same thing about you."

The gunman moved out of the shadows, the Greener in his hands rock steady and pointed right at the big marshal. "You know how it is, Matt," he said. "Never could cotton to sleeping at night, especially when the moon is full. I guess it's the lobo wolf in me."

Pollock jerked his chin toward the dead men. "Can't make 'em out from here. Who did you gun?"

Matt shook his head. "I didn't gun anybody. This

is Indian work, a Cheyenne Dog Soldier by the name of Iron Hawk."

Pollock smirked. "Hell, you telling me that drunken Injun took 'em both?"

"He isn't a drunk anymore, Roman," Matt said. "In fact I'd say he's downright sober. Plenty sober enough to lift their hair."

Pollock lowered the shotgun and stepped to Finley's body. He grunted and then moved to the dead Mexican.

"Hell, I ran these two off the place a couple of days ago," he said. "I can't abide to be under the same roof as a greaser. You know how it is, Matt."

"No, I don't know how it is," the marshal answered. He nodded to Finley. "What about him?"

Pollock shrugged. "It was only a matter of time before I plugged that damn farmboy. He was so dumb, he grated on my nerves."

The gunman took a step closer to Matt. "Where did you find them?"

Before the marshal could answer, a match flared as an oil lamp was lit in the cabin and Abbey Mc-Kenna called out: "Roman, who is out there?"

"Marshal Dillon," Pollock answered over his shoulder, his eyes on Matt. "He's brought in dead men."

Matt heard a gasp from inside the cabin, then the door opened, spilling a sudden rectangle of pale orange light on the snow. Abbey McKenna stepped into the yard, her brother close behind her.

Abbey stepped quickly to Matt, her eyes wide. "Marshal, whatever has happened?"

Matt touched the brim of his hat. "Two of your riders, ma'am. They've been killed and scalped."

"Scalped!" Abbey stiffened in horror. "By Indians?"

"One Indian," Matt said. "A Cheyenne Dog Soldier by the name of Iron Hawk."

Abe McKenna pushed his sister aside, his face white with shock. "Iron Hawk! You mean that stinking drunk Indian did this?"

Matt nodded. "Like I told Roman here, I'd say that recently he's become almighty sober."

Abe swallowed hard, his throat moving. "But why? I mean—"

"Because Iron Hawk remembered that the Mexican was in the saloon the night you had a two-dollar whore ride him like a horse," Matt interrupted, the sudden steel in his voice clear to everyone.

Abe looked stricken. "Where's the Army? It's time they rounded up that renegade and hung him."

"I reckon the Army has enough on its hands herding the Sioux and Cheyenne onto the reservations," Matt said. "The Army won't send the cavalry out after one man, and even if it did, a regiment of horse soldiers couldn't find him."

Abe opened his mouth to speak, but Abbey cut him off. "Marshal," she asked, "why did you bring those men back here?"

"They're your riders," Matt said. "I figured you'd want to bury your dead."

"But, Marshal," Abbey protested, her voice sweet, "Mr. Pollock ran those two off our place a few days ago." She smiled. "Practically speaking, you see, they don't work for me anymore."

Matt looked down at Abbey from the saddle. She wore an expensive dressing gown of blue watered silk, and the slippers of soft leather on her feet were brand-new. The marshal's eyes shifted to Abe. The suspenders of the man's black pants hung loose over his hips, and his worn and darned vest was faded to a pale pink. But the huge diamond ring on the little finger of his left hand sparkled in the moonlight whenever he moved and Matt guessed it had last been worn by the rich cattle buyer Justin Herrick.

It seemed to the marshal that the McKennas were indeed beginning to prosper mightily. But they were building their wealth on the bodies of dead men, and they no doubt thought there was no reason why they could not continue to do so in the future.

Abe's voice brought Matt back to the present. ". . . so take that carrion back with you to Dodge," the man was saying.

"They're your dead. You bury them," Matt said, his blue eyes suddenly hardening to a gunmetal gray, glinting in the darkness. "And one more thing, these two and five others were involved in the robbery of twenty-thousand dollars from the Lee-Reynolds stage earlier today. The shotgun guard was killed and so was a passenger, and another is probably dead by now. Jim Buck the driver was badly wounded."

Matt's eyes sought Abbey's in the gloom. "Where were your hands around ten o'clock this morning?"

"Marshal, is this another of your unfounded accusations?" Abe demanded. "Our hands were right here, with the cattle, where they belong."

Abbey put her hand on Matt's thigh. "Marshal, you seem to have a very low opinion of us. I can assure you, Finley and the Mexican acted alone." She smiled, her silk robe molding to her curves in the wind. "Like Abe says, all our hands were here this morning at ten o'clock. We have another herd coming up from Texas in a few days and half of our punchers are with the cattle."

The woman looked up at Matt and seductively touched her tongue to her full lips. "We're ranchers, not bank robbers."

"It was a stage that was robbed," Matt said evenly.

Abbey laughed. "See, I don't even know the difference." Her hand slid higher along Matt's thigh. "Now look at us. Do we really seem like outlaws to you?"

"Yes, you do," Matt said, deciding to lay it on the line, his voice harsh. "I believe you murdered Andy Reid for his land. I believe you murdered a man called Justin Herrick for the money he carried, and I believe you organized the robbery of the Lee-Reynolds stage and killed three people."

The big marshal's smile was bleak. "I can't prove any of these things, at least not yet, but now you know exactly where I stand. I plan to see all of you behind bars and some of you will hang."

Abbey jerked her hand away as though Matt's leg was suddenly red-hot. He saw it then: the icy flash of anger in the woman's eyes and the quick hardening of her mouth. Gone was the pretty young girl's face, replaced by the stony features of a ruthless killer.

"You believe all you like," Abbey snapped. "But you'll never prove a thing." The woman turned on her heel and stalked back into the cabin. Abe lingered for a few moments, opened his mouth to say something, then thought better of it and followed his sister into the cabin, slamming the door shut behind him.

The yard was once again plunged into darkness and Matt felt, rather than saw, Roman Pollock step beside him.

"You're pushing too hard, Matt," he said, his voice whisper soft but heavy with menace. "The McKennas hired me to stop folks like you pushing them, and they do right by me."

Pollock had made no move to level his shotgun, but Matt's hand dropped closer to this holstered Colt.

"You push much more, Matt," Pollock continued, his voice hissing like a snake, "and I'll start pushing back. On your best day you couldn't shuck a gun half as fast as me, and that's something you'd do well to remember."

Suddenly weary, Matt had had his fill of the McKennas and Pollock. He swung his horse around and then reined him in. "Bury your dead, Roman," he said.

Pollock nodded. "I'll see it done. But push me too hard, Matt, and there will be others to be buried."

As Festus and Matt rode from the cabin, the deputy turned to Matt, looked away, then gazed back at him again, one untidy eyebrow raised.

"All right, Festus, there's something stuck in your craw," Matt said. "Let me hear it."

"I was just thinkin' about what that Pollock feller said, about you being only half as fast as him. You don't believe it, do you?"

Matt rode in silence for a few moments, his head bowed. Then he said: "I've seen Roman Pollock draw on a man and he's as fast as chain lightning with a gun." The big marshal's face was set and grim. "No, Festus, I can't match that kind of speed. Not on my best day."

chapter 10

Miss Kitty Uncovers
a Secret

Like the yucca flowers out on the plains, Dodge was beginning to bloom. Gone were the brooding gray clouds that had hung, roof-high, over the town all winter. The days were growing warmer, the nights shorter, and red, white and blue bunting was once again draped over the doors of the saloons and stores along Front Street. Gamblers, pimps, whores and hundreds of rodent-eyed hangers-on were arriving daily by foot, horse, stage and the rattling Santa Fe steam cars.

Fresh from Denver, Luke Short, dapper and deadly but with a reputation for playing honest poker, had a table at the Alamo and the Masterson brothers were holding court at the Alhambra. Doc Holliday, always an unwelcome visitor as far as Matt was concerned, had blown in like a tumbleweed from Cheyenne, where, according to the *Dodge City Times*, he'd been involved in a cutting and had fled half a step ahead of the law.

Fast men and faster women could be seen everywhere. The sporting crowd, with their well-turned fingers, smooth talk and artistically waxed mustaches, shuffled and squared the decks at all of the town's seventeen saloons and six dance halls, and smiling whores, gaudy in scarlet, yellow or blue silk plumage, mingled with the men, painted hawk eyes hard, predatory and knowing.

The gang was all here and now all impatient Dodge could do was hold its breath and wait for the herds . . . and the hundreds of free-spending cowboys driving the cattle northward.

For the past two weeks Matt had been kept busy preserving law and order among this unruly throng.

A couple of gamblers at the Saratoga got into an argument over the dubious charms of a young whore who had just graduated off the line. Their talking done and no compromise reached, the pair drew derringers and cut loose. A total of nine shots was fired, with nary a hit on either side, but the combatants were again reloading their artillery when Matt banged the men's heads together and dragged them off to the calaboose.

A drunken bank clerk made the mistake of his life when he called Bat Masterson a liar. The gambler immediately cried foul and hauled iron. But a fight was avoided when the clerk promptly fainted. Matt let Masterson go after pointing out the error of his ways and giving him a stern warning about his future behavior.

Festus ran a goldbrick artist out of town after the man tried to outcon Mayor Kelley and then did the same thing to a hard-up foreigner who claimed to be the king of Russia. Then the deputy began to supervise—badly, the mayor would later accuse—a chattering Chinese work crew repairing the railroad water tank down by the stockyards.

There was still no reply to Matt's wire from Texas, and Abbey and Abe McKenna, driving a spanking new fringe-top surrey, were in town often but went out of their way to avoid the marshal.

"The latest McKenna herd arrived yess'tidy, Matthew," Festus said as he and Matt sat in the marshal's office over their morning coffee. "I hear tell eight hundred head."

"Anybody check the brands?" Matt asked, knowing that was unlikely.

But Festus' answer surprised him. The deputy sipped his coffee and laid the cup back on the desk. "Rafter V, all of them. Tom Cunningham was out by the Pawnee quail huntin' and he happened to look over the herd. Tom says what attracted him was the fact that they ain't longhorns, Matthew. They're Herefords, and nice ones too."

Matt sat forward on his seat. "Rafter V, huh? I guess I'll check that brand with the Cattleman's Association."

"Matthew, us deputies don't get paid enough for

all the stuff we do, but we do it anyhow," Festus
sighed. "I already checked on the brand. Them cows
belonged to an English outfit out of the Brazos country that goes by the name of the Victoria Feed and
Cattle Company. I guess they named themselves for
good ol' Queen Vic."

"You're one step ahead of me, Festus," Matt said.
"You learn anything else?"

"Only this—six McKenna riders headed south to
round up that herd. Only four of them made it back."

"Cunningham tell you that?"

The deputy shook his head. "Heard that my ownself. A couple of the McKenna riders were drinking
at the Long Branch and I overheard them talking.
Seems that the two who didn't make it were top
hands and the rest of them boys had a hard time of
it drivin' that many cattle."

Matt sat deep in thought until Festus asked: "What
you thinkin', Matthew?"

The big marshal didn't answer immediately, his
forehead furrowed. Then his expression cleared and
he said: "Festus, I'm willing to bet the McKennas
didn't buy that herd. It could be that the Herefords
were rustled and two of their riders were killed when
the shooting started."

"Or maybe they were caught an' hung," Festus
pointed out. "By times, them Limey ranchers are a
right hard bunch."

Frowning, Matt looked into his coffee cup. "What
I don't understand is why the McKennas would take

a chance like that, rustling another herd I mean. They must know all this robbing and killing could catch up with them sooner or later and they'll have some tough questions to answer."

Festus scratched his jaw. "Might be the case, but I reckon they think they'll get away with it, Matthew. As you said yourself, we can't prove that they did anything illegal. And it could stay that way. Maybe nobody else can prove it either."

"We could backtrack that herd along the trail, find out what happened," Matt suggested.

"We could." Festus nodded. "But with the cattle season startin' an' all, I don't think Mayor Kelley would cotton to the idea of leaving Dodge without peace officers while we go gallivantin' off down the Western Trail."

Matt thought that through, knowing Festus had the truth of it. Kelley would never agree. He'd say an investigation was up to the United States marshal. But the only way to get a marshal here—more likely an overworked and stretched-thin deputy—was to come up with some hard evidence against the McKennas.

A sense of defeat hanging heavy on him, Matt again faced the fact that he had no such evidence. And he was sure, if put to it, Abbey could produce a forged bill of sale for the Herefords. She was not the kind to slip up on a detail like that.

Matt drained his coffee cup and stepped across the office. He strapped on his gun and settled his hat on his head. "Festus, I'm going to take a turn around town," he said. "I guess you'd better get back to repairing the water tank."

Festus nodded, his eyes bleak. "Matthew, them Chinamen are a trial and a tribulation. I don't understand their heathen jabbering an' they don't speak a word of American. I'm plumb used up, an' that's a natural fact."

"Do the best you can, Festus." Matt smiled. "Mayor Kelley sets store by that tank."

Festus rose wearily to his feet. "I still say it should be up to the railroad to fix up the dang thing." The deputy stretched and yawned. "Well, I'll go find me a place in the shade and do my supervisin'. That is if'n them Celestials will let me be, always comin' up an' jabbering about this an' that. Wears a man out, fer sure."

After his deputy left, Matt stepped out onto the boardwalk. A creaking farm wagon rolled past and a solitary rider tied his horse to the hitching rail outside the Alamo and stepped inside.

The sober, industrious citizens of Dodge were awake and beginning their day, the men in somber black broadcloth and high celluloid collars, their womenfolk raising dainty parasols against the morning sun that was beginning to climb above the roofs of the saloons and stores along Front Street.

The shadier denizens of Dodge were still asleep and would remain so until sundown, when they'd suddenly emerge like a fluttering flock of bats, happy to have shunned the sunlight, at home in the darkness.

Across the street, the Long Branch had opened its doors and Matt decided it was time to talk to Kitty about Sam. Had she managed to talk her bartender out of marrying Abbey McKenna? That was unlikely, but now was as good a time as any to ask.

Matt walked across to the saloon and stepped inside. A swamper was mopping the floor and Kitty sat at a table, drinking coffee from a painted china cup, a newspaper spread out in front of her.

To the big marshal's surprise, Kitty was wearing a fashionable afternoon dress of blue taffeta and her hair was piled high with ribbons, her beautiful face already made up.

"Going somewhere?" Matt asked as he stepped to the table.

Kitty looked up and her eyes widened in surprise. "Matt, I didn't hear you come in."

The marshal smiled. "Next time I'll remember to wear my spurs."

Kitty rose to her feet, got up on tiptoe and kissed Matt on the cheek. "I'm not going anywhere, Matt. I'm expecting a guest for afternoon tea."

"Am I allowed to ask who it is?"

"Of course. It's Abbey McKenna."

Matt stiffened in shock. "Abbey McKenna! I don't understand. I mean, why?"

"Why? Because she's Sam's bride-to-be." Kitty smiled. "I want to find out if her intentions are honorable."

"Is that all?"

"No, it's not all." The smile fled from Kitty's lips.

"Matt, Sam gave me notice last night that he was quitting the Long Branch. He says he plans to spend all his time with his new bride."

Matt shook his head. "Then you couldn't talk him out of it."

"I didn't try. Sam is crazy about that girl. She's his sole topic of conversation, all he thinks about. I couldn't talk him out of marrying her if I tried."

Kitty's fingers touched Matt lightly on the chest. It was a very feminine gesture and one she used often, a slender bridge that not only linked their bodies but their two very different worlds. "Matt, I'm really worried," she said, her lovely eyes clouded. "Sam told me he plans to withdraw all his money from the bank. He says he wants to box it up and give it to Abbey as a wedding present."

"Money?" Matt asked. "I didn't know Sam had money. How does a bartender save money?"

"When it comes to his work, Sam is as honest as the day is long, but he's always been careful about what he spends," Kitty said. "Remember how Festus used to tease him about being such a tightwad?"

Matt nodded. "Festus says he's so tight he never throws him a free drink and he claims Sam's still got four cents out of every nickel he ever made."

"Festus could be right," Kitty said. "Over the years, Sam invested his money wisely, in railroad and shipping company stock mostly. A couple of years ago, when I was making improvements to the Long Branch, he offered me a loan. He told me then that he had over twenty thousand dollars in the bank, and I'm sure his balance has grown since then."

Kitty dropped her hand from Matt's chest, her worried eyes showing her concern. "Matt, after what happened to Andy Reid, you don't really think Sam's life could be in danger, do you?"

The marshal nodded. "Kitty, I'm sure of it."

"What can I do?"

"Have tea with Abbey McKenna. Sound her out. I don't know what she might tell you, but maybe she'll let something slip . . . anything."

"I'll try," Kitty said. Her face took on a mock-serious look. "Sometimes, when women get to talking over tea and cakes, deep, dark secrets are revealed."

Matt didn't smile in return. "Kitty," he said, "I have a feeling Abbey McKenna has plenty of those."

After Matt left the Long Branch, he angled across the street to Floyd Bodkin's bank. When he stepped inside, a clerk directed him to Bodkin's office and Matt rapped on the door.

"Come in," the banker said.

Matt stepped inside and Bodkin looked up and smiled. "Good morning, Marshal. What can I do for you?"

Bodkin waved Matt into a chair and the big lawman sat. "Floyd, I've got a question to ask."

The banker beamed a wide, professional smile. "Ask away, ask away."

"Did Andy Reid have an account at your bank?"

"Indeed he did, Marshal. He deposited gold, dust and nuggets, and had it converted into cash."

"How much was the deposit worth?"

Bodkin shrugged. "I can't remember the exact amount without consulting my ledgers, but I'd say it was close to thirty thousand dollars."

"Is the money still on deposit?"

Bodkin shook his sleek head. "Oh dear me, no. Mr. Reid withdrew every penny about a week before he died."

"Did Andy sign anything when he made the withdrawal, a piece of paper maybe?"

"Yes, he did. He signed a paper authorizing the withdrawal of his money. He didn't sign of course. He just made his mark. Andy couldn't write."

"Did he tell you he was going east to live with his sister?"

The banker laughed. "Marshal, he never mentioned a sister. Andy said he was going to get married and aimed to travel east with his bride. He planned to buy a home. In Boston, I believe."

"Did he say who he was going to marry?"

"No. All he'd tell me was that he'd just met a beautiful girl who made him feel like a youngster again. He was very excited and, if I may be allowed to say so, head over heels in love. At the time I thought that very strange in a man of his mature years."

Matt shrugged. "Love can change a man so you hardly recognize him as the same person."

"Indeed."

Bodkin settled clasped hands over his paunch and twiddled his thumbs. "Now, Marshal, is there anything else?"

Matt shook his head. "No, I guess you summed it all up for me." He rose to his feet. "Thanks for your help, Floyd."

The banker waved a hand. "Anytime, Marshal, just anytime."

Matt left the bank and walked along the boardwalk to his office, his mind working.

He had thought that Andy Reid would have run the McKennas off his property. He'd been wrong. Instead, old Andy had fallen deeply in love with Abbey and promised her marriage. The girl had no doubt convinced the old prospector to withdraw his money from the bank, telling him they needed it to make a fresh start back east as a married couple. Andy, too blindly in love to spot the danger, had eagerly agreed—and it had cost him his life.

Something similar had happened to Justin Herrick, though Matt suspected that lust rather than love had been involved. The result had been the same—a dead man with two bullets in his chest.

How to prove any of this?

As Matt stepped into his office, he admitted to himself that he had no idea.

Two hours later the marshal glanced out the office window and saw Abbey McKenna draw her surrey up outside the Long Branch.

Men jumped from the boardwalk and eager hands

helped the girl down from the carriage to the street. Gone was the patched and faded dress she'd worn when she first arrived in Dodge. Now she was decked out in an expensive emerald green dress of watered silk, the bustle fashionably large, a little boat-shaped hat of the same color on top of her piled-up hair. Emeralds glittered on the lobes of her well-shaped ears and a large ruby ring adorned the wedding finger of her left hand. The girl was breathtakingly beautiful, Matt thought, if you could get past the tightness of her small mouth and the hard light that glinted so often in her blue eyes.

But there was no suggestion of hardness in the dazzling smile Abbey flashed to the men who had helped her, as she played the role of a fashionable, sophisticated Texas belle to the hilt. A couple of bowing, eager-eyed men held open the doors of the Long Branch and the girl, head held high and proud, stepped inside.

Matt was surprised Abbey had so readily accepted Kitty's invitation. But then, Kitty Russell was a wealthy woman who had a great deal of influence in Dodge. Perhaps Abbey, who did little without an ulterior motive, felt it would be to her advantage to cultivate Kitty's friendship.

The girl left two hours later and Matt hurried over to the Long Branch. Once inside, Kitty motioned him to a secluded table and they both sat. "Drink, Matt?" Kitty asked.

The marshal shook his head. "No, thanks. Tell me what happened, Kitty."

"Why, we had tea and cakes."

Matt was disappointed and it showed. "That was it? That was all? You just had tea and cakes?"

"And conversation," Kitty said.

Reining in his eagerness, Matt took a deep breath and asked: "What did you talk about?"

"Oh, this and that."

The big marshal's patience snapped. "Kitty, I swear, if you don't tell—"

"I love to tease you, Marshal Dillon, because you're just so . . . teasable," Kitty laughed, laying her slender white hand on Matt's huge paw. The laughter slowly fled from her face to be replaced by a look of concern. "In fact, I learned a great deal about Miss Abbey McKenna."

Matt nodded, his eyes hard. "Let me hear it."

"Well, Abbey and Abe were orphaned at a very early age after their parents were taken by the cholera. After that, the kids were separated and sent to one foster home after another. Abbey says she was treated like a slave most of the time, overworked, beaten and underfed. Then, as she got older and began to grow into a woman's shape, she was used and abused by the men in the families, once by a father and six sons who used to take her in turns."

"And then?" the marshal asked.

Kitty's eyes searched Matt's and he knew she was looking for a suggestion of sympathy. There was none. Whatever terrible things had happened to Abbey McKenna in the past, she was a killer now, and that was what concerned him.

"And then," Kitty continued, "one day she stole some money and ran away. She later met up with Abe again in Abilene. They tried making it as ranchers, but it didn't work out."

"So how did they get their herd?"

"Abbey says she was once taken in by an old lady who was kind to her. But the woman had to let her go because she was leaving for Dallas to live with her brother. According to Abbey, the old lady died and left her money in her will, enough to buy a herd and pay for the hands to drive it north. And she says there was some cash left over to pay for the Herefords."

Matt shook his head. "All that sounds mighty thin to me. Maybe a shade too convenient. Besides, Roman Pollock isn't a puncher. He's a professional gunman and the price of his kind comes high."

Kitty shrugged. "I couldn't tell what was fact and what was not, Matt. Abbey conducts herself very well. She's very poised, very smooth."

"Did she say what she plans to do in Kansas?"

"In Kansas? Nothing. Abbey says that over the years she's grown to hate the West, that all her stored-up memories are too painful to go on living here. She says she plans to move east just as soon as she marries Sam and sells her herds. Abbey wants to live in a big city and be a fine lady with her own home and servants and carriages."

Matt's face was set and hard. "With the money she got from Andy Reid, Justin Herrick and the Lee-Reynolds stage robbery, she'll be able to do just that.

Add Sam's twenty thousand and she'll live high on the hog. At least for a while. Then she'll have to rob and cheat and kill again."

Kitty's eyes were guarded. "Matt, I've spoken to Abbey and she comes across like a really sweet person, despite the hard life she's had. Is there any chance you could be mistaken about her?"

The big marshal shook his head. "None, Kitty." He stood and looked down at the woman. "When is the wedding day?"

"Right after Abbey sells her herds, whenever that happens. Why?"

"Because the day Abbey McKenna becomes Mrs. Noonan is the day Sam's life isn't worth a plug nickel."

chapter 11

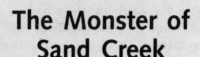

The Monster of
Sand Creek

The morning after his talk with Kitty, Matt was shaken out of sleep by Festus.

The marshal opened his eyes and saw his deputy's hairy, concerned face hovering over him. "Matthew, wake up!"

"I'm awake, Festus. How could a man be still be asleep with you shaking the life out of him?" Matt sat up and swung his legs off his cot. "What's the trouble?"

"Matthew, Abe McKenna and Roman Pollock are over to the Alhambra. They're rounding up a posse to go out after Iron Hawk. I reckon they've already signed up ten, twelve riders."

Matt yawned and stretched. "What time is it?"

"Almost ten." Festus' eyes were both accusing and puzzled. "You slept late."

The big marshal smiled and nodded. "Had some

trouble at the Alamo going on midnight. Must have been two in the morning before I got it all sorted out."

"Gun trouble?"

"No. The worst kind—woman trouble."

Festus' left eyebrow crawled up his forehead. "You sure don't seem too concerned about this here posse business, Matthew."

Matt shrugged. "They won't find him. Not with the kind of posse McKenna will put together at the Alhambra. All those drunks will do is ride in circles on the plains for a couple of hours, then come back when the whiskey jugs run dry or the sun gets too hot."

His words dropping like rocks into an iron bucket, Festus said: "Gus Fradette is scouting for them."

Matt jumped to his feet. "Fradette? Are you sure?"

Festus nodded. "Sure, I'm sure. He's drinkin' in the saloon with the rest of them, wearin' that buffalo coat o' his an' smellin' like he camped out in the stock pens."

Matt stepped to the stove, added some wood and set the coffeepot on top to heat.

Gus Fradette was bad news. The man was a hulking giant, over seven feet tall, and he carried a lot of solid meat on his arms and shoulders. He was said to be crazy in the head, but Matt considered him crazy like a fox or, more appropriately, a wolf.

Fradette had been with Chivington at Sand Creek in sixty-four, when the mad colonel's Third Colorado Volunteer Cavalry attacked a sleeping Cheyenne village and massacred three hundred people, most of them women, children and old men.

Along with the rest of Chivington's trash, recruited from the scum of the Colorado mining camps, Fradette had killed and raped, one of his victims a dying woman he had just sabered. He made his reputation as a scout and Indian fighter when he rode back into Fort Lyon with a child's head stuck on the point of his sword and told a crowd of drunken admirers: "We killed and scalped 'em all, big an' little. Nits make lice."

Afterward, Fradette hunted buffalo on the plains and had once been a skinner for Bat Masterson. But the fastidious Masterson finally became tired of the man's stench and filthy habits and ran him out of camp.

Fradette had been ready to draw down on Bat, but when he looked into Masterson's eyes and saw only cold blue ice, he thought better of it, pulled in his horns, silenced his rattles and rode meekly away.

Since then, Fradette had served as an Army scout from time to time and had carried out several contract killings. His proud boast was that he would cut any man, woman or child in half with a shotgun for fifty dollars.

Matt, who'd had run-ins with the man before, hated Fradette's guts—and the feeling was mutual.

The big marshal poured himself coffee. It was only lukewarm, but it tasted good, black and bitter, the way he liked it.

He admitted to himself that he was worried.

Without Fradette, Abe McKenna's posse was just drunken rabble who would head for the hills as soon as the first shot was fired.

But Fradette's presence changed everything.

The man was a born killer and no woman was safe from him, especially when he was drunk, whiskey turning him mean and violent and all too ready to kill or rape.

With a posse backing him up, Fradette would consider the settlers' wives, living out on the plains in isolated cabins, fair game. A coward at heart, he'd only act when he knew others would back his play, and McKenna's drunken rabble would be ideal for the task.

Festus' voice cut through Matt's thoughts. "Y'know, Matthew," he said, "one day I think I'm gonna put a bullet in ol' Gus, for everybody's sake."

Matt nodded, his face stiff and hard. "If I don't beat you to it."

The marshal stood in thought for a few more moments, then made up his mind. He drained the last of his coffee, dressed hurriedly and buckled on his gun belt.

"Festus," Matt said, "take care of things in Dodge. I may be gone most of the day."

"What do you have in mind, Matthew?"

"I don't want Fradette and the rest of that riffraff loose on the plains. I'm going with them."

"You step right careful, Matthew," Festus warned. "Ol' Gus is a back-shooter, and if I'm readin' his stamp right, so is Abe McKenna."

Matt nodded. "I don't plan to turn my back on either of them."

The big marshal settled his hat on his head, lifted his Winchester from the rack and filled his pocket with .44.40 shells.

He stepped out of the office, walked to the livery stable and saddled Buck, sliding his rifle into the boot.

Matt rode to the Alhambra and swung out of the saddle at the hitching rail. The sun was already driving away the shadows from between the buildings, and as it did to an aging whore, the harsh morning light was revealing Dodge's wrinkles.

Sticky beads of rosin were being forced from the warped, sun-bleached pine boards of the saloons, and the recent snow, long since melted, had done little to erase the dust that covered everything. The bunting that had been hung to welcome the returning cowboys drooped forlornly in the hot spring air like saggy drawers on a washline, and the flies were back, buzzing fat, ugly and bloated from the stock pens by the tracks.

None of this did Matt notice, and if he had noticed, he wouldn't have cared. Warts and all, Dodge was his home—and all things are beautiful if you love them enough.

His spurs chiming in the morning silence, the tall marshal walked into the Alhambra, as free striding and graceful as a cougar. A dozen men were lined up at the bar, including Gus Fradette, and standing beside the scout were Abe McKenna and Roman Pollock.

The other men Matt knew by sight. All of them were troublemakers of one kind or another, a work-shy bunch with shrewd and calculating eyes, as sly and opportunistic as outhouse rats. These men were drifters who arrived each spring just ahead of the herds. They preyed on the cowboys, taking advantage of the Texans' openhanded generosity—but they were always ready with club or knife when begging failed and a dark alley lay close.

A smile touched Matt's lips. And Abe McKenna and Roman Pollock thought they could hunt down a Cheyenne Dog Soldier with this sorry bunch! It was Pollock who saw Matt first.

His expression suddenly wary, he laid his beer down on the bar and asked: "You joining our posse, Matt?"

The marshal nodded. "Sure am, Roman. I don't want this drunken trash out on the plains without me being there to rein them in."

A lanky man in a threadbare gray suit and plug hat stepped away from the bar, his eyes ugly. "Here, who you calling trash?" he asked, his hand close to the Remington stuck into his waistband.

"You," Matt said pleasantly, "and the rest of this scum."

The man turned and spat, then faced Matt again. "You're wearing a gun. You shoot as slick as you talk?"

"Yes, he does, Hank," Pollock said quickly, quietly. "And if you draw on him, he'll kill you for sure."

Matt stood relaxed, smiling slightly, his right thumb tucked into his gun belt close to his Colt, his confidence loudly eloquent, a man primed and ready for whatever came next.

The man called Hank looked into the marshal's suddenly ice-cold eyes and didn't like what he saw. He'd been tense, ready to make his play and impress the others around him, but now Pollock had called it and he realized with terrifying certainty that if he went for his gun he could die. Right now. Coughing up his lungs on the saloon floor.

Matt saw the man's inward struggle and knew he didn't have the sand for it.

Finally Hank said: "Aw, the hell with it. I was only funnin', Roman." He stepped back to the bar. "But city marshal or no, he don't have the right to call a man trash and a low person."

Pollock's smile was thin and fleeting, his eyes on Matt. "Hank, he's got the right to call you anything he damn well pleases and there ain't a damn thing you can do about it." The gunman turned on the man, his blazing contempt obvious. "Now is there?"

Hank lowered his head, saying nothing, his face flushed, all at once finding something of intense interest at the bottom of his whiskey glass.

It was Abe McKenna who tossed words into the echoing silence.

"Now see here, Marshal," the man said, his handsome face purple with anger, "that renegade Injun out there killed two of my hands and you said yourself that he aims to come after me. I plan to find him and hang him."

Matt laughed. "With this bunch?" He nodded toward Fradette. "And that animal?"

So far the massive scout had said nothing and watched in silence as Hank ate crow. Now he pushed off from the bar, huge, hairy hands hanging loose at his sides. The man's brown hair hung in filthy tangles over his shoulders and an unkempt beard spread over his chest. The stench of him filled the room, feral and cloying.

"Dillon," he said, "one day very soon I'm going to nail your hide to the barn door."

Matt's expression—a thin smile still playing around his mouth—didn't change. "There's no time like the present, Fradette."

Fire ignited in Fradette's black eyes. "Damn you, I can't match your draw, but unbuckle that gun an' I'll show you something."

"Any way you want it, Fradette," Matt said, his fingers moving to the buckle of his gun belt.

Roman Pollock stepped between them. "No!" He turned to Fradette. "You're being paid to find that damn redskin and I don't want you all used up before we even leave Dodge."

Matt's laugh was without humor. "Roman, Fradette won't have to look far to find Iron Hawk. Believe me, the Cheyenne will find him." He jutted his chin toward the scout. "Show the boys your tobacco pouch, Fradette. Seems to me you've always been right proud of it."

The man hesitated, then snarled: "Damn right I'm proud of it." He reached into a pocket of his filthy buffalo coat and came up with a wrinkled brown sack tied with a rawhide string.

"Tell the boys what it is, Fradette," Matt said. The humor had gone from his face and his eyes were cold, hard and accusing.

The man grinned and held the sack above his head where everybody could see. "Boys, I made this here tobacco pouch from a Cheyenne squaw's teat I cut off'n her at Sand Creek. We showed them Cheyenne a thing or two that day, didn't we, boys?"

A few halfhearted cheers rang out from the men lining the bar, but Pollock's face was like stone and McKenna's gaze, fascinated yet horrified, was fixed on the pouch.

"Now you get my drift, Roman," Matt said. "Iron Hawk may have been a drunk, but plenty of times he saw Fradette show that pouch around the saloons and heard him boast about the children and women he'd killed at Sand Creek." The big marshal turned on Fradette, a smoldering rage building in him. "If he sees you out on the plains, Fradette, Iron Hawk will remember, and trust me, he'll come after you. He knows your name, Fradette. He knows your name."

The scout stared at Matt for a long moment, his face slowly draining of color. Then, aware that Pollock and the rest were watching, he retreated into bluster. "Let that Injun come, Dillon. I'll tack his damn hide to the barn door alongside your'n."

Matt nodded. "Could be, Fradette. But remember this. That's a Cheyenne Dog Soldier out there, maybe the last of them. You'll find him a lot harder to kill than women and children."

Mad clean through, the scout opened his mouth to speak, but Pollock cut him off. "Are we going to stand here jawing all day or are we gonna hunt down and hang that Injun?" He turned to the men at the bar. "What do you say, boys?"

A cheer went up from the posse and Abe McKenna waved a hand toward the saloon door and yelled: "Let's ride!"

Led by McKenna and Fradette, a dozen men brushed past Matt, leaving Pollock alone. "You still coming with us, Matt?" he asked.

The marshal nodded. "Like I said, Roman, I can't let Fradette and the rest of that rabble loose on the plains. There are helpless women and children out there."

Pollock studied Matt in silence for a few moments, then grinned. "Mount up, Matt. It's your funeral."

chapter 12

A Battle on the Plains

Fradette had sold McKenna on the notion that Iron Hawk could still be hanging around White Woman Creek, where he'd killed his punchers, so the posse rode east, Matt following close behind them.

The morning was cool with the crispness of spring, but the day would rapidly get hotter as the sun rose higher. A few thin clouds smeared the sky here and there, as though God had walked across a pale blue carpet with snow on his boots. The birds were out and jackrabbits bounded away from the horsemen, zigzagging around the blooming yucca. The plains stretched away on all sides, flat and empty, the always wind restlessly stirring the tall bluestem and Indian grass.

Matt rode through a broad patch of bright yellow prairie dandelions and looked ahead of him at the ragtag bunch of posse men. They were talking loud and boasting louder, passing a jug back and forth, half of them already drunk. What had motivated Mc-Kenna and Pollock to recruit this bunch?

In McKenna's case, it was fear. The man had been genuinely terrified the night Matt had ridden into his ranch with the dead punchers. And the marshal's warning that Iron Hawk would seek revenge was motive enough for McKenna to hunt down the Chey-enne and kill him.

Pollock had no such fear. His motivation was simple—McKenna paid him gun wages, and so long as the money kept coming, he would do what he was told. The grim, hard-bitten gunman had spent time on the plains and he must know that trying to hunt down a lone Indian in that vastness was an impossible task.

Fradette probably realized the same thing, but like Pollock he was being paid wages to take a leisurely ride in the sun and that was something he wouldn't kick against.

As for the rest, a few dollars and free whiskey were all the motivation they needed—that and the possibility that they might get the chance to string up an Indian from a cottonwood.

Matt shook his head and smiled. God help them if they ever caught up with Iron Hawk. This posse would discover that they'd grabbed a hundred differ-ent kinds of Hell by the tail.

It was still well shy of noon when they fetched up

to the White Woman. Rifles and a few shotguns slid from their boots and the posse spread out and approached the bend of the creek at a lope.

The wind stirred the branches of the cottonwoods and teased the tall grass into movement, but the creek itself was silent and deserted.

"He's lit out," Fradette said, stating what was obvious to everyone.

"Question is, which way was he headed?" McKenna asked.

Fradette shrugged. "Pick a direction. One's as likely as another."

McKenna was frustrated and it showed in the way his head swiveled on his shoulders, looking around him. "Damn it, if that Injun ain't here, he could be anywhere," he said.

"Calling it quits, Abe?" Pollock asked, his eyes malicious. "I told you it's better to let him come to us. Then I can deal with him."

McKenna ignored the gunman. "Fradette," he said, "at least take a damn guess."

The scout sat his saddle in silence for a few moments, then said: "We'll head north toward the Saw Log."

Pollock's eyes were ugly. "Why north, Fradette? Or don't you know?"

"After the Injun killed two white men, he'd reckon on getting as far away from the soldiers at Fort Dodge as possible," Fradette answered. "He'd head north. At least I think maybe he would."

" 'At least I think maybe he would'," Pollock spat,

mimicking the scout's voice. The gunman turned to McKenna. "Call this off, Abe. We're wasting our time."

McKenna shook his head. "We ride north, like Fradette says. I want that Indian dead."

The sun was hot, and Matt felt sweat trickle down his back under his shirt. He had said nothing, his only concern to herd this rabble back to Dodge. Their arguments were none of his business.

"Well, you can count me out."

All eyes turned to the man who had spoken, a thin towhead wearing a canvas duster and battered black hat. "This saddle is gallin' my hide," the man said. "I didn't plan on riding this far an' then even further."

There were a few sullen murmurs of agreement, but Pollock cut them off. "You'll stick," the gunman snapped, suddenly glad to find a target for his growing irritation. "If the rest of us are riding north, you will too."

"Damned if I will," the towhead said, anger flaring red on his cheeks.

Pollock's smile was thin and mean. "You'll head north, either sitting your saddle or hanging head down across it. Don't make no never mind to me."

The towhead reached carefully into the pocket of his duster and threw a few dollar bills on the ground. "Take back your damn money, Pollock. I told you, I'm through."

The gunman's expression did not change. "Clear your coat away from your gun," he said. "I plan on giving you an even break."

For a few moments the towhead sat motionless; then he slowly placed both hands on the saddle horn. "If I reach for my gun, you'll kill me," he said, the words coming hard, strangling in his throat.

"Damn right I will," Pollock said, thin lips peeled away from his teeth, his eagerness to smash and destroy a raw, ugly thing. "Now back down or make your play."

The towhead dropped his eyes. "I'll ride," he said.

Pollock turned to the rest of them. "Anybody else want to quit?"

There was no answer. "Right," the gunman said. "We ride north."

Now that the whiskey jug was empty and the day was growing hotter, the mood of the posse turned surly. To a man, they were afraid of Roman Pollock—and this manhunt wasn't turning out to be as much fun as they'd expected it to be.

Matt smiled to himself. These men were accustomed to slinking around Dodge under cover of darkness like gray ghosts. The bright light of day and the vast openness of the plains was making them uncomfortable, and like rats, they sought a hole into which they could bolt until the coming of night. They didn't know it then, but much worse lay in store for them—and a few would never see Dodge again.

McKenna and Fradette rode in the lead. Pollock, his face a study in barely suppressed rage, fell behind.

McKenna eagerly scanned the country ahead of him, and it seemed to Matt that the threat of Iron

Hawk had affected the man even worse than he'd first thought. McKenna was driven by fear. It was a dark force pent up inside him, and where there is fear, there is hate. McKenna wanted Iron Hawk dead as a release from fear, but it was his hate of the Cheyenne that drove him onward.

The posse rode through a shallow saddleback between two low rises topped by buffalo grass, then jumped their horses over a narrow, winding stream that ran off the Saw Log.

Shadows cast by clouds passing in front of the sun were chasing one another across the flat grassland as the creek came in sight. A few cottonwoods grew on both banks and a thicker stand mixed with willow obscured a bend where it made a sharp turn to the west.

Fradette reined up about a hundred yards from the creek and the others followed his lead.

"See anything?" McKenna asked, his eyes eager. "Fradette, did you see something?"

Fradette shook his head. "Seems all quiet to me."

Pollock kneed his horse alongside McKenna. "The Injun ain't here, Abe, and that means he could be anywhere. I've had enough. Let's head back to Dodge and get us a drink."

Doubt showed on McKenna's face. "Roman, we have to find him." Then, more to himself than anyone else: "Where the hell is that Indian?"

Fradette turned in the saddle to face McKenna. "I'll go check out the creek anyhow. Then we should turn back like Pollock says."

McKenna nodded silently and his scout kicked his horse forward. Matt watched Fradette as the man crossed the grass toward the stand of cottonwood and willow. Like Pollock, he doubted that Iron Hawk was there. It was too obvious a hiding place.

But in that, he was wrong.

When Fradette was about ten yards away, the Cheyenne suddenly walked his horse out from among the cottonwoods, the butt of his Winchester resting on his right thigh, his eyes fixed on the bearded scout.

Gone were his filthy buckskins and in their place Iron Hawk wore a simple breechcloth of tanned deerskin. His hair, washed with a natural soap of yucca leaf sap, hung glossy and black over his back and shoulders. He had used plant and earth dyes to paint the top half of his face black, and white lightning streaks ran down his chest. Around his waist the Cheyenne wore the red Dog Soldier's sash and a holstered Colt taken from one of the McKenna punchers.

Fradette yelled something and brought his rifle up fast. But Iron Hawk fired first, using his Winchester like a pistol, holding it straight out in front of him.

Fradette's horse went down and the man rolled away from the kicking animal, losing his grip on his rifle. He sprang to his feet, saw Iron Hawk riding at a walk toward him and panicked.

His face twisted in fear, throwing off his cumbersome buffalo coat, Fradette dashed toward Matt and the others.

To the marshal, it seemed that the next few moments lasted an eternity. Fradette ran, screaming to the posse for help. But Pollock and the rest sat their horses, as though turned into statues of stone by the scene unfolding in front of them.

Iron Hawk fired again and Fradette's right knee exploded in a scarlet burst of blood and bone. The man stumbled, then tried to rise to his feet. The Cheyenne's third bullet smashed into the scout's other knee and Fradette shrieked and fell heavily on his belly.

As Iron Hawk walked his horse toward him, Fradette lifted his head, his right arm extended in submission, and Matt heard him beg hoarsely for mercy, just as the women at Sand Creek must have done. But there was no mercy in Iron Hawk. His fourth bullet crashed into Fradette's open mouth, blowing out the back of the scout's head, a sudden scarlet halo of blood, skull and brain fanning around him.

Like a man rousing himself from a dream, Pollock yelled: "Get that damn Indian!"

The posse hung back, what they had just seen scaring them into immobility.

"Get him!" Pollock yelled again. He set spurs to his horse and charged at Iron Hawk, roaring Colts flaring, bucking in his hands.

The posse reluctantly followed and rifles and shotguns crashed as they fired.

Iron Hawk gave ground, swung his horse toward the creek and faded back into the trees.

Roman Pollock was closing on the Cheyenne's position fast. The gunman was a dozen yards from the cottonwoods, riding at a gallop, when a shot crashed from the underbrush. Pollock's horse cartwheeled, throwing the gunman over its head. Pollock fell hard in a tangle of arms and legs, and he lay on the ground stunned.

McKenna and the others galloped past the fallen gunman as Iron Hawk opened up from the cottonwoods, rapidly blasting shot after shot from his Winchester.

A rider went down, then a second. The rest pulled up their horses, wheeling into one another in their haste to get away from what had all at once become a killing ground.

McKenna yanked on the reins and his horse reared, then swung to its right. The man galloped back toward Matt, his face a wild mix of fear and rage. "Damn you, Dillon, help us!" he yelled, reining up in front of the marshal.

Matt shook his head. "This isn't my fight, McKenna," he said. "It's yours."

The man cursed and Matt added quietly, "You've got yourself in a helluva fix, haven't you?"

McKenna's riders were milling around him, and Pollock had gotten to his feet. The gunman was staggering, a Colt in one hand as he unsteadily cast about searching for the other.

The *Yip! Yip! Yip!* of the Cheyenne war cry rang out from the trees. Iron Hawk crashed through the underbrush at a run, his long-legged zebra dun covering the ground fast. He cranked his Winchester from the shoulder, slamming shots into the horsemen surrounding McKenna. A rider threw up his arms and tumbled out of the saddle. Next to McKenna, the towhead who had braced Pollock was hit in the right temple. A mess of blood and brain splattered across McKenna's face and the man shrieked in fear and horror. His fingers went to his cheek and came away bright red. McKenna stared at the gore on his hand, his eyes wide, shocked and unbelieving. The man turned terrified eyes to Matt, then frantically swung his horse away and spurred the animal into a run, fleeing to the south.

Pollock was firing at the Cheyenne, both his guns blazing. Matt saw Iron Hawk jerk as he was hit. Then the Indian was gone, galloping fast across the flat, rifle raised over his head, the *Yip! Yip! Yip!* of his war cry fading into the distance.

Matt rode forward at a walk toward the creek. Pollock looked up at him and Matt saw that the man was in a frustrated, killing rage.

"Where the hell is McKenna?" he demanded.

"Gone," Matt answered. "He headed south."

Pollock swore and looked around him. "How many did we lose?"

"Five," Matt answered. "And another burned across the shoulder."

Pollock's eyes were blazing. "I didn't see you in the fight."

Matt shrugged. "Like I told McKenna, it wasn't my war."

Behind Matt, what was left of the posse sat their horses, in a state of numb shock, faces ashen, unable to comprehend what had happened to them. As Gus Fradette had learned the hard way, they had now come to fully understand the difference between frightened women and children and an armed and ready Cheyenne Dog Soldier.

The ragtag posse, thinking it was going to be easy, had tangled with one of the greatest fighting men the world has ever seen—and it had cost them dearly.

Pollock stepped to his dead horse, shook his head and swore, then turned and looked around him. His eyes fastened on a tall man in a threadbare gambler's frockcoat and stovepipe hat sitting a fine-looking American roan.

"You," Pollock snapped, "get off that horse. Find yourself another one."

His nerves frayed, the man looked down at Pollock and snarled: "The hell I will. I stole this hoss for my ownself nigh on two year ago. Go steal one of your own."

The gunman smiled, a tight, humorless grimace. He stepped quickly to the roan, reached up and, with surprising strength, grabbed the man by the front of his coat and threw him out of the saddle.

The gambler landed flat on his back, lay there dazed for a few moments, then sprang to his feet. His flaring anger overcoming his good judgment, he yelled: "Damn you to hell, Pollock!" And he went for his gun.

Pollock had to make a half turn, but his draw was lightning fast. Both his Colts roared before the gambler had even cleared leather, two bullets thudding into the center of the man's chest only an inch apart.

The gambler's eyes were filled with horror and disbelief, unable to comprehend the fact of his own dying. He stretched up on tiptoe, teetered for a few moments, then crashed his length on the ground.

Pollock quickly shucked the empty shells out of his guns, reloaded, then spun the Colts back into the holsters. He turned and looked at Matt. "He should have given me the damn horse when I told him to," he said. "I can't abide incivility and a lack of generosity in a man."

Matt saw something in Pollock's eyes that disturbed him, that same, unholy black fire that he'd noticed earlier, but now it was brighter, glowing unnaturally.

In that instant the marshal realized that the disastrous battle with Iron Hawk had pushed Roman Pollock over the line between sanity and madness. And now the gunman would be more dangerous and unpredictable than ever before.

chapter 13

Day of the Bounty Hunter

"**A**nd you didn't arrest him, Matthew?"

"For what, Festus? I was out of my jurisdiction and besides, the other man drew down on Pollock first. He didn't give him much choice."

Festus nodded. "That feller ol' Roman killed was no bargain. His name was Newt Ransom and he'd gunned more than his share his ownself. It was him that shot Five Ace Johnny Kileen over to Topeka a year or two ago, an' Johnny was far from bein' a pilgrim."

The deputy's eyes searched Matt's plate and lighted on a lone strip of bacon. "You plannin' on eating that, Matthew?"

The big marshal shook his head and Festus deftly speared the bacon with his fork. "Well, there's one good thing," he said, talking around the food in his mouth. "At least ol' Iron Hawk got rid of Gus Fradette. The world will be a better place now his shadow's gone from it."

The door of the Sideboard Restaurant swung open and an elderly cavalry major stepped inside. His eyes swept the room and he touched his battered campaign hat to a couple of female customers, then strolled over to Matt's table.

"Sorry to intrude, Marshal, but do you mind if I join you?"

"By all means, Major," Matt said. "But we've just finished breakfast." He glanced at Festus, who was busily mopping bacon grease off his plate with a chunk of bread. "At least one of us has."

"I've breakfasted already," the soldier said. "But I could sure use some coffee."

Matt beckoned to a waitress, who filled the major's cup and he sipped appreciatively. Finally he laid his cup on the table and said: "My name is Anderson and I'm in command of three troops of the Sixth Cavalry. I understand you recently had a run-in with the renegade Cheyenne I've been ordered to capture."

Matt nodded. "Yesterday. The Cheyenne's name is Iron Hawk. He's a Dog Soldier."

"And a drunk if what I've been led to believe is true."

"He was," Matt said. "But since then I reckon he's signed the pledge and keeps almighty sober."

Anderson picked up his cup. "And you last saw him where exactly?"

Matt shifted his weight, the rickety chair groaning

under him. "Up on Saw Log Creek. I was with a posse that tangled with him. He bushwhacked us pretty good."

"Six men lost, I'm told."

"Five. The sixth was shot by one of his own kind during a disagreement over a horse."

The major shook his head. "We live in violent, dangerous times, Marshal, and no mistake."

Anderson drained his cup and said: "Ah, now I'm at least half awake." He stood and asked: "Which way was this Iron Hawk headed when you last saw him?"

"West," Matt said. "And he was wounded, though how badly I couldn't tell."

"Might slow him down some," Anderson said.

Matt nodded. "It might, Major, but don't count on it."

"Well, thank you for your help, Marshal," Anderson said. "Now I must go. My men are waiting."

After the door closed behind the soldier, Festus' eyebrow crept up his forehead as he thoughtfully scratched his unshaven jaw. "Three troops of blue-coat cavalry to round up one lone Injun, Matthew?"

Matt shrugged. "Three regiments wouldn't be enough. If Iron Hawk doesn't want to be caught, he won't be caught. That's a big prairie out there."

The marshal rose and dug into his pocket to pay his bill. Festus made no move to find money and Matt asked: "You broke again?"

"Matthew, you know us poor deputies don't make enough to eat in places like this," Festus said. "About all we can hope for are a few leftover scraps out the back door of the kitchen come closin' time."

Matt sighed and dug deeper. "Let's see, I had coffee and two eggs and bacon. You had a two steaks, a dozen eggs, bacon and two pieces of pie." The marshal laid two dollars on the table. "I hope that covers it."

Festus smiled. "It's always a real pleasure dinin' with you, Matthew."

Later in the afternoon, Festus stepped into the marshal's office and brought bad news.

"Guess who just drifted into town, Matthew?" he asked. "I mean as big and bold as you please?"

Still smarting over his deputy's extravagant appetite, Matt frowned and said: "I've no idea."

Festus grinned. "None other than the Missoula Kid his ownself!"

"The Missoula Kid? Here in Dodge?"

"Natural born and like I said, as big and bold as you like. I swear that ranny can strut sittin' down."

Matt was worried. He'd had dealings with the Missoula Kid in the past, and the man was pure poison. He was a bounty hunter out of the New Mexico Territory who didn't believe in taking his prisoners alive. "That way I don't have to feed 'em" was his unsmiling boast.

Nobody knew how many men the Kid had killed. Some said only a few dozen, others that his score ran into the hundreds and the truth was probably somewhere in between.

The Kid was a tall, arrogant man, lean and hard-boned, all the lard burned out of him by sun and long, difficult trails. As Matt recalled, he had the thin-jawed, deeply browned face, narrow waist and wide shoulders of the desert rider. A man who affected the drab dust brown clothes of the experienced manhunter, the Kid had eyes that provided an unexpected and vivid contrast to the rest of him; they were an astonishing emerald green shot through with flecks of gold.

Although he could use a Colt well, the Missoula Kid's preferred weapon was the Winchester in .44.40 caliber and he was an expert marksman. Most of his victims hit the ground dead before they heard the rifle shot.

That fact that the Missoula Kid was in Dodge was mighty bad news—for somebody.

And Festus confirmed Matt's thought.

"Know what Percy Crump tole me?" the deputy asked. Then, without waiting for an answer, he continued. "The Kid says to Percy to get ready for an embalmin'. 'Fer who?' says Percy. 'Fer a man who ain't dead yet but soon will be,' says the Kid. Then he tells Percy he wants him to build a lead-lined coffin on account of how he plans on takin' the deceased back to the Arizony Territory on the steam cars."

Matt leaned forward in his chair. "Did he give Percy a name?"

"Sure did." Festus scratched his jaw, his eyes wary. "Matthew, you ain't gonna believe this."

"Try me."

"The name the Kid give Percy was Roman Pollock."

Matt slammed back in his chair. "Pollock? Then the Missoula Kid must have a wanted dodger with Roman's name on it. I imagine there's plenty of them out there."

"I guess he must. Otherwise he wouldn't be here," Festus said.

Matt stood. "Where is the Kid now?"

"Last I seen him he was over to the Long Branch. You gonna talk to him, Matthew?"

The marshal nodded. "I sure am. I'm going to try and head off another killing."

When Matt stepped inside the Long Branch, the Kid was standing at the bar, his rifle on the counter in front of him. It was still too early for the sporting crowd and apart from the day bartender there was no one else in the saloon. Matt looked around but there was no sign of Kitty.

The Missoula Kid turned as he heard the chime of Matt's spurs and at once his eyes became guarded. "Howdy, Marshal," he said. "It's been a long time."

Matt nodded. "I'd say it's been a fair spell, Kid. How you been keeping?"

"Oh, fair to middling. The kind of business I'm in can wear on a man."

The Missoula Kid wore a brown coat, and shirt and pants of the same color. His battered hat was also brown and there was nothing about him that would shine or glitter in the sun. The man looked to be in his mid-forties, but he could have been ten years older or younger.

The bartender glanced from Matt to the Kid and, being a knowing kind of man, stepped quietly to the end of the bar.

"Business is why I'm here," Matt said. "I hear you've got business with Roman Pollock."

The Kid nodded. His fingers went to the edge of his coat. "May I?"

"Slow, Kid," Matt said, his hardening eyes signaling that he was tense and ready. "I mean slow as molasses in January."

"You're not a trusting man, are you, Marshal?" the Kid said.

"Live longer that way."

The Kid opened his coat and slid his hand into an inside pocket. He brought out a folded piece of paper that he straightened out, then held up for Matt to see.

"Recognize the likeness on that?" he asked.

Matt nodded. "It's Roman Pollock all right."

"Read what it says."

"Says he's wanted dead or alive for the murder of a deputy sheriff in the town of Lost Nickel in the Arizona Territory. Says the reward is five thousand dollars."

The Kid nodded. "Lost Nickel is a cowtown down to the Mogollon Rim country." He smiled. "Now five thousand might seem a lot for a tin-star deputy, but the man had a whole passel of kinfolk and friends and they put up the reward money."

"And you intend to take Pollock back to Arizona?"

"The only way I ever take 'em back—dead," the Kid said. "I've already ordered his coffin."

"I heard," Matt said. "Only it isn't going to happen in Dodge." The big marshal took a step closer to the bounty hunter. "What you do out on the plains is not my concern, but this is my town and what goes on here interests me a great deal. You want to kill Roman Pollock, you do it well away from Dodge." Matt's blue eyes were cold, uncompromising. "Kid, I want your rifle and belt gun. You can pick them up at my office when you leave."

Matt knew that the Missoula Kid was a man who played the odds and right now the odds were stacked against him. The Kid was not a glory-hunting youngster anxious to make a reputation as a gunfighter. He was a businessman, and if business forced him to use a gun, then he'd use it, coldly and indifferently, as a tool of his trade. The Kid operated within the law, often with its full cooperation, and drawing down on a cowtown marshal was not good for business. Matt saw the acceptance of that fact in the sudden quieting of the man's eyes.

The Kid hesitated for only a moment longer, thinking it through, then shrugged. "Take my guns, Marshal. I'll be by to pick them up tonight."

Matt took up the bounty hunter's rifle, then told him to lay his Colt on the counter. The Kid lifted the gun free with the tips of his fingers and laid it front of the marshal.

Matt shoved the Kid's Colt into his waistband and

said: "Kid, I guess you know Roman Pollock is no bargain. He's a hard man to kill."

Again the Kid shrugged. "I've hunted hard men most of my life. When it comes right down to it, Pollock will die as easy as any other."

"I wouldn't go counting on it," Matt said.

The day was shading into night when the Missoula Kid came to pick up his guns. Without a word, the man holstered his Colt, then walked out of the office to his waiting horse.

Matt stood on the boardwalk and watched the bounty hunter leave. After the Kid was gone, Matt remained where he was, the evening sky touching the flat planes of his rugged, handsome face with scarlet.

Darkness crowding in from the prairie surrounded Dodge, and a silence fragile as broken glass lay on the town. The lamps were being lit along Front Street, and on the boardwalks, respectable men in broadcloth suits stepped through dancing pools of orange light as they hurried to cross the tracks, anxious for dinner. A saloon girl at the Alhambra picked out a Chopin nocturne with one finger, stripping the melody down to its unadorned beauty, a lost, lonely and haunting sound in the echoing quiet.

Matt lingered for a while on the edge of the boardwalk, enjoying the coming of the night and the darkness and the yap of the awakening coyotes out on the grassland.

He was about to walk back into the office when

the tiny calico cat stepped into view and quickly blocked his path. The cat stood and looked up at him, defiant and still, its eyes on fire.

"Will you give me the road, cat?" Matt asked.

The little creature did not move. The tall marshal nodded. "Then I'll give you the road." He gave a small bow, sweeping his arm along the boardwalk. "After you."

The calico lifted its nose disdainfully and walked slowly away, its tail an erect, triumphant flag.

Matt watched the cat go and shook his head in puzzlement. What the heck did that animal have against him?

He was still trying to puzzle out the answer to that question as he walked into his office and lit the lamp, for the first time in days feeling relaxed and at ease with himself.

But as he carried a cup of coffee to his desk and sat, he had no way of knowing that the light of day would bring a horror to Dodge that he could never have imagined . . . not in his worst nightmare.

chapter 14

The Headless Horseman

"**I** guess you heard that Abe McKenna has demanded protection from the Army," Kitty Russell said, holding her coffee cup poised at her mouth with both hands, her beautiful eyes on Matt.

The big marshal nodded. "Spoke to a cavalry major yesterday. The Army has three troops out."

"Think they'll find that Indian?" Kitty asked, laying her cup back on the saucer.

Matt shook his head. "No, I don't. Not unless he wants to be found."

"Big Bertha left on the morning stage," Kitty said. "She told me she wants to keep her hair. The word is getting around that Iron Hawk is after Abe McKenna and the others who were in the saloon that night."

"McKenna is about the only one left, him and Roman Pollock."

Matt and Kitty were sitting at a corner table in the Sideboard, meeting as they often did for lunch, knowing that when the herds arrived both would be too busy for social occasions.

The restaurant was full, mostly the town's businessmen and their wives. A farmer, his plump wife and seven hungry youngsters were crowded around a table in the center of the room, sharing a heaping platter of boiled chicken and potatoes.

"How is Sam doing?" Matt asked.

Kitty smiled. "Full of plans for his wedding. He says he's looking forward to living back east with Abbey." Kitty's eyes slanted to the farmer's kids. "He says he and Abbey plan to have at least three children."

"Somehow I can't see Sam Noonan as a family man," Matt said.

"I can," Kitty said. "I think with the right woman he could settle down just fine."

Matt smiled without humor. "Is Abbey McKenna the right woman?"

Kitty shook her head. "Matt, I don't know. I just don't know. Maybe—"

The door slammed open and Festus stomped into the restaurant, his face ashen, eyes haunted, like a man just wakened from a terrible dream. He glanced around the room, then hurried to Matt's table.

"Matthew, you better come see this," he said, his voice trembling. "Big trouble."

One look at his deputy's stricken face convinced Matt that this wasn't one of Festus' exaggerations. He stood, found his hat and apologized to Kitty. Then he quickly followed Festus outside.

Roman Pollock sat the roan horse in the middle of Front Street, gaping, horrified townspeople crowding the boardwalks around him.

"This man," Pollock roared, "tried to kill me. But I done for him. Let this be a warning to all of you. My name is Roman Pollock and I will not be pushed, I will not be slighted and I will not tolerate bounty hunters laying for me."

Blood ran over Pollock's right hand, turning it into a glistening scarlet glove. The blood trickled down the length of a slender tree branch about ten feet long that the gunman grasped tightly in his fist. The branch had been sharpened into a spike at the top, and rammed onto this spike was the bloody, grinning head of the Missoula Kid.

Behind Pollock stood the bounty hunter's horse, the Kid's decapitated corpse hung over the saddle.

"Roman!" Matt yelled, walking toward the gunman. "I think we need to talk."

Pollock drew with his left, his Colt flashing into his hand. "Stay right there, Matt Dillon," he said. "I won't be crowded by you or anyone else. Take one more step and, I swear, I'll drop you where you stand."

People were gathering around Pollock at a safe distance, but Matt was aware that if lead started flying there would be dead on the street.

Roman Pollock was insane, no longer able to distinguish between what was real and what was not, and that made him unpredictable and dangerous.

Matt stopped and turned to his deputy. "Festus, get those people back," he said. "Clear them off the street."

Pollock sat motionless on his horse, his gory trophy waving above his head. The Missoula Kid's eyes were wide open, staring into nothingness, his thin hair lifting in the wind.

"He came at me, Matt," the gunman said, his deranged smile a twisted, bizarre grimace. "He lay out all night on the long grass and when I stepped from the bunkhouse he cut loose. He missed, damn him, but I didn't."

"Roman," Matt said, his voice soft, coaxing, like he was speaking to a child, "climb down and come into my office. We'll have coffee and talk this thing through. What you're doing here is wrong."

The gunman shook his head. "Don't push me, Matt. You know I won't be pushed."

"I'm not pushing, Roman," Matt said. He unbuckled his gun belt and let his Colt drop to the ground. "See, no guns. All I want to do is talk."

Pollock's face was black with anger and hate, the very building blocks of hell. "No talk. I'm all through talking. Now, if anybody comes at me or tries to push me, I'll do all my talk with my guns."

"Roman," Matt said, "maybe you should see Doc Adams. He can—"

The gunman ignored Matt's words. He swung his

horse around, gathered up the reins of the Kid's buckskin and walked along the street to Percy Crump's funeral parlor. The undertaker stood on the boardwalk outside his door, shoulders rounded, his face gray. Even though he was a man used to violent death in all its forms, this was beyond even Crump's vast experience and he looked deeply troubled.

Pollock stopped and studied Crump for a few moments. He threw his bloody trophy at the undertaker's feet. The Kid's head flew off the sharpened end of the tree branch and bounced in the dust of the street. "Bury that," the gunman said. He waved a scarlet hand toward the headless body. "And that. Put him together and bury him in the coffin he ordered for me."

Pollock, seeing the surprise in Crump's eyes, nodded. "Oh, yes, he lived long enough to tell me about it. He was gut shot but couldn't believe he was really dying and I guess he still hoped to take me back to Arizona." The gunman's face took on a sly look and he chuckled. "But Roman ended all his hopes when he summed everything up with another bullet. Then Roman cut off his head and put it on a spike."

The gunman swung the roan away from Crump. "You bury him," he said. "In the coffin, like I said." He kicked the big horse into a lope and headed along Front Street toward the open prairie.

Matt picked up his gun belt and ran after the man. "Roman!" he yelled. "Stop right there!"

The gunman reined up and sat still in the saddle for long moments, his back turned to the marshal, his head bowed like he was deep in thought. Then Pollock savagely yanked the roan's head around, the animal rearing as he drew his Colts.

Letting out a shrill, high-pitched scream, the man fired fast from both guns, half a dozen bullets kicking up startled exclamation points of dust around Matt's feet. Pollock holstered his guns, fought his rearing horse, then swung the roan around and galloped out of Dodge and into the grassland.

Matt had not drawn his gun.

Pollock, whatever his demented reasoning, had not shot to kill. But Matt knew with chilling certainty that if he'd drawn his Colt he'd be lying dead on the street.

A showdown with Pollock was coming—the marshal realized it was now inevitable—but today had not been the time nor the place.

Matt buckled on his gun belt, then smiled as Kitty ran into his arms.

"I was so terrified," the woman gasped. "It was . . . it was horrible . . . that head . . ." She laid her head on the marshal's chest. "Matt, when Pollock started to shoot I thought . . . I thought I'd lose you."

Matt held Kitty close, feeling the pounding of her heart. "He didn't try to hit me, Kitty," he said. "Why, I don't know." His smile grew wider. "Maybe because of old time's sake."

Kitty sobbed softly, her tears staining the front of Matt's shirt. "Don't make jokes about what happened, Matt. I . . . I couldn't go on living my life if you were not part of it."

Matt bent his head and his lips found Kitty's. "I'll always be a part of your life," he whispered. "Today, tomorrow and the next day and the day after that, for as long as I live."

"Now what in tarnation was all that about, Marshal?" Matt turned and saw Mayor Kelley stomping toward him, chewing angrily on an unlit cigar. Kelley gave a perfunctory touch of his hat to Kitty, then said: "I was taking me afternoon nap when I heard all the shooting and hollering."

In as few words as possible, Matt described how Roman Pollock had killed a bounty hunter and paraded the man's severed head through the town.

"Sweet Jesus and his Blessed Mother and all the saints in Heaven preserve us," Kelley gasped, all the superstitious dread of the native-born Irishman bubbling to the surface. "It's a wonder we were not all murdered in our beds."

The mayor chewed on his cigar, frowning, for a few moments; then his face cleared as he came up with a suitable punishment for Pollock. "Right then, that's it. Matt, from now on, himself is banned from Dodge for thirty days. We don't need his kind here."

Matt nodded. "I'll see to it, Mayor."

"Make sure you do," Kelley said. "Cuttin' off heads indeed. I've never heard the like in me entire life." He crossed himself quickly and asked: "Is Percy Crump picking up . . . er . . . the pieces?"

Matt nodded toward the funeral parlor. "Look over there. He's working on it."

"Saints preserve us. What next?" the mayor asked

of no one but himself, his eyes wide as he saw Crump and his assistants shove back the crowd and get busy on their grisly task.

Kelley shook his head and began to walk away, then stopped and turned. "One more thing, Matt. You'd better speak to your deputy about finishing the work on the water tower before the cattle cars start arriving in the next few weeks."

"It's not finished yet?" Matt asked.

"No, it's not finished yet, far from it. Festus has made those Chinamen as lazy as himself. I went over there this morning and he was lying in the shade, sleeping like a pup, a half dozen pigtailed heathen snoring away alongside of him."

"I'll talk to him, Mayor," Matt said, knowing that anything he said would fall on deaf ears.

After the mayor left, Matt looked along Front Street to where a large crowd was still gathered outside Percy Crump's office. One of the undertaker's assistants gingerly lifted the Missoula Kid's head by the hair and stuffed it in a burlap sack while a couple more manhandled his corpse into the funeral parlor.

Beside him, Matt felt a tremor go through Kitty's body. He glanced down at her and saw that her eyes were staring into the distance, as though she was looking intently at something he could not see.

"Matt," Kitty said, shivering, "be careful. Be very careful."

"Woman's intuition?" the marshal asked, smiling.

"Yes," Kitty said, her face like white marble. "Yes, it is."

chapter 15

Cowboy Fandango

There was money in beef in the 1870s. Big Money. But not a red cent of it came easy. The eastern cities with their burgeoning populations were hungry for meat, and there was a ready market for all the steer a rancher could raise. But the markets were a thousand miles away from south Texas and the ranges—a thousand miles of dust, river crossings, stampedes, heat, rain and madness. An owner only got top prices for top cattle, so the herds had to get to Dodge in excellent shape. That was the responsibility of the thirty-a-month cowboys, hard men born to a hard land in a hard time, men who expected trouble at every bend of the trail and nine times out of ten found it.

These were the men who drove the herds into Dodge. They came from all corners of the world and differed in race and creed, but most were Texans, their soft, drawling speech and relaxed, almost indolent movements betraying their Southern heritage. But with that birthright came energy, intelligence, courage and swift action when the occasion demanded.

The cowboys loved danger and hated work and had a deep-rooted aversion to soap and water. All affected the wide-brimmed sombrero, jinglebob spurs, leather chaps to protect the legs from the thorny scrub of south Texas and handmade, high-heeled boots. The finishing touches to a puncher's costume were the flaming bandanna knotted around his neck and the holstered Colt that rode high on his hip, the butt between wrist and elbow, the horseman's mode of carry.

After the first herds were packed into the stock pens at Dodge, the cowboys headed for the barbershop and were shorn of six months' growth of hair and beard. Their next stop was the general store, to buy a new shirt and pants, and from there to the crowded saloons and dance halls.

With the influx of the herds, Matt had his hands full coping with the Texans, and for a while, he forgot about Abbey McKenna and Roman Pollock.

All the saloons were roaring, gorgeously adorned with diamond-dust mirrors imported from France, cut-glass chandeliers and long mahogany bars. Mayor Kelley had ordered new lamps to line the town's boardwalks. These had great polished reflectors that threw yellow light far out onto the street, and the mayor was heard to boast that he'd forever banished darkness from Dodge City.

Down by the depot, clanking locomotives hissed and steamed, their shunting boxcars clanging and clashing, and day and night, the drumbeat thunder of hooves on the loading ramps could be heard all over town.

Festus had finally finished work on the water tower, but the Santa Fe Railroad engineers complained that it leaked like a sieve. Festus indignantly told an enraged Mayor Kelley that he was a deputy marshal, not a carpenter, and besides, half of his Chinaman crew had quit to open a laundry and the surviving half didn't know a thing about carpentry either.

Matt stepped into the breach by calling in a favor and got a real carpenter to make the necessary repairs, but for a few days, relations between the deputy and the mayor were tense.

The marshal spent most of his daylight hours, sputtering pen in hand, trying to catch up on the mountain of paperwork that always accompanied the arrival of the herds, and he was at his desk when the office door swung open and Sam Noonan stepped inside.

It had been three weeks since the first of the cowboys hit Dodge and the Long Branch was so busy that Sam had not yet quit.

"Do you have time for a word, Matt?" the bartender asked. "I know you're busy, but—"

Matt's smile was warm. "For you, Sam, anytime."

Sam wore a flowery brocaded vest over a white-and-blue-striped shirt, the sleeves and wristbands protected by calico cuffs. He wore sleeve garters embroidered with the motto THE LADIES, GOD BLESS THEM, black pants and a pale blue four-in-hand cravat held in place by a diamond stickpin.

Kitty always prided herself on the splendid appearance of her bartenders, the mixologist profession at that time having the same prestige and social status as that of lawyer, doctor or banker.

"This won't take long, Matt," Sam said. His hair was neatly parted in the middle and slicked down, flat and shiny on either side of his head. "I guess you can tell that I'm due to go on duty at the Long Branch in ten minutes."

The marshal laid down his pen. "What can I do for you, Sam?" Feeling vaguely uneasy he waved the bartender into a chair.

Sam sat, then said: "Well, Abbey has found a buyer for both her herds, and her hands will be driving the cattle to Dodge within the next couple of days."

"Glad to hear it," Matt said, empty words for politeness' sake since he genuinely liked Sam, an easygoing, affable man who never had an unkind word to say about anybody.

Sam's smile was slightly embarrassed. "The thing is, Matt, with Abbey's herd sold, we don't see any need to postpone the wedding any longer."

"When's the happy day?" Matt asked.

"A week from today."

"Congratulations," the marshal said, wishing his voice sounded a lot more sincere.

But Sam had not detected Matt's feigned sincerity, because his next words shook the big lawman. "The thing is, Matt, well . . . you and I have always been friends, and I've got a favor to ask of you." The bartender squirmed a little in his chair, then asked: "Will you be my best man?"

Matt opened his mouth to speak, but Sam cut him off quickly. "I know this is short notice, what with Dodge being full of cowboys an' all, but I'd count it a favor, Matt. To me and my bride." Sam hesitated, then added: "You would honor us."

It was not in Matt Dillon's nature to hurt or belittle a man, and he would not do it now. After a few heartbeats of hesitation, he smiled and stuck out his hand. "The honor is all mine, Sam. I'll be delighted to be your best man."

Sam grinned, took the marshal's hand and shook it vigorously. "Thank you, Matt." His grin widened, and his eyes slowed. "Just wait until I tell Abbey."

Matt nodded. "Yes, Sam, just wait." He hesitated a few moments, then asked: "Are you still planning to move east?"

The bartender glanced at the clock on the office wall and stood. "We sure are, Matt. Abbey wants to live in a big city. She says she doesn't want to raise our kids in a wilderness."

"How about Abe? Is he going with you?"

Sam's grin lingered on his lips but the warm light fled from his eyes. "Yes. Abbey says she lost track of her brother for years and now she wants to keep him close."

"You get along with Abe?"

Sam looked uncomfortable. "I have to be going, Matt," he said. "And thank you again. You have no idea what this means to Abbey and me."

He stepped to the door, hesitated for a moment, then turned, his face bleak. "Matt, Abe McKenna is weak and I think he's yellow. But like a lot of cowards, he's got a cruel, vicious streak in him. You asked me if we got along, and the answer is no. But I will put up with him for Abbey's sake, if that's what she wants and needs."

Before Matt could say anything further, Sam stepped through the door and was gone.

Matt picked up his pen and dipped it into the inkwell.

He sat, deep in thought for a long while, the pen forgotten in his hand. He'd agreed to be Sam's best man, and had Sam been marrying any other woman than Abbey McKenna, he would have considered it an honor.

Could he go through with it?

Matt shook his head. When the time came, he'd have to make an excuse and back out of even attending the wedding—but that would mean breaking his word to Sam.

There had to be another way.

And there was. He could see to it that Sam Noonan didn't marry Abbey McKenna.

The only question was—how?

chapter 16

Trail of the White Buffalo

During the cattle season, Matt Dillon often slept in his office, forgoing the dubious comforts of the room he reserved year round at the Dodge House. The morning after his talk with Sam Noonan, he was wakened from a sound sleep by a loud hammering on the office door.

Matt swung his feet off his cot and glanced up at the clock, blinking against the light. It was not yet seven.

"It's open, damn it!" Matt yelled, irritated at being wakened so early.

A small, dapper man in well-cut range clothes stepped inside, a huge grin on his face. "Didn't want to barge in on you, Matt. Never know when a man has a lady friend visiting."

"Bat, what do you want?" Matt asked sourly. "You know what time it is?"

Bat Masterson's grin grew wider. "It's early, I know, Matt, but you won't want to miss this. Why, when I heard about it, I said to myself, 'Ol' Matt would never forgive me if I didn't tell him about it.'"

Matt stood and stretched. "Tell me about what?"

Masterson stepped over to the stove and tested the coffeepot. It was cold and empty and his face fell.

"Tell me about what, Bat?" Matt asked again. "And this had better be real good."

"It is good," Masterson said, his round, handsome face shining with enthusiasm. "I was talking to Clem Goldberg in the Alamo last night and—"

"You mean Clem Goldberg the peddler?"

"The very same. Anyhow, Clem says he was out by Mattox Draw a couple of days ago, and . . . well, Matt, guess what he saw."

The tall marshal stepped to the gun rack, shucked his Colt and made a show of spinning the cylinder and checking the loads. "This had better be real good, Bat," he said again.

"It's better than good," Masterson said. "It's great! Clem says he saw a white buffalo out there in the draw. Matt, it was all by itself and as white as milk."

"Did you wake me up to tell me that?" Matt asked.

"You mean you don't want to see it? Matt, a white buffalo happens maybe once in a man's lifetime. I've seen thousands, millions of buffalo, but I never did see a white one."

Matt thought for a few moments, then holstered his gun, the natural curiosity of the frontiersman strong in him. "White as milk you say?"

"Uh-huh. Or snow. Now I recollect, I think maybe Clem said white as snow."

Despite himself, Matt was intrigued. "Could be it's the last buffalo," he said.

Masterson nodded, smiling from ear to ear. "The last buffalo on the plains and it happens to be snow-white. Now don't that blow your hat in the creek?"

"You don't plan on killing it, do you?" Matt asked.

The man shook his head. "Hell no. I've done killed my share of buffalo. I just want to see it, something to tell my grandkids about."

Bat, a man who had worn a lawman's star a few times himself, saw Matt's hesitation and said quickly: "We can ride out to the draw, see the buffalo and be back before dark. Hell, nobody's gonna wake up in this town until then."

The big marshal was silent, thinking it through, then made up his mind. "All right, we'll head out as soon as I dress and saddle my horse."

Bat Masterson rubbed his hands together with glee. "This is gonna be great!"

Matt left a hurried note for Festus and propped it against the coffeepot, where the deputy would be sure to see it. He stepped back, read it over and smiled. Festus would puzzle over it for a long time.

GONE BUFFALO HUNTING. BE BACK BY SUNDOWN.

After Matt dressed, he followed Masterson onto the boardwalk, then stopped, a scowl on his face. "You didn't tell me he was coming," he whispered.

"He wanted to see the buffalo, Matt, same as us." Masterson smiled. "Looks like hell, don't he?"

"When a man is saddling his horse when decent folks are going to bed, how can he look any other way but like hell?" Doc Holliday asked, his pale, thin face irritable. The gambler's cold blue eyes went to Matt. "How you doing, Marshal?"

Matt nodded. "Just fine, Doc. And you?"

Holliday shrugged his skinny shoulders. "I die a little more with every tick of the clock. I guess that's why I want to see the white buffalo. If a man wants to die happily, he should learn how to live. And if a man wants to live happily, he should learn how to die. Me"—Doc's smile was touched with genuine humor—"I've learned 'em both."

Despite the heat of the brightening morning, Doc wore a long coat of gray wool, with a yellow muffler knotted around his neck. His large, sweeping dragoon mustache hid most of his thin mouth and his eyes under the shade of his hat brim were bright with the fever of his illness.

Matt thought to himself that Bat was right. Doc Holliday looked like hell, an animated cadaver, the death shadows already gathering dark in his hollow cheeks and under his eyes.

Doc leaned his weight on the saddle horn and smiled. "You don't like me much, do you, Marshal? Is it the shooting scrapes I've been in that bother you?"

Matt nodded, deciding to lay it right on the line.

"Those, and the fact that you don't have just a mean streak, Doc—you're poison mean all the way through."

Doc was pleased and it showed in the wide grin that suddenly took ten years off him and for a moment revealed the young man he'd once been. "Damn right," he said.

Matt shook his head. Doc was a hopeless case. The man was an unrepentant rogue and proud of it. "We'd better get moving," the marshal said. "It's a fair piece out to the draw."

Ten minutes later the three riders trotted out of Dodge under a light blue sky streaked with bands of scarlet and jade, then swung to the northwest.

Bat Masterson, never a man to skimp on his comforts, had a wicker picnic basket strapped to the back of his saddle, and he now and again reached back to steady it.

"What you got in there, Bat?" Matt asked.

The gambler smiled. "Had it made up at the Sideboard. Got us some roast beef on fresh sourdough bread, a couple of bottles of Bass Ale and half a dried apple pie. Oh, and I brought a coffeepot. I haven't had my morning coffee yet and that can wear on a man."

Bat insisted they stop at Buckner Creek to boil up his coffee, and when the cottonwoods lining the banks came into view, he turned to Doc, a huge smile splitting his face and said: "Hey, Doc, do you recollect? This is where we dressed up like Injuns and spooked that prune-eating sodbuster and his fat wife." Bat laughed and slapped his thigh. "Hell, them two fogged it out o' here like a couple of buck-shot coyotes."

Doc smiled and nodded. "I recall they told the marshal here that a thousand Cheyenne were after their hair."

"And I recall that I was going to run you two out of town for disturbing the peace," Matt said, a reluctant smile tugging at his lips.

"Marshal," said Doc solemnly, "like a true Solomon of the plains, your justice is surpassed only by your mercy."

"Don't count on it, Doc," Matt said.

The three men drank their coffee in the shade of the cottonwoods; then Bat threw the dregs on the fire and they swung into the saddle again.

Mattox Draw lay to the northeast, a shallow depression five miles long and a mile wide that was usually dry, but now and then channeled floodwaters off the Arkansas. The grazing around the draw was good, and Bat figured it was the prime grass that had attracted the white buffalo to the location.

"One time I saw a herd of five, maybe six hundred thousand buffs in the draw," he told Matt. "My brother, James, and me and another hunter by the name of Wyatt Earp killed two hundred in one morning. Took the skinners days to collect the robes."

"And now there's only one," Matt said, allowing himself to feel a momentary pang of sadness—as did so many other Western men—at the passing of the great herds.

"We're making history here today, gentlemen," Doc said. "We could be the last people on earth to see a white buffalo. There may never be its like again." `

Bat nodded as though Doc had fairly stated the matter. "I never figured," he said, "that I'd go down in history."

As the sun climbed higher in the sky, the three riders crossed a gently rolling landscape of shallow rises and fast-flowing streams. The grass was studded with pink, yellow and violet wildflowers and air smelled clean, the wind blowing long from the west, carrying with it the remembered scent of tall mountains and pines.

The riders followed a narrow game trail for a couple of miles, then swung sharply to the north across wide open country, a vast sea of green, the only splashes of color the flowers of wild onion growing among blossoming yucca.

"I reckon the southern mouth of the draw is about a mile ahead," Bat said. "Time to keep your eyes skinned."

Matt reached behind his saddle and took his field glasses from his saddlebags. As he rode, he scanned the country ahead of him, but the land was seemingly empty of life. Nowhere was there a sound or movement, the birds and animals gone to ground, sheltering from the heat of the noon sun.

The three riders drew closer to the draw, dry now that the Arkansas was no longer swollen from snowmelt. Bat, who knew the way of the land around him and the habits of buffalo, suggested they ride into the draw.

"Could be that buff wants to stay out of sight," he said. "The draw would be a natural hiding place for him, and there's plenty of grass and low-lying pools of water."

The riders spread out a little and entered the draw. It looked more like a large, sunken meadow than the kind of steep-sided, rocky gorge found in hill country.

After ten minutes, Bat swung out of the saddle and checked out an area of flattened grass, the ground around it freshly kicked up and disturbed.

"He rolled here and not too long ago," the gambler said, holding on to the reins of his horse. "I figure he must be right close."

Bat stepped into the saddle. "Ride slow, boys," he said. "We don't want to go stampeding him."

Ahead of the riders, the draw took a slight turn to the west and a narrow ledge of land about six feet high and a hundred yards long jutted out from the shallow bank, its crest covered in tall-growing Indian grass.

Bat in the lead, the riders rounded the spur—and almost rode right up on the grazing buffalo.

The massive animal lifted its huge, shaggy head, snorted angrily and then, its black eyes showing wary arcs of white, quickly trotted away from them.

Matt glanced at Bat and the man's shocked face

was a crestfallen study in disappointment. Beside him, Doc coughed, spat into the grass, and growled: "Well, don't that beat all."

The buffalo wasn't white. It wasn't even close. Patches of dirty gray hair clung to the animal's brown flanks and ran in a narrow streak along its back—unusual certainly, but a far cry from the rare snow-white beast described by the always voluble Clem Goldberg.

Bat shook his head in disgust, watching the buffalo as it faded into the distance. "Damn it all," he said. "I feel like a bride that's just been left at the altar. We rode all the way out here to see a white buffalo and all we got was a paint."

Doc spat again. "Hell, it isn't even a paint, Bat. Paint hoss has a heap more white on him than that."

Matt kneed his horse along side Bat. "Well, look on the bright side," he said, smiling. "At least now we get to eat that lunch you packed for us."

"Matt, I'm sorry I dragged you out here on a wild-goose chase," Bat said, shaking his head. "It's surely downright discouraging."

"Like smelling whiskey through the jailhouse door," Doc added, his grin mischievous. He glanced quickly at Matt, judging any possible reaction, then added: "Bat, when we get back to town remind me to have a word with Clem Goldberg."

"Get in line behind me, Doc," Bat said. "That windy yarn of his had us fishing with an empty hook."

Bat's mood improved after he ate, though Doc refused food and instead drank a pint of bourbon he'd stashed in his coat pocket.

"Every man should have at least one good friend," he explained, slapping the bottle, "and this here is mine."

After an hour, the three men swung into the saddle and headed back for Dodge.

The day was wearing into late afternoon when they reached Saw Log Creek and let their horses drink.

Matt had his foot in the stirrup, preparing to step back into the saddle, when he heard the sudden rattle of distant gunfire. He hesitated, listening. A few moments later a wide dust cloud rolled toward the creek. As the dust got closer, the marshal saw that it was being kicked up by a herd of wild-eyed, stampeding cattle.

They could only be Abbey McKenna's cattle.

chapter 17

Iron Hawk Strikes Again

The herd ran toward the creek and most of the longhorns charged straight across. A few tumbled down the steepest part of the bank and were trampled by those following. Others broke to the north and south, scattering over the prairie, several hard-riding horsemen trying to head them off.

A tall man on a buckskin pony rode close to the creek. From somewhere behind him a shot rang out and the man suddenly threw up his arms and splashed into the water, a widening red stain on his back. The buckskin reared, lost its footing on the bank, then crashed on top of the floundering rider. The saddle horn rammed into the man's chest, and he screamed once and was silent.

Matt heard the *Yip! Yip! Yip!* of Iron Hawk's war cry and saw the Cheyenne emerge from the dust, his Winchester firing fast from his shoulder.

A couple of the McKenna riders jumped out of the saddle, kneeled and fired at the charging Indian. Iron Hawk veered to his right, still shooting, and one of the McKenna punchers yelled, his rifle spinning away from him as his shoulder was shattered by a bullet.

"What the hell!" Doc yelled. "Indians!"

He spurred his horse across the creek, then mounted the far bank and hit the flat at a run, a roaring Colt bucking in his hand. Bat Masterson, never one to stay out of a fight, followed, sliding his rifle from the boot under his knee as he spurred his mount into a gallop.

Matt watched them go, aware that their tired horses would never catch up to Iron Hawk's fast dun. The Cheyenne was already galloping across the plain, fading into the distance, and Doc and Bat were lagging far behind.

The big marshal stepped into the creek and waded toward the buckskin and its rider. The man was dead, floating head down in the water. The buckskin's leg was broken, so Matt drew his gun and put the animal out of its misery.

He punched out the spent shell and was feeding another into the chamber when a short, wiry man in a ragged duster rode up to the bank on a lathered horse.

The man glanced down at the body floating in the creek and asked: "Is he dead?"

Matt nodded. "He was shot and then his horse fell on top of him."

"That makes one dead and"—he jerked a thumb toward the man with the wounded shoulder—"and one bad hurt by the look of him." The rider stood in the stirrups and eased a crick out of his back. "Damn cattle are scattered to hell and gone. Take us a week to round 'em up—that is, if we can hire the men."

Matt stepped out of the creek and gathered up the reins of his bay. "What happened?"

The stocky man shrugged. "We was heading Miz McKenna's herd for Dodge when the Indian hit us. We didn't see him coming. He just rose up out of the ground like a phantom and started shooting."

"That's an old Cheyenne trick," Matt said. "A warrior will make his horse lie on the ground and he'll lay right alongside it with his leg over its back. When the horse gets up, he's mounted and ready to go. If the grass is long enough to hide him, a Cheyenne can stay like that for hours, waiting his chance." Matt shrugged. "I've seen Apache do it too, come to that."

The McKenna rider leaned from the saddle and spat. "He fights like a damn Apache."

"Uh-huh," Matt said. "Iron Hawk is a Dog Soldier, and you're right: he's a handful."

The marshal turned as Bat and Doc rode back, their horses blowing hard.

"Lost him," Bat said. "He left us in his dust."

"I think maybe I winged him," Doc said.

Bat shook his head. "You didn't wing him, Doc. You weren't even close."

"Well," Doc said defensively, "I sure enough saw blood on his shoulder."

"That was an old wound, Doc," Matt said. "It was Roman Pollock who winged him."

Doc looked surprised. "Hell, I never knew Roman to miss like that."

"He was in a hurry," Matt said.

The McKenna rider had left to check on the wounded man, and now he came back. "Marshal, will you take Slim back to Dodge? I don't think he can ride that far without some he'p." The man nodded toward the other puncher, who was remounting his horse. "Bill and me are the only ones left and I reckon we should start trying to round up the herd."

The man's face was suddenly bitter. "Abe McKenna was with us, but he took off as soon as the Injun started shooting." The man spat. "I guess he's a runner, not a fighter."

Matt glanced up at the sun. It was still a couple of hours until dark and the wounded man would not slow him that much. "Sure," he said, "I'll take him back. Doc Adams can dig the bullet out of his shoulder."

The wounded man gave his name as Slim Brower and said he was from the Texas Big Bend country. His face ashen, the man complained about the pain in his shoulder, but his bitterest gripes were directed at Abe McKenna.

Looking like he'd just been kicked in the stomach, Brower turned to Matt as they rode and said: "Abe talks tough, but when it comes right down to it, he's plumb yellow. When the shooting started he flapped his chaps for Dodge and left us." The man winced as pain stabbed at him, then grumbled: "As soon as the doc fixes me up, I'm gonna ask McKenna for my time. Then I'm hauling my freight. I ain't gonna work for a boss who'll only stand his ground if'n he's buried standing up."

The day was starting to shade into evening as Matt and the others rode into Dodge.

Matt helped Brower into Doc Adams' office, just as the physician stepped out of his surgery. Doc's eyebrow rose as he looked at the wounded man. "You do this, Matt?" he asked.

The marshal shook his head. "Not guilty this time, Doc. That's a Cheyenne bullet in him."

"Silly old me. When it comes to bullets, I didn't realize there was a difference," Doc said. He put his arm around the wounded man's waist, helped him to the surgery door, then turned to Matt. "I'm pretty sure I can handle it from here."

"Anything you say, Doc," Matt said, realizing the physician was in one of his cantankerous moods and best left alone.

The marshal closed Doc Adams' door behind him, swung onto his bay and crossed Front Street, heading for the livery stable. Dodge was awake and had changed into her party duds, and the saloons and dance halls were filling with cowboys. The biggest crowd was at Chalk Beeson's Saratoga, where there was a seven-piece orchestra. Chalk had retained a Mr. Lawson from Baltimore for the entire season, and the tenor's renditions of "The Lakes of Killarney" and

"The Winsome Widow's Lament" were always enthusiastically received by the sentimental punchers.

Matt unsaddled the bay, rubbed him down with a piece of sacking, then gave the big horse a handful of oats and forked him some hay. He returned to his office, put on coffee and busied himself with paperwork. In an hour or so, it would be time to make his round of the saloons.

The clock on the office wall stood at seven after eight when Festus opened the door and stepped inside. The deputy crossed to the stove, found a cup and poured himself coffee. He sat opposite Matt, scratched his jaw and said: "I hear tell the white buffalo was a sure enough disappointment, Matthew."

Matt nodded. "Who told you?"

"Bat Masterson. Ol' Bat's over to the Long Branch, so down in the mouth he could eat oats out of a churn. He set store by that buffalo."

"Bat tell you about Iron Hawk and the McKenna riders?"

"Darn tootin' he did. Maybe that's why Abe McKenna is at the Alhambra, mean drunk and tellin' anybody who'll listen that he needs a lot more protection from the Army."

Matt picked up his pen. "Keep an eye on McKenna, Festus," he said. "There's no man more dangerous than a coward with a gun."

The deputy finished his coffee and left, and for the next hour, Matt slowly and laboriously worked his way through a stack of official correspondence.

It was after nine when Festus returned, a worried frown on his face. "I've been keepin' an eye on ol' Abe like you said, Matthew, an' it's been a chore. When I left him, he'd just quit cussin' and discussin' with that Slim Brower feller you brung in, the one that got his shoulder broke by Iron Hawk's bullet."

Matt was concerned. "What were they arguing about?"

Festus scratched his hairy jaw. "Well, it seems Slim wanted to draw his time, but Abe said there would be no money until the herd is sold. Abe told Slim, broke shoulder or no, to go help round up the cattle, and then he'd get paid."

"And then what happened?"

"Well, then Slim said, 'You're heeled, McKenna. Haul your iron and we'll have this out right now.' That's when I stepped in an' told them boys to cool off. Then Abe finished his drink an' left."

"Where is Abe now?"

"His hoss is tied up outside the Alamo, so I reckon he went there."

Matt rose, crossed the room and buckled on his gun belt. "Time for me to make my rounds, Festus. I want to make sure McKenna doesn't bump into Brower again tonight."

The deputy nodded. "That Slim feller looks mighty peaked, Matthew. I don't reckon he's really up for any gunfightin'."

"Maybe so," Matt said. "But I aim to make sure."

Outside a single gunshot roared above the racket

of the saloon pianos and the yells of the celebrating cowboys.

Matt yanked open the office door, stepped quickly onto the boardwalk and looked around. Front Street was crowded with riders moving from one saloon to the next, cowboys never walking anywhere they could ride a horse, and a solitary farm wagon drawn by an ox team trundled past the Long Branch.

The shot seemed to have gone unnoticed, because gunfire was not unusual in Dodge during the cattle season, and Matt decided it must have been some drunk rooster letting off steam.

He was about to go back inside when a young clerk in a too-tight suit and high celluloid collar pounded along the boardwalk toward him.

The man skidded to a stop and pointed back toward the Alamo. "Marshal," he said breathlessly, "a man's just been shot."

"Where is he?" Matt asked.

"Well, right now he's lying in the alley between the Alamo and the hardware store and I don't think he's planning to go anywhere else."

Matt reached inside the door, grabbed his hat and followed the clerk along the boardwalk to the Alamo. A couple of cowboys, whiskey glasses in hand, stood outside the saloon, looking around.

"What's going on, Marshal?" one of the punchers asked.

Matt ignored the man and stepped into the alley. A body was lying facedown across a tumbled stack of empty bottles. There was no mistaking the fat bandage around the man's left shoulder—it was Slim Brower. The McKenna rider had been shot in the back, a single, well-aimed bullet between the shoulder blades that had broken his spine.

Matt turned as Festus stepped to his side. "Get Doc Adams," he said. "Though I doubt Doc can do anything for him."

The physician confirmed Matt's opinion when he arrived a couple of minutes later. Doc rose from the man's side and shook his head. "Dead when he hit the ground." He turned to Matt, his eyes bleak in the gloom. "All my work wasted. Just another senseless killing."

The marshal left Festus to get the undertaker and walked quickly to the Alamo. The saloon was so crowded when he stepped inside it took him a few moments to locate Abe McKenna at the bar. Matt walked toward the man, elbowing revelers out of the way.

McKenna had a glass of whiskey in front of him and it seemed like he'd barely touched the drink. He turned when he saw Matt, then warily looked up at the tall marshal towering over him.

"McKenna," Matt said, his eyes shading from blue to gunmetal, "how long have you been here?"

McKenna's soft, petulant face flushed. "How the hell should I know? An hour maybe."

Matt reached over the bar and grabbed one of the bartenders as the man rushed past, foaming schooners of beer in both hands. He pointed at McKenna. "How long has this man been standing here?"

The bartender shook his head. "I don't know, Marshal. Look around you at the crowd in this place. I only serve 'em. I don't memorize their faces." The man looked down at Matt's big hand on his arm. "Now will you let me pass?"

Matt released the bartender and turned to McKenna. He reached down, slid the man's gun from the holster and smelled the barrel. "This gun has been fired recently," he said.

The crowd, sensing trouble brewing, was gathering around McKenna and the tall lawman. Over in the corner, the piano player struck a last few, faltering notes, then fell silent. Then he turned on his stool to watch the drama unfold.

"Of course it's been fired," McKenna said, his voice loud in the sudden, expectant silence. "You know I was jumped by an Indian. I fired it then."

Matt opened the Colt's loading gate and spun the cylinder. "Only one round has been fired. You shot just one time at the Indian?"

His eyes guarded, McKenna nodded. "That's right, once. Then I hightailed it for Dodge."

Matt decided to lay it on the line. "McKenna, I believe about ten minutes ago you fired that one shot into the back of one of your riders in the alley outside, a man who called himself Slim Brower. Then you snuck back in here and mingled with the crowd. There's so many people in the saloon, nobody saw you leave and they didn't notice you come back inside."

McKenna's expression was stubborn and belligerent. "I told you, I've been here for an hour and I never left."

As though he hadn't heard, Matt said: "Somebody in this saloon warned you that Brower was headed over here to renew the quarrel you had with him earlier. You laid for him in the alley and shot him in the back."

Matt shoved McKenna's Colt into his waistband. "McKenna, I'm arresting you for murder. If I was you, I'd think real carefully before I said anything else."

McKenna spat, his anger flaring. "I never shot anybody, and if you say I did, you're a damned liar."

The big marshal smiled and slowly shook his head. "I told you to think real careful before you said anything else."

Matt's right fist flew straight from the shoulder, crashing into McKenna's chin. The man's eyes rolled back in his head and he dropped like a slaughtered steer.

The marshal reached down, grabbed McKenna by the back of his shirt collar and dragged him out of the saloon and the length of Front Street, an excited, laughing crowd following at his heels.

Matt threw the still unconscious McKenna in a cell, then stepped back into the office and tossed the man's fancy gun into a desk drawer.

He knew his case against McKenna was thin. Could he make it stick? That would depend on Judge Brooker and Matt planned to cross the tracks and talk to the old man right away.

The marshal opened the office door and stepped

onto the boardwalk. A gun blasted and the guttering lamp on the wall beside his head instantly exploded, showering shards of shattered glass into his face, drops of blazing oil cascading over the pine boards like a fiery rain.

The location of the hidden gunman seemed to be directly across Front Street. Matt drew his Colt and sprinted into the narrow alley beside the Long Branch. He stopped, listening. Footsteps pounded in the distance and he heard a faint clink as the running man's toe hit an empty bottle. Matt walked further into the alley, then stepped into an open area between the back of the saloon and the corral of Moss Grimmick's livery stable.

Crouching low, Matt crossed the open ground, his gun hammer back and ready.

A freight wagon was parked at the far corner of the corral, its tongue raised, and the marshal stood behind a steel-rimmed wheel, his eyes trying to probe the crowding darkness.

Beyond the corral lay another open area of ground, ending at the hulking black shape of a two-story warehouse and beyond that a few scattered shacks, then the open prairie. A piano was playing in the Long Branch, its notes mingling with the constant clank of glasses, and Matt heard a woman laugh. He left the shelter of the wagon and stepped out into the open. A rifle flared orange from the corner of the warehouse, and the bullet whanged off the rim of the wheel where he'd been standing only a moment before.

Matt thumbed off a fast shot, aiming at the spot where he'd seen the stab of flame from the rifle muzzle, then fired once more to the right and left of the hidden bushwhacker's position.

As the racketing echoes of his shots faded away, the marshal walked toward the warehouse. Stepping carefully, he punched out the spent shells from his Colt and reloaded.

Something was coming toward him! A shadow detached itself from the inky backdrop of the darkness and moved in Matt's direction. The marshal's gun was level and ready, but he waited. Only a fool would shoot before he had identified his target.

The shadow moved closer and the big marshal tensed.

"Wha—wha's all the shootin' about?"

Matt relaxed. He knew that voice. It was Louie Pheeters, staggering drunk as usual.

The man got closer and stopped, swaying on his feet, blinking like an owl. "Oh, it's you, Marshal," he said, raising his battered plug hat. "Shootin' at out—outlaws, are ye?"

"Louie get away from here," Matt hissed. "You'll get your fool self killed."

"Now, listen here, Marshal," Louie slurred, his index finger raised. "I got the right to go . . . to go anywhere I please."

His eyes on the warehouse, Matt tried to step around Pheeters, but the man stumbled against him, stopping the big lawman in his tracks.

From somewhere behind the warehouse, Matt

heard the thud of hooves. He pushed Pheeters away from him and sprinted toward the sound. As he rounded the corner of the building the hoofbeats were already fading into the distance, rider and horse cloaked by the prairie darkness.

The wind tugging at him, Matt stood until the sound of the running horse was gone, then walked back, holstering his gun.

Pheeters had disappeared and the marshal made his way into the alley beside the Long Branch. He stopped as his nose detected an unexpected smell. The alley was narrow, sheltered from the wind, and the acrid bite of powder smoke still hung in the air . . . but there was something else, much more subtle, elusive and delicate.

It was the faint, flowery scent of a woman's perfume.

chapter 18

War Drums

"**M**att, you can hold Abe McKenna until after the inquest tomorrow morning. Then you'll have to let him go." Judge Brooker shook his gray head. "Sorry, but there's no alternative."

Matt's eyes searched the judge's face, trying to find something in the man's expression that would offer even a glimmer of hope. There was none.

"Judge," Matt said, "I know that earlier tonight Abe McKenna laid for Slim Brower and shot him in the back. He'd quarreled with Brower over money and the puncher challenged Abe to a gunfight. Later McKenna bushwhacked him and got even the only way he knows how."

"Maybe so, Matt," the judge said, pulling his dressing gown closer around his narrow chest, "but knowing is one thing, proving is another. Did anyone see McKenna in the alley around the time Brower was killed?"

Matt shook his head.

"Then did anyone see McKenna leave the Alamo saloon around the time of the murder?"

"No, sir," Matt replied miserably.

"You don't have a case, Matt. With the kind of circumstantial evidence you have, even a kid right out of law school could get McKenna acquitted on a murder charge."

The judge's milky blue eyes were sympathetic, but there was no give in them. "I'll hold the inquest tomorrow morning at ten. I warn you, the verdict is a foregone conclusion—murder by person or persons unknown. You will then release your prisoner, Marshal. You will have no legal right to hold Abe McKenna longer."

Matt rose, his hat in his hands. "Well, thank you for your time, Judge. I'm sorry to have gotten you out of bed so late."

Brooker waved a white, blue-veined hand. "Think nothing of it, Matt. I just wish I could have been of more help."

The big marshal's smile was tight. "So do I, Judge. So do I."

As he'd been told to expect, Matt heard Brooker exonerate Abe McKenna at the inquest next morning, the judge concluding that Slim Brower had met his death at the hands of an unknown assassin.

When Matt returned to his office, Abbey McKenna was waiting for him outside the door. The girl wore a stylish riding habit of dark blue velvet, English lace at the collar and cuffs, a top hat balanced on her piled-up curls. She looked fresh and breathtakingly lovely, marred only by the hard light in her eyes and what appeared to be an angry scrape across her left cheekbone.

Matt touched his hat brim. "What can I do for you, Miss McKenna?"

The girl's smile was brief and without warmth. "I'm here to take my brother home."

"You were at the inquest?"

Abbey nodded. "Yes, I left right after the verdict was read. It was dreadfully hot in the courtroom."

Matt opened the door and followed the girl inside. He waved her into a chair, found the cell keys, and returned with Abe McKenna. The man's jaw was bruised and he had a bad hangover, but otherwise he seemed unaffected by his night in jail.

Abbey immediately rose and rushed into her brother's arms, and the two clung close to each other for long moments, their seeking mouths joining.

Matt Dillon was no prude, but Abbey's display seemed to go far beyond the normal affection of a sister for her brother and it both disturbed and intrigued him.

The big marshal gave a half-embarrassed cough and the McKennas parted, Abbey's face flushed, her eyes alight.

As they stepped away from each other, Abe

reached out and touched the girl's cheek. "What happened?" he asked. His face suddenly turned ugly. "If a man did this to you, I'll kill him."

Abbey laughed. "It wasn't a man, silly. I was riding and caught my cheek on a dry cottonwood branch. That was all."

Matt reached into the drawer and found Abe's gun. He ejected the shells and passed the Colt to the young man, then dropped the ammunition into Abe's hand. "You can load it when you leave Dodge," he said.

McKenna holstered his gun and looked into Matt's cold, hostile eyes. "For what it's worth, Dillon, I didn't kill Slim Brower," he said.

"There's nothing you can say that's worth a hill of beans, McKenna," Matt said. "I hear the words, but I'm not listening."

Abe opened his mouth to speak again, but Abbey cut him off quickly. "Marshal, Sam told me you've agreed to be his best man. I'm so glad. It means a lot to my future husband."

Matt nodded. "I've known Sam for a long time. It was the least I could do."

"Did he tell you we're pushing forward the date of the wedding?"

"He did. In a week he said."

Abbey flashed her dazzling smile. "Now it's just four days—isn't that wonderful? We plan to travel east right after the wedding and honeymoon in Boston."

"What about your herd?" Matt asked. "The last

time I saw your cattle, they were scattered to hell and gone.''

"Oh, Abe plans to hire some cowboys to help round them up. A lot of the punchers are already broke and they'll jump at a chance to earn a few dollars. I've also sold the Herefords and the cowboys will bring those in too.''

"When?'' Matt asked.

Abbey smiled again. "Well, hopefully by the day after tomorrow. Sam and I want the herds sold and gone by the time we leave for the east.''

"Where is Roman Pollock?'' Matt asked suddenly.

The girl's smile slipped. "I don't know where he is.'' She shrugged her shapely shoulders. "Roman has not been well recently. One day he just rode away from the ranch and we haven't seen him since.''

"Good riddance, I say,'' Abe snapped. "Maybe him and that crazy Indian will meet out on the plains and kill each other.''

Abbey picked up her riding crop from Matt's desk. "Well, Marshal, we must be going. I'm so sorry you and Abe had a little misunderstanding. Slim Brower was such a nice man. I'm sure you'll find his killer.''

Matt nodded, his eyes hard. "I'm sure I will.''

As the pair stepped to the door, Matt asked: "Miss McKenna, where were you last night around ten o'clock?''

The girl turned, her face as pretty and innocent as that of a celluloid doll. "Why, I was on my way home to the ranch.''

"You were in Dodge?''

"Yes, I was. When I heard that Abe had been attacked by that horrible renegade Iron Hawk and had sought safety in Dodge, I rode here to make sure he was all right. I spoke to my brother outside the Alhambra and told him I wanted him to come home with me."

"I was drunk, Marshal, as you know," Abe said, rubbing his jaw. "I told Abbey I wanted to stay in town and get even drunker. That's how much the damn Indian is beginning to wear on me."

Abbey smiled. "We had a little quarrel I'm afraid, and I left for home alone." The girl looked at Matt, her eyes calculating. "Why did you want to know?"

Matt shrugged. "I was just curious."

As Abe opened the door for his sister, Matt said: "Watch out for those dry cottonwood branches, Miss McKenna. Sometimes they can whip across your face like bullets."

After the McKennas were gone, the subtle scent of Abbey's perfume lingered in the air. It smelled like fresh flowers.

The young lieutenant was exhausted.

Matt could tell by the way the officer slumped in the saddle, his head hanging, nodding with every step of his horse. At his side rode a grizzled corporal, a fat white bandage around his head, and behind trailed a dozen troopers, Buffalo Soldiers who looked to be as worn-out as their officer. A Pawnee scout in a calico shirt and black vest was out in front, a rifle across his saddle horn.

Matt sat his bay, his eyes on the patrol as it got closer. The big marshal had left Dodge an hour earlier, planning to check on the cowboys Abe McKenna had hired to round up his herd. The six punchers were all young and this had been their first trip up the trail. The last thing Matt wanted was green youngsters like these to tangle with Iron Hawk or Roman Pollock. Skilled as they were with cattle, nothing in their experience would have prepared them for the kind of slick gunplay and sudden, deadly violence the Cheyenne or Roman could offer.

The cowboys were holding the McKenna longhorns at the big bend of Buckner Creek, an area of good grass hemmed in on three sides by steep banks and cottonwoods, and so far they'd rounded up close to fifteen hundred head. There was still six hours of daylight, and one of the hands Matt had spoken with said they expected to pick up the Herefords and drive both herds into Dodge before dark.

Unlike the border trash who had come up the trail with the McKennas, the cowboys, all top hands, worked efficiently and well, just two of them holding the cattle within the bend with ease.

Three or four of the surviving McKenna punchers were helping the others with the roundup, but they were surly and uncommunicative and Matt had not spoken to any of them.

The marshal had looped a little ways south of the Buckner, scouting the area. He reined up his horse when he saw the patrol.

Now he waited as the soldiers drew closer. The

lieutenant, who looked to be still in his teens, jerked up his head, saw Matt and halted his men. He glanced at the star on the big lawman's vest and threw him a snappy salute. "Good afternoon, Marshal. Riding out?"

Matt nodded. "Just keeping my eye on a cattle roundup." His gaze went from the stone-faced Pawnee to the soldiers sitting stooped and weary in their saddles. "You look to have been though the mill, Lieutenant."

The young officer nodded. "Tangled with the Cheyenne yesterday, west of here. Lost a man and a horse and my corporal was wounded. We chased them across the south fork of the Pawnee but they outdistanced us. We fired on the hostiles, but I don't believe we caused any casualties."

Matt was surprised. "Lieutenant, you said 'them.' You mean there's more than one?"

"We counted at least twelve." The officer saw that Matt was puzzled and added: "Old Black Snake's band was camped at Fort Dodge awaiting relocation to the new reservation in the Oklahoma Territory. Last week a number of young warriors broke out to join this man Iron Hawk."

Matt nodded. "Lieutenant, Iron Hawk is a Dog Soldier, maybe the last of them, and he can still attract a following."

"Colonel Vanderhoff moved quickly to prevent another breakout," the young officer said. "All the warriors of fighting age are now securely penned up within the fort."

"With a Dog Soldier leading them, twelve Cheyenne is plenty to handle," Matt said. "I'd say you have a war on your hands."

The lieutenant stiffened. "We'll soon run them down, Marshal. Colonel Vanderhoff has asked for a full infantry regiment to reinforce his cavalry. I assure you that within the next week, Iron Hawk and the others will be taken to Fort Dodge in chains."

Matt smiled and shook his head. "I hope you're right, Lieutenant, because—"

"Dust, Sir!" the corporal yelled, looking over his shoulder.

The marshal rose in the stirrups and studied the land to the west. A huge purple-and-black cloud was rising into the air, flickering red glare at its base, stretching across the entire horizon.

"That's not dust," Matt said. "It's fire!"

The prairie was ablaze . . . and the Pawnee, understanding its significance, was already preparing his weapons and chanting his death song.

chapter 19

Run, Boys, Run!

"Lieutenant, the Cheyenne will be coming right behind that smoke," Matt said, sliding his rifle from the boot. "With your men as tired as they are, I suggest you hightail it for Fort Dodge."

"The Indians deliberately set the grass on fire?" the young officer asked.

"All but a singe pathway they'll use to ride through and attack," Matt said. "The Indians have burned the prairie for countless generations as a way of starting new growth to attract buffalo. The herds would travel hundreds, sometimes thousands of miles to graze on the fresh green shoots.

"The Cheyenne called prairie fire the Red Buffalo because of the way it could suddenly change direction very quickly, and now and again they'd use it as a weapon of war." The marshal gathered up the reins of his bay and pointed toward the racing smoke and flame. "And that's a weapon of war."

"Directed at my patrol?"

Matt shook his head. "Lieutenant, for reasons I haven't time to go into, Iron Hawk is fighting his own war against a man named Abe McKenna. McKenna's herd is up on the bend of Buckner Creek and I think Iron Hawk plans to burn him out."

"Is there anything I can do?" the young officer asked.

"Yes. If you plan on staying around, keep the Cheyenne busy until I can warn the punchers and get that herd headed for Dodge."

The soldier needed no other instruction. He swung his horse and waved his men forward, toward the smoke. The Pawnee hung back a little, thinking it through. Then, his mind made up, he galloped beside his officer.

The smell of the billowing smoke was heavy in the air and Matt could hear the crackle of burning grass as he headed the bay north toward the creek.

Behind him, rifles crashed and the Cheyenne were already yipping their war cries.

When Matt rode up on the creek, the fire was about a half mile away and coming fast. A young freckle-faced cowboy in batwing chaps rode toward him and the big marshal yelled to the man.

"Get the herd running for Dodge!"

The puncher shook his head. "We'll run too much beef off of them."

Matt pointed to the racing prairie fire. "Hell, man, look at that! In another five minutes you won't have a herd."

The cattle were already milling, rolling their eyes, scared by the smell of the smoke. A lanky brindle steer had forced his way through the rest of the herd, tossing his eight-foot-wide horns, snorting, ready to lead the stampede.

All the cowboys and four McKenna riders were with the cattle. The freckled cowboy turned and saw the fire burning closer, and his shocked face showed that the logic of Matt's order had finally hit home.

"And there's a bunch of Cheyenne coming right behind the smoke," the marshal yelled, laying it on the line for the man.

Now the young puncher had heard enough. "Move 'em out!" he shouted. He drew his gun and blasted a shot into the air, then another.

Led by the brindle steer, the herd immediately broke into a run, covering ground very fast, the punchers on the flank riding hard, turning them southeast toward Dodge.

Matt watched the longhorns go, the skilled Texas cowboys managing to keep them bunched and headed in the right direction. The cattle would run off plenty of beef, but at least the herd would survive.

The marshal had no idea why he'd saved the McKenna cows. Now, when he asked himself the question, he realized that his years in Dodge had given him the instincts of a cattleman—and he could not stand idly by while a herd, any herd, was needlessly destroyed.

The young cowboys were also a consideration. Hired by the day, they had taken no part in any of the McKenna lawlessness, and he could not let them be destroyed either.

West of the creek, the Red Buffalo was much closer, columns of spiraling smoke rising high into the air. To the south, the cavalry patrol was spread out in a skirmish line, backing toward him at a walk, the troopers blazing away with their Colts.

Iron Hawk and his Cheyenne rode through a break in the fire and swung wide of the soldiers, charging toward the creek. Their war cries changed to howls of frustration and rage when they saw that the herd was gone, and now they concentrated on the lone rider who stood in their path.

A bullet split the air above Matt's head and another kicked up dirt in front of his horse. Matt's fight was not with the Cheyenne, but if he turned his back and tried to outrun them, he'd be shot out of the saddle.

The big marshal threw his Winchester to his shoulder and fired at the closest warrior. The man threw up his arms and fell backward over his horse. Working the lever of his rifle, shooting rapidly from the shoulder, Matt poured fire into the oncoming Indians.

He scored no more hits, but as the warriors began to take fire from the charging cavalrymen, they suddenly broke and turned to the north. A bullet from the patrol hit another warrior and he went down with his horse. The man's paint pony hit the dirt headfirst, somersaulted onto its back, then crashed on top of the screaming Cheyenne. Led by the lieutenant, the patrol thundered past Matt at a gallop, firing their revolvers, the Pawnee yelling his war cry.

The Red Buffalo had reached the creek and the lawman gave ground, backing up his nervous, prancing bay.

Racing flames reached the Indian Matt had shot. The wounded warrior cried out in terror and crawled toward the marshal, desperately trying to outpace the fire. Matt watched in horror as the rushing wall of flame caught, then enveloped the man, embracing him with searing scarlet arms. The fire held the shrieking Indian for long, terrible moments, then roared past. Through the moving red-and-gray curtain of fire and smoke, Matt saw the warrior on his hands and knees, his head hanging. The Cheyenne's arms were charred black to the elbow, his hair was burned to the scalp and his face was a blistered, melted nightmare, no longer even vaguely human.

Matt raised his rifle, sighted carefully and fired once. The warrior's body jerked and he fell flat on his belly, rolled and lay still.

"I hope you would have done that for me," the marshal whispered as he slid his rifle into the boot and swung his horse away from the fire. Matt spurred the bay in the direction taken by the herd and the big horse's long-striding gallop quickly opened up some ground between himself and the fire.

When he looked back, he saw no sign of the cavalry or Iron Hawk's warriors. The flames of the Red Buffalo had not jumped the creek and already the fires were burning themselves out across the prairie, the spring grass not yet dry enough to feed the flames. A sullen smoke cloud hung in the air but it was being slowly shredded into long gray streaks by the wind.

Like the fire, the stampeding McKenna cattle had also burned themselves out. When Matt caught up with the herd it was strung out along the banks of Duck Creek just north of Dodge.

For a few moments the marshal watched the cattle drink; then he rode up to the freckled cowboy, who was sitting his horse under the shade of a spreading cottonwood.

"How many did you lose?" Matt asked.

The young cowboy reached into his shirt pocket, found his tally book and quickly checked his numbers. "We'd rounded up twenty seven hundred and sixteen head before the fire hit. We lost none after that."

Matt nodded. For all intents and purposes, the McKenna herd had survived intact.

The cowboy's glance was quizzical. "Never seen a single herd with so many different brands, Marshal. If a man was riding for the McKennas, he'd sure get his head turned around. One of them brands I recognize, seen it on a yearling steer down to Webb

County one time, had a D on its left shoulder and a K on the left hip. Cow belonged to a cranky old cuss by the name of Deacon Kraus. I recollect he paid his hands badly an' fed them even worse."

Matt tried to conceal his interest, asking casually: "What happened to Kraus?"

"What happened to him? Why I heard tell he married some pretty young filly. Then a couple of weeks later he ups and disappears. Some say the old coot was so wore out, he just dropped dead out on the range someplace. His body was never found—I know that."

"Would you say Kraus was a rich man?"

The cowboy shook his head. "There was a rumor going around that the old man had enough paper money to burn a wet mule. But judging by the wages he paid an' how he fed his hands, I doubt it. He had a run-down two-by-twice outfit and never could keep anybody working for him. Every rancher needs a few steady punchers."

Matt nodded. "I guess he does." He touched his hat brim. "Well, I got to be moving on. If I see you around Dodge, I'll buy you a drink."

The cowboy grinned. "Name's Perry Owens, an' broke as I am, I'll surely take you up on that offer."

As Matt rode toward Dodge, he felt strongly that Deacon Kraus had been the first of Abbey McKenna's many victims. It was likely she'd heard the rumors and married the old man believing him wealthy. When she discovered he wasn't, she'd had him murdered and then taken his small herd and whatever else she could find. And judging by how poorly Abbey was dressed when she first arrived in Dodge, Kraus hadn't been worth much.

Since then she'd come far.

She'd murdered two more men for their money and organized a highly profitable, and bloody, stage robbery. Now both her herds were sold and when she got her claws into Sam Noonan's nest egg, she would move east and live the kind of elegant life she craved.

There were now just three days remaining until the wedding. His face bleak, Matt realized that for Sam—and himself—time was running out fast. . . .

chapter 20

The Haunted Alley

Matt left his bay at the livery stable and found Festus waiting for him in the marshal's office.

The deputy had put on the coffee and Matt poured himself a cup and sat at his desk. Briefly, he told Festus about the desperate flight of the McKenna herd from the prairie fire and described his battle with Iron Hawk and his Cheyenne.

"You think them bluecoat soldiers ran them down?" Festus asked.

Matt shook his head. "I doubt it. The patrol's horses were tired. They wouldn't run very far."

Festus was silent for a few moments; then his eyes took on a haunted look. "Matthew," he said, "I got me a real problem."

The marshal smiled. "Not woman trouble, is it?"

"Nah, nothing like that." Festus leaned forward

and dropped his voice to a confidential whisper. "It's them danged Chinamen."

"But the work on the water tank is done," Matt said.

"It is, but you'd never know it by the way them Hindoos and all their kinfolk foller me around, Matthew. I reckon they think I'm some kind of a god or somethin'. It's plumb wearin' on me."

Matt suppressed a smile and said with a straight face: "Now where would they get a crazy idea like that?"

"I dunno. But they do. They fall into line behind me everywhere I go and one that can speak some American keeps jabbering, 'New jobee, boss man. New jobee.' "

Matt nodded. "I guess they liked working for you, Festus. You gave them the notion that the way to handle hard work is to lie down beside it and sleep like a pup."

Festus sat back in his chair and scratched his hairy throat, his left eyebrow crawling up his forehead. "Matthew, for your information, hard work ain't good for a man. It can give him the rheumatisms somethin' terrible, to say nothin' of the croup."

"So what are you going to do about the Chinese?"

"I dunno. I haven't taken dead aim at a notion yet. But I've learned how to shake 'em off. I suddenly cut to my left or right, depending where I'm walkin', an' step up that alley where ol' Black Buffalo shot hisself. The Chinamen won't come after me in there, say the place is haunted by evil spirits."

Festus leaned forward in his chair again. "Matthew, I think maybe it is, a ha'nt, I mean. When it's dark, that alley is spooky enough to hair-lip the governor."

The marshal recalled that Festus had once punched cows along the Canadian, and the deputy still retained the cowboy's deep dread of the supernatural. Now Festus confirmed Matt's thought.

"I recollect another ha'nt like that one time," he said. "It was way back, afore I was a Ranger. I worked at ranch where lighting killed a cowboy and his pony as they was coming home drunk from the saloon one night.

"Well sir, the poor puncher's hat was blown clean off'n his head an' it landed right in the middle of the trail. Nobody wanted to pick it up after that. And it come about that we'd ride a mile around the hat so we didn't have to see it when we passed by. That ten-dollar Stetson stayed right where it was on the trail for four, maybe five years."

"What happened to it?" Matt asked. "Somebody finally take it?"

Festus shook his head. "Nah, one night a big wind came an' picked up the hat an' carried it away. But, Matthew, that spot on the trail was always ha'anted by the ghost of the dead cowboy and his hoss, just like the alley over yonder across the street."

Matt smiled. "Festus, you're carrying a big ol' forty-five on your hip. You shouldn't be scared of the boogerman."

"You can poke fun at me all you want, Matthew,

but there's plenty of spooky alleys in Dodge. Just ask them Chinamen. The one that speaks some American, he says he saw an evil spirit in the alley by the Alamo t'other evenin', just afore Abe McKenna shot that puncher an' now can't be hung on account of—"

Matt jerked upright in his chair, asking quickly: "What did he see, Festus?"

The deputy was taken aback by the marshal's quickening interest, and it took him a few moments before he answered. "Matthew, the Chinaman didn't see Abe McKenna if'n that's what you're thinkin'. It's kinda hard to make out what that heathen says most of the time, but he claims he laid an eye on a female spirit standing in the alley afore Slim Brower was shot.

"He says she was wearing a black cloak and her name is Kwan Yin, that's the goddess who escorts the souls of the dead to the other world." Festus slammed his hand on the desk. "Dang it all, Matthew! See how them Hindoos is learnin' me to talk all kinds of heathen stuff. Anyhoo, the Chinaman was so scared, he took one look an' hightailed it out of there."

As Festus rose to pour himself coffee, Matt sat deep in thought.

The Chinese laborer said he'd seen a female goddess in the alley beside the Alamo just before Slim Brower was killed. It had been no spirit, but a woman of flesh and blood.

Matt had no doubt that it was Abbey who'd shot at him the night before. But until now he'd hadn't linked the girl to the murder of Brower. If Brower had gone looking for Abe, it would have been an easy matter for Abbey to lure the man into the dark alley. Broken shoulder or no, an invitation from a pretty girl was one that the puncher would eagerly have accepted.

Perhaps Abbey had let him kiss her and then suggested they go somewhere more private, and she'd asked Brower to lead the way. When the man turned his back on her, she'd shot him.

After that, Abbey had made her escape and staked out Matt's office, knowing he'd eventually be called to investigate the murder. And her plan might have succeeded had her aim been just a shade better.

Abbey must have been worried that the marshal was getting too close. All she needed was a few more days to attain her goals. If she succeeded in killing Matt, her future was assured because there was no one else who could stop her.

Could the big marshal stop her now?

Matt shook his head. Given time maybe. But time was now on Abbey's side.

By noon the next day, both McKenna herds had arrived safely in Dodge and Abbey had been paid in cash by the buyer, a man named Canfield.

Matt ran Canfield down at the bar of the Alhambra and the man readily produced bills of sale the McKennas had given him for both herds. There were seven in all, six for the mixed herd of longhorns and one for the eight hundred Herefords.

Each bill of sale was written in the same fine cop-perplate hand. Only the signatures were different, including, Matt noticed, one for six hundred yearling longhorns signed by Deacon Kraus.

"What kind of prices did the McKenna herds real-ize?" Matt asked.

Canfield, a square, powerful man with a stubborn jaw, reached into the pocket of his coat and produced a small ledger. "Prices are only fair to middling this year, Marshal," he said. "Though Miss McKenna made out quite well." He hesitated a few moments, then asked: "Is she a friend of yours?"

Matt nodded. "We're acquainted."

"Fine girl," Canfield said. "Very fine young lady indeed." He thumbed through the ledger and found the page he wanted. "Ah yes, here it is. Both herds were mostly young stuff. I paid nine dollars a head for the yearlings, fourteen for two year olds and fif-teen for the rest. The Herefords brought twenty-three dollars a head. The total was forty thousand and nine hundred dollars." Canfield beamed. "A tidy sum, Marshal."

"I guess it is," Matt agreed, "especially since Miss McKenna keeps her overheads low."

When Matt left the Alhambra, he glanced up the street and saw Kitty window-shopping outside the New York Hat Shop. Kitty wore a cool, lacy white dress, a small parasol shading her from the blazing sun.

His spurs ringing on the boardwalk, the tall marshal walked toward the woman, and Kitty turned, startled. "Why, Matt, I didn't see you on the street. Where did you come from?"

"The Alhambra," Matt said. "Just some official business." He glanced into the shop window. "Thinking of buying a hat?"

"Yes." Kitty turned and smiled. "Sam asked me to be Abbey's maid of honor and of course I agreed."

"I'm to be his best man," Matt said, his face revealing nothing of how he felt.

"I know. Sam told me. Isn't it wonderful? The two of us together like that." Kitty took the big marshal's hand. "Now you're here, you can help me choose."

Matt took a step back, confused. "Kitty, I know nothing about women's fixin's. The only hat I ever bought is the one I'm wearing."

"Oh nonsense, Matt. I need your advice."

The marshal opened his mouth to object, but Kitty pulled him toward the doorway of the store. "It will only take a minute."

Forty-five minutes and a score of hats later, Kitty still hadn't made up her mind.

"I thought modom suited the wide-brimmed white perfectly," the salesgirl said hopefully. "It highlights modom's fair complexion."

Kitty picked up the hat and settled it on head, and immediately Matt's heart skipped several beats. The first time he ever laid eyes on her, he thought Kitty the most beautiful woman he'd ever seen. And nothing had happened since to change his mind.

"Oh, I just don't know," Kitty sighed. "Matt, what do you think? Does the wide brim make me look kind of short and dumpy?"

Sensing the trap, Matt carefully stepped around it. "I reckon it makes you look as purdy as a field of bluebonnets," he said. "You'll put the bride in the shade."

Kitty flashed a delighted white smile. "Well, that settles it then." She gave the hat to the salesgirl. "I'll take this one."

The young salesgirl's eyes slanted gratefully to Matt as she laid the hat in a pink box, then tied the box with a white ribbon and walked over to the counter.

Kitty's eyes were filling up as she stepped beside Matt and lightly placed her hand on his wide chest. "Will you one day help me choose a hat for our wedding, Matt?"

It seemed to the marshal that the very mention of matrimony, even when they weren't getting hitched themselves, made females go dewy eyed, and Kitty, though a levelheaded, successful businesswoman, was apparently no exception.

But Matt made no attempt to back away from this one. "Of course I will," he said. He inclined his head, kissed Kitty's soft, yielding mouth and added: "You can count on it."

They stayed close, the unspoken love they felt for each other making the space around them sacred for a few fleeting moments.

It was the salesgirl who broke the spell. "Ah-hem,"

she coughed politely, "is there anything else I can do for modom?"

Kitty smiled, looking up at Matt's face. "No, that will be all," she said. Then, after a heartbeat's pause: "At least for the time being."

Matt was walking back to his office, the lingering memory of Kitty's lips still on his own, when a rider thundered down Front Street on a lathered horse. The marshal recognized the man as one of the punchers who had come up the trail from Texas with the McKennas.

The man reined in his mount, the pony's skidding hooves kicking up a cloud of dust, and vaulted from the saddle. "Marshal," he yelled, "the McKenna cabin is being attacked by Indians." He ran toward Matt, his face panicked. "I don't think they can hold out much longer."

"Who's at the cabin?" Matt asked.

The man gulped for breath, then said: "Miss Abbey rode in just before the attack. Abe's there and another three hands. The Cheyenne have them penned up in the cabin tight as Dick's hatband. Unless they get help, there ain't nobody comin' out of there alive."

Whatever his personal opinion of the McKennas, Matt's conscience would not allow him to stand idly by and let them be needlessly killed. He made up his mind quickly, told the rider to find himself a fresh horse, then looked for Festus.

Matt found his deputy eating chicken and dumplings at the back of the Chinese laundry, surrounded by a crowd of admiring Celestials. As Festus gulped down the remainder of his food, skillfully demonstrating a recently acquired talent, the use of chopsticks, Matt had to elbow a path for them both through protesting Asians before he started to round up a posse.

The only males awake in Dodge were the town's respectable citizens. But despite their broadcloth suits and celluloid collars, they were tough men who handled guns like they'd been born to them. Most had fought in the War Between the States and a few, like the gunsmith Newly O'Brien and Howie Uzell, the clerk at the Dodge House, had fought Indians in the past.

Mayor Kelly, a fighting Irishman with no backup in him, volunteered his services. Kelly was chronically shortsighted and his shooting could be erratic and highly dangerous to his own side, but what he lacked in gun skills, he made up for in sheer guts and determination.

The only member of the sporting crowd the marshal roused from slumber was Bat Masterson. He had two reasons, the first being that Bat was a skilled gunhand who had helped defeat a large Comanche and Kiowa war party at Adobe Walls in Texas a few years before. And the second was a little payback for the white buffalo debacle. Matt still resented being so rudely shaken awake by the dapper little gambler.

Though Bat grumbled that no honest man gets up at two in the afternoon, he nonetheless armed himself, saddled his horse and within minutes was wide-awake and ready for the trail.

Half an hour after the McKenna rider had asked his help, Matt led a posse of fifteen men out of Dodge and north toward the Pawnee.

chapter 21

The Return of
Roman Pollock

The McKenna cabin on the Pawnee River lay almost thirty miles to the northwest.

Matt figured the posse could get there by late afternoon if they took the most direct route northwest, across Duck, Saw Log and Buckner creeks, then past the lower fork of shallow, winding Sand Creek.

It was fine country for riding, with nothing but flat grassland as far as the eye could see. As they crossed the Saw Log, the posse startled a large herd of antelope, which fled in a panicked run to the south, vanishing into the eddying cloud of their own dust, and jackrabbits constantly bounded away from them in every direction.

The sun was dropping lower in the cloudless sky when Matt led the posse to the Buckner. The riders watered their horses in a shallow draw just off the creek and the men who smoked built cigarettes or lit cigars.

After ten minutes' rest, Matt led the posse to the northwest again, setting the pace at a distance-eating lope, Festus on his durable mule effortlessly riding alongside him.

If the McKennas were still holding out, dusk might put an end to the siege, since the Cheyenne didn't like to fight in the dark. But Indians were notional, and if put to it, they would attack at night, especially if there was some tactical advantage to be gained.

Matt decided grimly that if his posse didn't get there in time, it would be a serious mistake for the McKennas to place their trust in the darkness.

When the posse reached Sand Creek, Matt led it north for a ways along an old, overgrown buffalo trail. He crossed the creek where a trickle of water flowed between swelling sandbanks and then swung almost due north.

Matt glanced at the sky. To the west the blue was fading into a pale rose and a few smears of purple cloud were tinted along their bottom edge with gold. The marshal calculated there were still a couple of hours until dark, plenty of time to effect a rescue—if the McKennas were still alive.

Ahead of him Matt heard the faint report of a rifle, followed by another.

"I guess it ain't over yet, Matthew," Festus said, sliding his rifle from the boot under his knee.

"Sounds like," Matt answered.

A low rise covered in short buffalo grass lay about a quarter mile in front of them, at its base a small pool with a solitary willow trailing its branches into the water. Matt threw up a hand and reined in his bay, the posse crowding around him.

"When we top the rise, we'll see the cabin," Matt said. He smiled. "Anybody want to play general from here?"

"I do," Bat Masterson hollered. He kneed his horse forward until he was opposite Matt. "I say we spread out in a skirmish line and just go a-hornin' over the rise," he said, his face eager. "Take them redskins by surprise that way."

Matt nodded. "Anybody else got a better idea?"

The only voices raised murmured approval of Masterson's suggestion, and Matt slid his Colt clear of the holster. "Then we play it Bat's way." He kicked his horse into a gallop and called over his shoulder: "Remember the Alamo, boys!"

The posse spread out and took the rise at a run, Matt in the lead.

A few yards ahead of the marshal, a Cheyenne suddenly jumped up from the long grama grass and threw his rifle to his shoulder. Matt fired, missed, then fired again and the warrior went down. Behind and on both sides of Matt, rifles and shotguns banged and Matt saw another warrior run toward the cabin, then fall on his face on the grass.

Iron Hawk, recognizable by his waist-length hair and black war paint, rode from behind the cabin, three other warriors galloping close behind him. Iron

Hawk fired, and beside Matt, Mayor Kelley's horse collapsed. The little Irishman was thrown clear, but he rolled, then sprang to his feet, his Colt blasting.

Matt and the other posse members reined up their horses and concentrated their fire on Iron Hawk and his mounted warriors. A young Cheyenne threw up his hands and tumbled off his pony, his naked chest suddenly splashed with scarlet.

The cabin door swung open and two of the Mc-Kenna punchers ran outside, guns blazing. Another Cheyenne fell, then another. Iron Hawk swung his horse away from the cabin, a solitary warrior following him, and galloped away to the north.

There was no cowardice in the act, since Indians saw no logic in continuing to fight a losing battle. Iron Hawk had been surprised by the arrival of the posse and today the odds were not in his favor. Tomorrow, or the next day, that could all change. Better to run away and live to fight again when he had the advantage.

Festus, as he surveyed the smoke-streaked battle-field, was disappointed and it showed in the dejected slump of his shoulders. "Heck, Matthew," he said, "I figured ol' Iron Hawk would pin himself to the ground with that sash o' his'n and fight to the death. I'd loved to have seen that."

Matt's smile was thin. "I guess he felt there was nothing around here worth dying for, Festus. He had no women or children to protect, no village lying open and vulnerable behind him. I'd say he plans to stay alive long enough to exact his revenge on Abe McKenna."

Mayor Kelley stomped toward Matt, cursing like a muleskinner. "Damn it all, that Injun is hell-bent on setting me afoot," he yelled. "He stole me best horse an' now he's killed me second best, the red devil."

"I'm sure Miss McKenna will lend you a horse, Mayor," Matt said.

Kelley scowled. "Well, that's all fine and dandy, Matt. But damn that redskin's eyes, it's the principle of the thing."

Bat Masterson rode up beside the marshal, waving a hand toward the posse members, who were now dismounted and standing around the Cheyenne dead. "We count four Cheyenne killed and another who's wounded but breathing his last," he said. The gambler smiled. "Matt, that charge of mine really buffaloed 'em."

Bat was expecting congratulations and Matt, who considered Masterson a scoundrel but a first-class fighting man, was not about to disappoint him. But then Abbey McKenna stepped out of the cabin door and walked toward him and what the marshal had to say died on his lips.

The girl's dress was splashed in blood and her face was streaked black from powder smoke. Her eyes had a haunted, faraway look and Matt could see that she'd been badly frightened.

"Thank you for getting here in time, Marshal," she said, her voice shaking a little. "Our ammunition was running low and I don't think we could have held out much longer."

Matt Dillon was by nature a caring man, but there

was in him hard, tempered steel which would not even now allow him to unbend.

"Are you wounded?" he asked, his voice curt.

Abbey shook her head and looked down at her dress. "This isn't my blood," she said. "Early in the fight, Tom Stockton had his lower jaw shot away. I . . . I was standing next to him when it happened."

"Where's Abe?" Matt asked.

The girl's eyes went to Matt, then slid uneasily away. "He's all right. Abe took sick after the firing started. I told him to lie down on the floor."

Abbey stepped close to Matt's horse and looked up at him with frightened eyes. "I want to go back to Dodge with you and the others, and so does Abe. I'm to be married the day after tomorrow and I don't want to stay out here a moment longer. I know that Indian will come back looking for us."

Matt nodded. "You're welcome to ride back with the posse. I'm sure you can find a hotel room in town. In the meantime, these men need coffee and food if you have some. They've ridden far and have another long ride ahead of them."

Without another word, the marshal swung out of the saddle and led his horse to the front of the cabin. Both windows had been shattered by bullets and the pine boards along the front were pockmarked with holes.

The Cheyenne had laid down a heavy fire and the defenders were lucky to have gotten away with only one man wounded.

Matt was about to step into the cabin to check on

the badly injured Tom Stockton when Howie Uzell yelled: "Rider coming."

Matt followed the man's pointing finger and saw someone on a tall horse approach at a walk through the gathering twilight. There was no mistaking the alert, stiff-backed way the rider sat his saddle.

It was Roman Pollock.

The gunman rode up to the front of the cabin and gave Matt a nod; his cold eyes scanned the members of the posse, rested briefly on Bat Masterson, then dismissed him.

Pollock touched his hat brim to Abbey. "Evening, Miz McKenna," he said.

The girl's suddenly frightened glance went to Matt and then to Pollock. "It's nice to have you back with us, Roman," she said, her voice weak and uncertain.

"Good to be back," Pollock said. His quick eyes ran over the curves of the girl's body, the woman hunger naked in him. "Had Injun trouble, I see," he said finally. "Heard the guns from a long ways off."

"The marshal and his posse arrived just in time, Roman," Abbey said. She tried a smile, but it didn't quite reach her eyes. "I was just about to make coffee. Would you like some?"

The gunman shook his head. "No, I don't want coffee. I'm here for something else."

Men had gathered around Matt, and Mayor Kelley was looking at Pollock like he would a rattlesnake that had just crawled out from under a rock.

"Do I have something of yours?" Abbey asked.

Pollock nodded. "I heard you sold both herds. I'm here to claim my share."

"I'll make up your wages right away," Abbey said.

The gunman shook his head. "I don't want wages. I want half."

One of the McKenna punchers, a tall, skinny man with a bobbing Adam's apple and hound dog eyes, took a step toward Pollock. "If that's going to be the way of it, then we all should have equal shares. I buried two men after we took them Herefords."

Alarmed, Abbey's eyes darted to Matt. "Mike," she snapped, "shut your mouth."

"I'll be damned if I will," the man said, his long face flushed and belligerent. "Pollock wants half, but I say equal shares for all."

Matt saw the quick hardening of Pollock's eyes and knew he would soon have to stop a shooting. He led his horse forward to place himself between the two men, but stopped . . . as a living, breathing horror stepped out of the cabin.

Tom Stockton's entire lower jaw was gone, leaving only a gaping hole of raw, bloody meat and broken teeth in which his tongue lolled. The front of the man's shirt was covered in a thick crust of blackened blood and he staggered a little when he walked. Stockton held a Colt in the fist that hung at his side, and his eyes were wild, fevered, suffering a pain that was beyond pain, yet he seemed unaware that he was already dying.

Stockton tried to talk, a hoarse, guttural sound

without meaning that made blood bubble up in his shredded throat. The man stumbled toward Pollock, his fixed gaze, accusing and terrible, on the gunman.

"What the hell is he saying?" Pollock asked.

The man called Mike tried to grin and failed, the terrible sight of the wounded man stripping the bark off him. "I think he's objecting to your share, Roman."

For a few moments Pollock sat perfectly still in the saddle. Then, in a swift blur of movement, his hands flashed to his guns. Both Pollock's Colts roared and Stockton staggered under the impact of the two bullets that crashed into his chest. The man took several steps backward, then fell on his face and lay still.

"I'd say ol' Tom doesn't have an objection anymore." Pollock smiled.

Matt went for his gun, but Pollock swung his Colt around fast and covered him. "Don't try it, Matt," he whispered, his eyes burning. "Or by God I'll shoot you right where you stand."

The marshal had not cleared leather and now he let his gun slide back into the holster.

"Wise move, Matt," Pollock said. "If you'd tried to complete your draw, you'd be lying dead in the dirt right now."

"This is an outrage," Mayor Kelley spluttered. "That was cold-blooded murder." He stomped toward Pollock. "I have almost twenty men here and I demand your surrender."

"I won't be surrendering today, Mayor," Pollock said, backing his horse, his guns covering the posse.

"Masterson," he said, "you know me. You know what I can do. Advise the rest of these men to give me the road."

"Do as he says, boys," Bat said, his face bleak. "We can get him, but he's poison fast and he'll leave five or six of us dead on the ground."

Pollock turned quickly to Abbey McKenna. "Woman, this isn't over, not by a long shot," he said. "I'll be back to claim what's mine."

The gunman backed up his horse, swung the animal around and spurred into a gallop. Matt stepped into the saddle and followed, his tired bay still willing to move out eagerly.

Pollock headed toward the north fork of Sand Creek, his leggy roan eating up distance. Matt followed as best he could, but he sensed Buck's tiredness and a couple of times the big bay stumbled.

As the space between them opened up, the gathering darkness swallowed Pollock, and Matt knew he had no hope of catching him. The gunman could ride in any direction and fade like a wraith into the night.

Reluctantly Matt pulled up his horse and turned back for the McKenna ranch.

Now he knew he would have to deal with Roman Pollock. And Bat Masterson was right—Pollock was fast. Very fast.

chapter 22

Sam Noonan's In-law Problems

The McKennas loaded up their surrey with luggage—including, Matt noted, a locked strongbox—and rode out with the posse. The three surviving hands had elected to stay at the ranch and Abbey told them she would pay them their wages before she left on her honeymoon.

The man named Mike, who had let slip about the fight for the Herefords, took this news with ill grace and vowed to be waiting outside the church to make sure he was paid his due.

Abe, who looked green around the gills, held the reins of the surrey and drove in the wake of the posse.

Both men and horses were tired and the short, sharp battle with the Cheyenne and the killing of Tom Stockton seemed to be weighing on them. Even Bat Masterson was silent, and he was by nature a talking man.

With Matt and Festus in the lead, the posse rode across the flat grassland under a bright full moon, which touched both men and horses with an unearthly silver light.

Abbey McKenna sat beside her brother, her eyes fixed on the unseen distance ahead, biting her lip now and then as though deep in thought.

Matt knew Iron Hawk's attack had scared the girl badly, as it had her brother. Now her only concern was to marry Sam Noonan and get as far from Kansas as possible.

The only problem, Matt thought bitterly, was that Sam's money would go east with Abbey but Sam would not. The McKennas would murder him somewhere between the Dodge rail depot and Boston, probably while they rode the steam cars.

Once away from Dodge, Sam would be on his own. Matt could do nothing for him, and that thought rankled.

The McKennas found rooms at the Dodge House and the posse broke up, a few trailing after Masterson to the bar at the Alhambra.

Matt rode to the livery stable, rubbed down the bay and fed him a bait of oats and a generous amount of hay. That done he returned to his office along roaring, brightly lit Front Street. Competing pianos cascaded a cacophony of sound into the night, and the tangled notes were accompanied by the hoarse yells of drinking men and the silken laughter of women.

A few minutes later Festus stepped into the office

and announced his intention of crossing the Deadline to patrol the lace-curtain side of town.

"How about the Chinese?" Matt asked. "They still following you around?"

Festus scratched his throat and looked thoughtful. "They sure are, Matthew. But know something? I'm starting to get used to them. There's something about Celestials that just kinda grows on a man."

Matt nodded, smiling. "Just so long as they don't interfere with your duties. You know Mayor Kelley sets store by letting the respectable citizens see a star across the tracks."

"They will, Matthew. Like I told you, I'm on my way over there right now."

Ten minutes after Festus left, Mayor Kelley barged into the office. The little man was still mad about the death of his horse, and he pitched into Matt concerning his deputy.

"Do you know what's going on across the Deadline?" he asked. Without waiting for a reply, he answered his own question. "Festus is walking about over there with a dozen jabbering, blathering Chinamen trailing behind him."

Matt fought back a smile and said: "I know, Mayor. Apparently they think Festus is a god."

Kelley stiffened in shock. "May all the saints in Heaven preserve us! What kind of god? You mean they think he's the great Poobah or something?"

"Or something," Matt agreed. "They figure he's their work god."

"Work god! The man's never done a lick of hard

work in his life. Mention manual labor to him and he thinks you're talking about a Mexican."

"Well, over to the water tower, Festus taught the Chinese how not to work and still get paid for it. I guess they reckon that's mighty powerful medicine."

For a moment it looked to Matt like Mayor James H. Kelley was about to have an attack of apoplexy. The mayor stuck a cigar in his mouth, snatched it out again, then shoved it back. Speaking around the stogie, his voice strangling in his throat, he finally managed to choke out a few words.

"Then tell Deputy Marshal Festus . . . Festus . . ."

"Haggen," Matt supplied.

"Deputy Marshal Festus Haggen that I don't want pigtailed heathen across the tracks any more than I want cowboys over there."

"I'll tell him," Matt said.

"And tell him one more thing. Tell him that the next time the water tower needs repairing, I'll be doing the supervising me ownself and he'll be doing the work." Kelley nodded his head vehemently. "Tell Mr. Haggen to put that in his pipe and smoke it."

"I'll make sure he knows, Mayor," Matt said.

"Humph," Kelley said. The little Irishman turned on his heel, stomped to the door, then turned and stabbed his cigar at the marshal like a dagger. "And another thing, do something about the damn stray curs running all over town. Shoot them on sight, and that's an order."

Before Matt could reply, Kelley stormed out the door and slammed it shut behind him.

The big marshal sat for long moments, thinking, then slowly shook his head. "Who," he wondered aloud, "is the great Poobah?"

Arm-in-arm, Abbey McKenna and Sam joined the traditional nightly promenade along the boardwalk of Front Street, the bartender beaming as passersby stopped and offered their congratulations on his upcoming marriage.

Matt stood outside his office and watched the couple stroll past the Long Branch, Sam acting like he'd suddenly grown to ten feet as he proudly showed off his beautiful bride-to-be.

Abbey had changed into a silk gown of dazzling yellow, the bustle huge, as befitted a fashionable Dodge City belle. The neckline was cut low and tight, revealing the generous swell of her breasts, which were separated by deep, shadowed cleavage. By contrast, Sam wore a suit of somber black broadcloth, a white shirt and a string tie. He was the very picture of a soon-to-be respectable Easterner.

As Matt watched, the couple lingered for a while at the darkened window of the hat shop, Abbey excitedly pointing something out to Sam. The bartender laughed, said something in return and then bent his head and kissed Abbey's willing mouth, the woman clinging close to him.

The couple was still locked in a passionate embrace, heedless of the smiling people who passed them on the boardwalk, when Abe McKenna, drunk and belligerent, stepped out of the Long Branch.

McKenna looked up and down the street, saw Sam and his sister, swore loudly and lurched toward them. "You!" he yelled when he was still twenty feet away. "Take your dirty paws off her!"

Surprised, Sam turned and Matt saw the man's face pale as Abe stomped toward him, his spurs ringing loud in the quick, shocked silence that had descended around them.

Abe stopped, his hand on his gun, his face black with anger. "Damn you!" he shouted again. "I told you, Noonan, let her be!"

Matt stepped into the street and angled fast toward the hat shop. The promenading couples, for the most part gamblers, cattle buyers and cowboys escorting painted and feathered saloon girls, had stopped to watch.

The marshal knew that Sam never carried a gun, and he was also aware that McKenna would have no compunction about shooting down an unarmed man.

Alarmed, Matt had almost reached the boardwalk when Abbey, her face as angry as that of her brother's, broke away from Sam and ran quickly toward Abe. "Go back to the hotel, you fool!" she yelled. "You'll spoil everything!"

Abe shook his head, bloodshot eyes looking past Abbey to Sam. "I've had enough, Abbey," he said. "I won't stand by and watch another man paw you ever again."

Matt stopped, waiting to see how the girl would react. Her response was instantaneous and violent. McKenna's head jerked as Abbey slapped him hard across the face, the crack of the blow loud in the quiet. "Go back to the hotel," she hissed through tightly clenched teeth. "I'll deal with you later."

A thin trickle of blood ran from the corner of McKenna's mouth as he looked at Abbey in shocked disbelief. People stood around watching—people who knew Sam Noonan well and were acquainted with his bride-to-be and her brother. Their stunned faces revealed that they were desperately trying to come to grips with what was happening.

Like a man waking from a dream, Abe McKenna suddenly allowed his pent-up fury to erupt. He roughly pushed his sister aside, slamming her against the wall, and paced toward Sam, drawing his gun. The bartender's face paled, but Sam had plenty of sand and he showed no fear. He slowly opened his coat. "I have no gun," he said.

McKenna's Colt slid from the holster. He thumbed back the hammer.

"McKenna!" Matt roared. His left arm was thrown straight out, a finger pointing at Abe. "Stop right where you are!"

McKenna hesitated, his gun still leveled at Sam.

"Pull that trigger, McKenna, and I'll drop you," Matt said, his voice suddenly low and iron hard.

McKenna paused, uncertain and wary, for a couple of tense heartbeats. He turned toward Matt and raised the gun threateningly. And that was his mistake. Matt's right hand blurred as he drew and when McKenna saw the Colt flash into the big marshal's hand he almost fell over from shock.

"Ease the gun back into the holster, then unbuckle and step away," Matt said quietly.

Abe dearly wanted to shoot. Matt saw it in the man's eyes. He wanted to swing up his gun and cut loose. But he knew if he tried he'd die, and McKenna wanted badly to live.

Carefully, his face like stone, the man slid his Colt back into the holster, then, with trembling fingers, began to unbuckle his belt.

Matt watched McKenna closely. Abe was a man of no courage, a bully and a braggart, but it is always a dangerous mistake to take such men too lightly. The man's gun belt thudded to the boards at his feet and he took a step back, then another.

Abbey rushed to her brother's side and put her arms around him. "Please, Abe," she said, "go back to the hotel."

The couples on the boardwalk, deciding the excitement was over, were beginning to resume their promenade. Perry Owens, the young Texas cowboy who had headed the McKenna roundup, was walking with one of Kitty's girls from the Long Branch. Matt saw Owens' eyes slant to McKenna, wondering at him. Owens, a man who lived a hard life among hard men, was obviously amazed that anyone who felt himself man enough to buckle on a gun could come up so short on grit.

A smile tugging at the corners of his mouth, Matt decided right there and then that Perry Owens, for all his easygoing ways, could be a handful.

"Marshal," Abbey McKenna said, letting go of her

brother and stepping to the edge of the boardwalk, "do you intend to press any charges against Abe?"

Matt picked up McKenna's gun belt; then his eyes bored cold and hard into Abbey's. "I have plenty of charges," he said, his voice bitter. "It's making them stick that's the problem."

The girl looked like she'd been slapped. She opened her mouth to speak, but Sam interrupted. "Matt, I'd take it as a favor if you'd let Abe walk away from this tonight." The bartender's face was bleak, but he had evidently not understood the deeper meaning of Matt's reply to Abbey. "Tomorrow is my wedding eve, and I think enough damage has already been done."

"Oh, don't say that, Sam," Abbey said, rushing into the man's arms. "Abe is drunk. He . . . he doesn't know what he's saying."

Abe McKenna stood still as a rock on the boardwalk, bloodshot eyes watching his sister in Sam's arms, a killing rage still burning in him.

Matt looked over to the bartender. "I'm letting it go, Sam. Call it an early wedding present." He turned to McKenna. "You can pick your gun up in the morning when you're sober."

Abe's eyes were ugly. "Someday, Dillon. You just wait. Someday I'll cut you down to size."

Matt smiled and shook his head. "No, you won't, McKenna, because I don't intend to ever turn my back on you."

Abbey disentangled herself from Sam's arms and

stepped beside her brother. She turned and said: "Until tomorrow, Sam. Is that all right with you?"

The bartender nodded. "I can wait until then."

Abbey flashed Sam her sweetest smile, then said to Abe: "I'm taking you to the hotel. We have to talk."

A sly awareness crept into Abe's eyes. "That's right." He grinned. "We have to talk about a lot of things."

chapter 23

Kidnapped!

Matt walked back to his office and hung Abe McKenna's cartridge belt and holstered Colt on the gun rack. Suddenly tired, he let his shoulders slump, the long ride out to the McKenna ranch and the fight with Iron Hawk finally catching up with him.

But it was just after midnight and the noisy saloons and dance halls were in full swing and there could be no question of seeking his blankets until after first light.

The fire in the stove had burned down to gray ash but the coffee was still hot. Matt poured himself a cup and wearily sat at his desk. A short break and he would have to begin making his round of the saloons.

On the office wall the railroad clock ticked slow seconds into the room like drops of water falling into a bucket and the restless prairie wind explored around the building, softy sighing to itself as it sought secret ways inside.

The big marshal's head drooped until his chin lay on his wide chest. His breathing slowed and his chair creaked against the burden of his weight. Matt drifted, sleep crowding in on him like the night darkness from the plains, and soon his mind drew a shade across the events of the day and he gave way to slumber. . . .

The marshal woke with a start to the sound of booted feet thudding along the boardwalk outside.

A quick glance at the clock told Matt he'd been asleep for an hour and he rose to his feet just as the office door swung open and a big, rough-looking man with a broken nose and a wide, hard-boned face, stepped inside.

"Marshal," the man said, getting right to the point without any preamble, "I need your help. My partner's been robbed and I think maybe he's dead."

"Where is he?" Matt asked.

"He's laying behind the Comique Theater. Me an' Bill was over there to hear Dora Hand sing, and when the show was over, Bill went out back. He was a long time returning and I went looking for him. I found him lying on the ground, his pockets turned inside out, so I came here for you."

The man wore a dirty red shirt and tan canvas pants tucked into scuffed, knee-high boots. He carried a revolver and a bowie knife on the belt around his middle and Matt pegged him as a muleskinner, one of dozens who made supply trips to Dodge every week during the cattle season.

The marshal stepped across the room, put on his hat and turned to the man. "Go get Doc Adams. Tell him to meet me behind the Comique."

The muleskinner nodded. "Name's Jake Lloyd by the way."

"Pleased to meet you, Jake," Matt said. "Now go get the doc like I told you."

Matt walked up Front Street to the Comique Theater. Called the Comikew by the cowboys, the two-story lumber building was saloon, dance hall, gambling house and theater all in one.

A few patrons were standing outside the front door when Matt turned up the alley alongside the building and walked around the back. A pale rectangle of flickering yellow light spilled on the ground from the window of the performers' dressing room, enough for the marshal to see a pair of booted feet, the rest of the man's body stretched out of sight in the darkness.

The shadowy outline of a wagon with a pair of mules in the traces stood nearby, and one of the animals, sensing another human presence, restlessly blew through its nose and stamped its foot.

Matt stood for a few moments and looked around. Nothing moved. It wasn't unusual for a wagon to be parked behind the theater, since there were regular deliveries of beer and food to the saloon inside.

Had the wagon been driven by Jake Lloyd and his partner? It seemed likely. Maybe Bill had left to check on the mules when he was bushwhacked. A faint groan came from the fallen man and the big marshal quickly walked over and kneeled beside him.

"Bill, are you all right?" he asked, his eyes trying to penetrate the gloom to see the man's face.

The man called Bill groaned again and whispered something Matt couldn't hear. The marshal bent his head lower and said: "Say that again."

"Sure will, Mary Ann!"

Suddenly the man on the ground moved and something hard crashed against the side of Matt's head.

And he knew no more.

Matt Dillon woke to pain. His head throbbed and the taste of blood was thick in his mouth.

The marshal opened his eyes and tried to move. He couldn't—and when he attempted to shift his position again, the ropes that bound him hand and foot only cut deeper into his wrists. He was in a cramped sitting position on the floor, his back against a wall, knees drawn up, trussed tight and secure by someone who knew his business.

Slowly, so not to be noticed, Matt turned his head and looked around him.

He was in a small sod cabin with a dirt roof and a single window. Two men sat at a rough pine table, playing poker with a well-thumbed, greasy deck, a smoking oil lamp sputtering above their heads. A cot lay against one wall and an unlit stove stood close to where Matt lay. There was no other furniture.

But what caught and held the marshal's attention were the two men who sat at the table. The one facing him was Jake Lloyd and the other was his partner, the man he'd called Bill.

Matt looked down at his holster. It was empty. But the slight movement of his head had attracted Lloyd's attention.

"So," the man said, "you're finally awake. For a spell there I figured ol' Bill had done for ye."

"Must have a hard head, I reckon," Bill said. "I sure buffaloed him good."

"What did you hit me with?" Matt asked, wincing against the pain that hammered inside his skull.

"Used my forty-four and it can surely put a hurt on a man if'n you hit him right." Bill's bearded lips twisted into a smile. "An' I hit you right."

"Where am I?" Matt asked.

Jake Lloyd's laugh was ugly. "Just like a lawman, always askin' questions. Ask too many more, Marshal Dillon, and I'll stuff one o' Bill's dirty socks in your mouth."

"That is, if we don't close your mouth permanently with a bullet," Bill said, drawing his Colt and laying it on the table in front of him.

"Would have done that afore now," Lloyd said, "except that we're good Christians and will send no man to the grave until he makes his peace with God."

"Good Christians as ever was, an' that's a natural fact," Bill agreed, nodding. "So say your prayers quick, Marshal, 'cause I intend to plug you after I play a few more hands o' poker."

"Who set me up?" Matt asked, bitter words tumbling from a mouth that tasted like smoke. "Was it Abbey and Abe McKenna?"

"Now that would be telling," Lloyd said. "Let's just say that our employer asked us to keep you out of the way for a few days, or kill you, whichever we preferred." The man looked over at Bill. "And we prefer to kill you."

"Indeed we do," Bill agreed. "Leave no witnesses, I always say. That way a man doesn't have to be always fussin' and frettin' and forever checking his backtrail."

"How much are the McKennas paying you?" Matt asked.

Bill shook his head. "I'm not saying it was the McKennas mind, but the wages was fifty dollars if we kept you alive, a hundred if we didn't. We took the hundred."

" 'The laborer is worthy of his hire'—that's what the Good Book says," Lloyd stated in a reverent tone. "And we will prove worthy."

"Amen and amen," Bill agreed. "Two pair, queens and tens to beat," he added.

"Damn it!" Lloyd snapped, throwing down his cards. "That's five in a row."

Bill shook his head. "Tut, tut and tut, Jake. Be not hasty in your spirit to be angry, for anger rests in the bosom of fools. That's also from the Good Book." He rose from his chair, tested Matt's bonds and then returned to the table. "It's getting close to sunup. Two more hands, then we'll gun our prisoner and be on our way."

"I'll deal this time," Lloyd said. He picked up the deck and then looked over the table at Bill. "Who's going to gun him, me or you?"

Bill shrugged. "Makes no never mind to me, Jake. Whatever Heaven ordains, I say. If'n you want your bullet in him, go right ahead."

Lloyd began to deal the cards. "I'll do it. I haven't shot anybody, man, woman or child, in a six month, and that can tell on a feller."

"Indeed," Bill agreed. "The more reg'lar you kill, the easier it gets. Them's words of wisdom."

Lloyd nodded. "As ever was spoke, Bill."

Matt tried to work a hand out of the rope around his wrists. But the rope was knotted tight and he succeeded only in flaying off a layer of skin. He looked around the room, trying to find another way—and out of the corner of his eye caught a flicker of movement at the cabin window.

Matt's whole attention concentrated on the window, but it was once more just a blank rectangle of darkness. It must have been a night bird. Or a stray leaf blowing in the wind.

There it was again!

This time the top of a battered hat appeared, slowly moving up the cracked glass until a hairy, puzzled face appeared under the hat brim. It was Festus' face.

As Matt watched, another head appeared beside

that of the deputy's, this one old, wizened, expressionless . . . and unmistakably Chinese.

Quickly Matt glanced over to the two men at the table. But they were engrossed in their cards and hadn't noticed.

Festus' eyes swept the room as Matt mentally yelled at him to keep his fool head down. The deputy scanned the cabin a second time; then his eyes found Matt and stayed on him for a few moments. Slowly, inch by inch, Festus' head lowered and disappeared from the window.

A few minutes ticked by and Matt began to wonder if his deputy had considered the odds too even and gone back to Dodge for help. He was ashamed of the treachery of his thought as soon as it entered his head.

Festus might have been lazy and shiftless by times, but he had sand, and when he put his mind to it, he could be an enduring and dangerous fighting man. Right now, he was probably hatching a plan, something that didn't come real easy to him.

All at once, Bill said: "Three queens to beat," and threw his cards on the table.

Lloyd swore again. "All I've got is a lousy pair of tens. I've had enough of this—"

The cabin door slammed open and Festus burst inside, a Colt in his fist. Bill saw him first and rose, clawing for the gun on the table in front of him. Festus fired, then fired again, and the man slammed backward, hitting the wall hard, then sliding to the floor, his eyes open and jaw hanging slack.

Lloyd whirled, drawing as he did so, but he never cleared leather. A rifle crashed from outside the cabin door and a bullet thudded into the man's chest. Lloyd rose up on his toes, cleared his gun and tried to bring it level. Festus fired, and at the same time, the rifle roared a second time. Hit twice, Lloyd screamed and fell on his back across the table. He looked up in stunned disbelief at the guttering oil lamp, as though trying to find in its orange flame the reason for his dying. The man groaned deep in his throat and rolled to his right. He toppled off the table, hit the floor with a crash that shook the cabin and lay still.

Festus quickly stepped through a gray pall of powder smoke and kneeled beside Matt. He got out his pocketknife and cut the marshal free.

Matt rose to his feet, rubbing his wrists, and grinned. "I'm sure glad to see you. Where am I and how did you find me?"

Festus fed shells into his gun and answered: "As to where you are, Matthew, this is an abandoned settler cabin on Mulberry Creek. I'd say we're pretty much due south of Dodge. As to how did I find you, well, you've got a Chinaman to thank for that."

Festus stepped to the cabin door and called out: "Hey, Liang!"

An impossibly ancient Chinese man, a smoking Winchester in his hands, appeared in the doorway and asked: "The Great Idle One summoned me?"

"This is who found you, Matthew," Festus said proudly, slapping the old man on the shoulder. The deputy's smile was almost shy. "I don't set store by it, but Liang is one of them Chinamen that reckons I'm a Great Idol."

"Festus," Matt began, "I think—"

"Tell the marshal how you done it, Liang," Festus said, interrupting. The deputy thought about it for a few moments, then said: "Nah, that'll take too long. I'll tell him my ownself."

Festus told Matt that he'd come back over the tracks looking for him and that somebody said he'd seen the marshal walk behind the Comique Theater.

"Well, I beat the bushes back there but couldn't find hide nor hair of you," Festus continued. "Then Liang here suddenly quit his jabbering and went quiet for a long spell. Then he said, 'Idol One, the marshal is no longer in Dodge.' He pointed south, toward the Mulberry, and said, 'He has been taken in that direction.'"

Warming to his subject, Festus put his arm around Liang's shoulders and added: "Ol' Liang here was a great doctor in his own country, kinda like Doc Adams, and he has the gift of second sight, just like them black-eyed hill women back to Tennessee, where I growed up. Somehow he knowed you wasn't in Dodge and he led me right here to you."

Matt stuck out his hand. "Mr. Liang, I'm grateful. If it wasn't for you, I'd be dead by now."

Liang shook Matt's hand and nodded. "A friend of the Idle One is a friend of mine. He is teaching us the way."

"Maybe later you and me should have a serious

talk about that, Mr. Liang," Matt said. He turned to Festus: "Recognize these two?"

The deputy stepped over to Bill's body and then kneeled beside Jake Lloyd. He rose after a few moments, then shook his head. "They're both dead as they're ever gonna be. I don't know them, but I've seen these fellers around town. Mostly they were always broke and looking for work." He nodded to Lloyd as he handed Matt his Colt. "This was in his belt."

Matt nodded and dropped his gun into the leather; his face settled into hard lines. "They found work, Festus. I think Abbey and Abe McKenna hired them to kill me, or at least keep me away from Dodge until the wedding is over."

"So what do we do now, Matthew?"

"Is there a mule wagon belonging to these two outside?"

Festus nodded. "It's pulled behind the cabin."

"Then we'll load up the bodies and take them back to Dodge."

"And after that?"

"After that, I'm going to prevent Sam Noonan from marrying Abbey McKenna. I don't know how, at least not yet, but stop the wedding, I will."

chapter 24

A Letter from the Rangers

Sam and Abbey's nuptials were set for three in the afternoon at the Baptist church across the tracks, refreshments to follow at the Long Branch.

The bartender was a well-liked and respected man and the *Dodge City Times* reported that a large turn-out was expected, adding: "*The Times*, metaphorically speaking, throws its old shoe after the happy couple and wishes them a long and prosperous life."

Matt tossed the newspaper onto his desk in disgust and glanced at the office clock. It was a few minutes before nine—just six hours to go.

The door opened and Floyd Bodkin the banker stuck his head inside. "Busy?"

"Never too busy to talk to you, Floyd." Matt smiled.

Bodkin stepped up to Matt's desk and shrugged. "This is probably nothing, Matt. But you were interested in Andy Reid, so I thought I should let you know that I've lost another major depositor."

"Who?" Matt asked, already guessing what Bodkin's answer would be. The banker shifted uncomfortably from one foot to another. "It's Sam Noonan. Late yesterday afternoon he cleaned out his entire account, just over twenty-three thousand dollars."

Matt leaned forward in his chair. "Did he say why?"

The man nodded. "Yes, he did. He said he wanted to surprise Abbey McKenna by giving her the money as an early wedding present. He said Abbey had already told him they'd need cash to hand when they arrived in Boston, prices being what they are, and that he should withdraw his deposit before they left on honeymoon. I told Sam I could transfer his account to any Boston bank he cared to mention, but he insisted on taking out every last penny."

Bodkin's face was apologetic. "As I said, Marshal, it probably means nothing. But after what happened to Andy Reid, I thought you should know."

Matt came at the banker from another angle, surprising him. "What do you think of Abbey McKenna, Floyd?"

It took the banker a minute, and when he spoke, his eyes were guarded. "I think it strange that she's sold both her herds but hasn't made a bank deposit, not in my bank or any other." The man paused again, then added: "You asked me what I think of her, and the answer is simple. I think she's an extremely ambitious young woman who will go far. As to how many lives she will ruin in the process, I don't know." Bodkin shook his head, a small sadness in him. "The evil thing about ruthless ambition is that it never looks back at the mess it leaves behind."

"Are you attending the wedding, Floyd?" Matt asked. "According to the newspaper it's shaping up to be the social event of the year."

The banker's face hardened. "I think I'll forgo that pleasure." He took his watch from his vest, thumbed open the case and glanced at the time. "Goodness, I'm late. I must be going."

As Bodkin reached the door, Matt called out after him: "Thank you for the information, Floyd."

The banker waved a hand. "I hope it helps." He turned and faced the marshal. "I'm just trying to make sure that Sam Noonan doesn't lose"—he hesitated, then finished—"everything."

A few minutes later Matt stood on the boardwalk outside his office, looking up and down Front Street.

At the Long Branch, Kitty had erected an archway of white flowers and silver-painted wedding bells. And the members of the five-piece orchestra she'd hired from the Comique were already lugging their instruments inside.

The sky was bright blue, clear of clouds, and the sun was beginning its climb over Dodge, washing out the night shadows from the alleys and the corners of the buildings. A cattle train drawn by a chugging locomotive was pulling out of the rail depot heading east, its whistle wailing, the loaded boxcars clashing as they gathered speed along the uneven iron track.

Matt was about to step back inside when he saw Abe McKenna, wearing a brand-new black suit and plug hat, stroll along the boardwalk toward the Long Branch. The man glanced casually across the street, saw Matt and stopped, his eyes popping wide in shocked surprise.

The big marshal's slight smile was grim. Apparently McKenna didn't yet know that he'd brought in two dead men late last night—the men he and his sister had hired to kill him.

McKenna stood rooted to the spot for a long moment, his eyes on Matt, then turned on his heel and hurried away toward the Dodge House. Soon Abbey would learn that her plan to get the marshal out of the way had failed.

As to what she might do next, Matt had no idea. Brazen it out probably, trusting that he had still not found any evidence to arrest her.

Briefly Matt considered riding out to the McKenna ranch and searching the cabin to see if he could find anything that would tie them to the murder of Andy Reid or the robbery of the Lee-Reynolds stage.

He dismissed the thought at once. By the time he got back, the wedding would be over, and Sam and Abbey would be man and wife. Besides, none of the McKenna riders who'd threatened to picket the nuptials were in town. It was likely that Abe had paid them off, but if they were still at the ranch, they wouldn't let him near the place without a fight.

A sense of defeat growing in him, Matt stepped back into the office. He glanced at the clock. A little more than five hours to go . . . and it seemed there was nothing he could do prevent the marriage.

The marshal sat at his desk and pulled some of his paperwork toward him. He dipped his pen in the inkwell but laid it down again when Kitty walked inside, her face wreathed in a smile.

"Not dressed yet?" she asked.

Matt shook his head. "A bit too early. The wedding isn't until three."

Kitty sat on the edge of the desk. "You'll escort me to the church, of course." She smiled, her eyes shining. "I just know that everybody will look at us and say, 'Now there goes a handsome couple.' "

Despite his frustration, Matt laughed. "I never laid much of a claim to being handsome. But if you say so, Kitty, then it sets just fine by me."

Kitty leaned over and kissed him. "You'll always be handsome to me, Marshal Dillon."

As Floyd Bodkin had done earlier, Kitty saw the time and exclaimed: "Goodness, I must be going! I only have five hours to get ready." She stepped to the door and turned. "Pick me up at two thirty, Matt. I want to get to the church in plenty of time."

"How is Abbey McKenna getting there?" Matt asked quickly.

"Oh, her brother is driving her over there in the surrey. Abbey doesn't want Sam to see her wedding dress until she arrives at the altar."

For the next two hours Matt busied himself with

paperwork, trying to take his mind off what was happening. In large part he succeeded, but by noon he laid down his pen and realized that he had to face the inevitable.

He couldn't stop it now. The wedding would go on as planned.

Matt had but one go-to-meeting suit and that was in the wardrobe at his room in the Dodge House. Kitty would expect him to wear it, as would Sam. He rose and found his hat. He felt depressed, an emotion strange to him. But he accepted it for what it was, just his anger spread thin, and he knew all he could do now was steel himself for what was to come.

Crossing the street, Matt stepped into the lobby of the Dodge House. Howie Uzell was behind the desk and the marshal gave the man a nod as he headed for the stairs.

"Wait, Matt," Uzell called out. "I have a letter here for you." The clerk handed over a long white envelope. "This came a couple of days ago, but what with the fight with the Cheyenne an' all, I plumb forgot about it until now."

Matt thanked Uzell, immediately opened the envelope and read. He had to read Texas Ranger Captain Lee McNelly's letter a second time before its full impact hit him.

Dear Marshal Dillon,

I received your wire several weeks ago and resolved to respond by letter just as soon as my health would allow, being then under the care of a physician and confined to bed by sickness.

The woman about whom you inquired, Abbey McKenna, also goes by the names Ann Grant and Esther Keene. She and her husband, Abe McKenna, are wanted in the state of Texas for murder, robbery and cattle rustling.

Six months ago, Abbey bigamously married an elderly rancher named Deacon Kraus of Webb County and shortly afterward the old man disappeared. His cabin was ransacked and the McKennas appropriated his herd.

We have evidence that as they left Texas, the couple, aided by others, rustled a large number of cattle from several ranches. We have also reason to believe that six men, identified by eyewitnesses as working for the McKennas, later stole eight hundred head of prime Herefords. During the commission of the latter crime, four cowboys working for the Victoria Feed and Cattle Company were murdered.

The body of Deacon Kraus was recently discovered in an arroyo near his ranch. Although the corpse was much decayed, the coroner established that the cause of death was a single .36 caliber ball to the back of the head.

On subsequent investigation, a drifter and sometime cowboy by the name of Charlie McCoy confessed that he had been paid twenty dollars by Abbey McKenna to kill the old man. McCoy has now begun a thirty-year sentence for murder,

and has expressed his remorse and complete will-
ingness to testify against the McKennas.

Please detain Abbey McKenna and her husband
and hold for the United States marshal. Although
I am currently too infirm for travel, representa-
tives of the Texas Rangers are being dispatched
to Dodge City to offer testimony at the court of
inquiry and subsequent trial.

I am, sir,

Yours respectfully,

Leander H. McNelly (Capt.)

Matt looked up from the letter. Abbey and Abe
were husband and wife! That explained much, including the strangely close, passionate bond between
them. Uzell, seeing the sudden hardening of the marshal's face, asked: "Matt, is there anything wrong?"

Matt nodded. "Yes, Howie, there's plenty wrong."
He glanced up the staircase. "What's Abbey McKenna's room number?"

"Eight," the clerk replied. "But she's not there.
Miss McKenna and her brother left a couple of hours
ago." Uzell smiled. "They said they were taking a
drive in the surrey to calm their wedding day nerves.
I imagine they'll be back soon if you'd care to wait."

Matt shook his head. "Howie, I don't reckon
they're coming back—ever." Ignoring Uzell's startled
questions, the marshal stood for a few moments
thinking it through. Sam had surprised the couple by
giving Abbey his money as an early wedding present, so there had been no need to go ahead with the

sham marriage. Matt guessed they hadn't left last night because too many people were in the streets. The McKenna surrey heading into the darkness of the prairie would have raised eyebrows if not outright suspicion. The marshal decided that after Abe saw him standing outside his office, he and Abbey had panicked and elected to make a run for it a shade earlier than they'd intended.

But a run to where?

Was there anything at the ranch they would want? Matt recalled the strongbox Abbey had loaded into the surrey. No doubt they had brought their money with them to Dodge. But they still might require clothing and other items. Since they had no way of knowing that Matt kept a room at the Dodge House, they probably thought their absence would go unnoticed until the time of the wedding. With a four or five hour head start on any pursuit they might figure there was plenty of time to visit the cabin and pick up what they needed.

Only Matt's reluctant visit to the hotel and Howie Uzell remembering the letter from Captain McNelly could wreck their plans.

Matt was aware that he had strung together a lot of maybes concerning the intentions of the couple, but thin as his suspicions were, they were all he had to go on. He also realized that time was fast running out and his first inclination was to saddle his horse and ride hard after the McKennas.

Frustration tugging at him, he knew he couldn't leave just yet. He wouldn't let Sam stand forlornly at the altar, waiting for a bride who would never arrive, with at least a hundred people in the church watching and whispering. A man Matt considered a friend could become a pathetic object of pity—or even worse, a laughingstock.

Matt shook his head. There was no other way. Before he went after Abbey and Abe McKenna, he'd have to break the bad news to Sam.

The bartender had a room upstairs at the Long Branch, and when Matt knocked on the door, Sam answered in his underwear, his face covered in soap, a razor in his right hand.

The man smiled and looked at the marshal from head to toe. "Matt, not dressed yet? We're due at the altar in less than an hour."

Matt did not return Sam's smile. "Can I come in?" he asked.

"Sure," the bartender said, grinning, opening the door wide. "Come to ask what your best man duties are?"

"Not that," Matt said, shaking his head. He closed the door behind him.

"Sam, there's no easy way to tell you this"—he held out the letter—"so maybe you should just read."

"What's it all about?" Sam asked, his face puzzled, as he looked down at the sheet of paper.

"Just read it—that's all. Just read it."

Sam looked into Matt's bleak eyes and what he saw troubled him. He took the letter and sat down on the corner of the bed.

As Matt had done earlier, the bartender read the

letter, then, more slowly, read it again. When he was done, his face drained of color, he looked up at the tall marshal standing over him. "There's some mistake, Matt? The Ranger captain made a mistake maybe?"

Matt shook his head. "No mistake, Sam. In fact I'd guess that what's in the letter isn't the half of it."

The paper trembling in his hand, Sam nodded. "I see." The man was silent for a few moments, too shocked to speak, then managed, his voice choking: "Hard thing for a man to learn on his wedding day." He glanced up at Matt again. "Where has she gone?"

Aware of how cruel the cuts inflicted by his words would be, Matt answered: "Abbey and her husband have left town. I'm about to round up Festus and we're going after them. We'll get your money back, Sam."

The bartender shook his head. "I don't care about the money. I only care about losing Abbey."

"I know," Matt said. "It's a mighty hurtful thing." Gently he took the razor from Sam's shaking hand, wiped the blade on the towel the man had draped over his shoulder. Then he folded the razor closed. "I have to be going, Sam," he said, laying the razor on the dresser. "Will you be all right?"

The bartender nodded without speaking.

Matt stepped to the door, then turned as Sam whispered: "Matt, about Abbey. Please . . . please don't harm her."

"I won't," the marshal said. "I reckon there's been enough harm done already."

chapter 25

Bushwhacked!

Matt found Festus asleep at the rear of the Chinese laundry. He roused the deputy and on the way to the livery stable explained what had happened. "Reckon we kin catch up to them, Matthew?" Festus asked.

Matt shrugged. "I don't know, but we're sure going to try."

The marshal tightened the girth on his saddle and turned to find Liang at his elbow. "What are you doing here?" he asked.

The old Chinese man nodded toward Festus. "I go where he goes."

"You got no call to do that, Liang," Matt said. "Where we're going there could be much danger."

Liang shrugged. "The person who risks nothing does nothing, has nothing and is nothing. I will go."

"Aw, let him tag along, Matthew," Festus said.

"The old coot sees stuff other people don't, so maybe he can put us on the trail of the McKennas." The deputy led his mule from the stall and clapped a hand on Liang's shoulder, grinning. "Besides, they're really cute little fellers once you get to know them."

Matt nodded. "Just stay out of the way if shooting starts, Liang. You're not being paid to be a lawman."

"You could deputize him, Matthew," Festus suggested.

Matt shook his head. "I have enough troubles with the deputy I already have."

The sun had passed its highest point in the sky when the three riders left Dodge and headed north toward the cabin on the Pawnee.

Around them the long-riding country was green, streaked with stands of wildflowers, and ahead a shimmering heat haze at the horizon merged sky and land into one.

After they crossed the bend of Saw Log Creek, Festus picked up the twin tracks of the surrey wheels. "Drivin' north, Matthew," he said. "Headed right for the cabin like you thought." The deputy's eyebrow rose. "Figger they might still be around?"

Matt shook his head. "I doubt it. But we can pick up their tracks from there."

Liang kicked his swaybacked pony alongside Matt's bay. "Danger, Marshal." The old Chinese pointed vaguely ahead of him. "Out there."

"Where?" Matt asked.

Liang shook his head. "This I do not see. I only feel."

The marshal turned to Festus. "You set store by what he says?"

The deputy shrugged. "I dunno. But Liang is a powerful wise man, Matthew. Seems to me when people talk to him, he hears one word an' understands two."

Matt made up his mind. He slid his Winchester out of the boot and laid the rifle across his saddle horn. "Then we'll ride real careful. Maybe he senses something, maybe he doesn't, but I don't want to bet the farm that he's wrong."

Under a hot sun, the three men watered their mounts at Buckner Creek. The flat plain stretching away from them in all directions was shadowless, the only shade cast by the cottonwoods, the dark silhouettes of their windblown leaves dappling the ground in restless movement. To the west, black scars from the flames of the Red Buffalo still streaked the grama grass, but already green shoots were thrusting up everywhere and the hardy, stubborn yucca was again in bloom.

Matt swung back into the saddle and led his small posse north, across the hot, still land; the only sounds were the fall of their mounts' hooves and the hum of insects in the grass. Ahead of them lay Sand Creek, a good-sized stream with many twists and turns, both its banks lined with clumps of trees and plum bush.

The riders reached the creek and followed it north for a mile along a narrow game trail, fetching up to a small pond, where water had collected in a shallow sink. The banks surrounding the pond were muddied by the hooves of deer and antelope that had gathered here to drink, along with paw prints of the wolves and coyotes that preyed on them.

Matt and the others crossed the creek just north of the sink, skirting around a stand of cottonwood and plum bush, clumps of tall Indian grass and tangled brush growing up around their trunks.

The three riders had just cleared the trees when a fusillade of shots violently hammered apart the silence of the afternoon. Beside him, Matt heard Festus yell as a bullet struck him and the deputy tumbled off his mule, hitting the ground hard.

A bullet burned across the thick muscle of Matt's biceps as he swung his horse around, his rifle coming up to his shoulder. Festus, game and as tough as rawhide, was on his feet, staggering, his shirt splashed with blood. The deputy had lost his rifle when he fell from his mule but he was thumbing off shot after shot from his Colt.

Matt fired at a puff of smoke beside the trunk of a cottonwood and he heard a man yelp in surprise and pain. Liang's Winchester fired, then fired a second time, forcing one of the bushwhackers to start up and make a run for better cover. Matt saw the man, fired and nailed him low in the left side. Before the man fell, the marshal cranked another round into the chamber and shot him again.

Matt glanced around him quickly. Festus was down, lying on his back, Liang kneeling beside him. A terrible rage in him, Matt shoved his rifle into the boot, drew his Colt and spurred toward the trees. Ahead of him a tall, skinny man stumbled from the brush, blood staining his pants below his belt buckle. Matt recognized the man as the McKenna rider named Mike, the puncher Abbey had tried to hush after he let slip about the Herefords.

The man had a six-gun in each hand and he screamed curses at Matt as he stumbled toward the marshal, his guns blazing. A bullet split the air beside the lawman's cheek as he returned fire, getting off three fast, accurate shots. Hit hard, Mike took a step back, his face twisted in fury. He tried to bring up guns that suddenly appeared to be as heavy as anvils.

Matt fired again and Mike went to his knees. The gun dropped from his left fist and he tried to bring his remaining Colt to eye level with both hands. Matt fired another time, and the puncher rocked under the impact of the bullet, then fell on his side, thudding lifeless onto the grass.

Warily Matt rode up to the trees, then scouted the area. One man sprawled beside the tree where Matt had shot at him. Another, hit twice by the marshal's bullets, lay still, half hidden in the brush.

All three of the men were McKenna hands, and all three were dead. Swinging out of the saddle, Matt kneeled beside the skinny man named Mike. He searched the man's pockets and found what he suspected he'd find. Among the loose change and crumpled bills were five newly minted double eagles.

A quick search of the other bodies revealed that

all carried the same amount of money in brand-new gold coins—obviously part of the bank shipment taken from the Lee-Reynolds stage.

Abbey and Abe had met these men at the ranch and then paid them to bushwhack anybody who might be chasing them. A grief growing in him, Matt looked across to the still body of Festus, his head and shoulders held gently in Liang's arms. The ambush had failed, but the McKenna riffraff had succeeded in shooting down a man who was infinitely better than any of them.

Matt rose and stepped beside Liang. "How is he?" he asked, fearing the answer to that question as soon as he asked it.

"The Idle One will live. A bullet passed through the left side of his chest and broke many ribs." The old Chinese man smiled. "But I will take care of him, and the gods willing, he will soon be well again."

Matt kneeled beside Festus and grinned. "I think Doc Adams will have something to say about that."

The deputy opened one eye, his brow crawling up his forehead. "Tell me the truth, Matthew. Am I dying?"

Matt shook his head. "Liang says a bullet went right through your side and busted some ribs. But you'll live."

"I'm very weak, Matthew." Festus's voice quavered. "So, so very weak. I'm gonna need a lot of bed rest and a powerful amount of tender, loving care. Matthew, you'll have to bring me my meals from the Sideboard three times a day and make sure

there's always a bottle of good whiskey by my bed-
side and maybe the odd cigar." Festus coughed, then
coughed again. "Otherwise," he said, "I'll just fade
away."

Fighting back a smile, Matt nodded. "I'll see what
I can do." He turned to Liang. "Can he ride?"

"He has lost blood, but the Idle One is strong and
not worn-out by hard work." The old man nodded.
"Yes, if we go very slowly, he can ride."

Festus laid a hand on Matt's arm. "Matthew, go
after them McKennas an' do what you have to do.
Ruth will take me where I want to go. She can be
right gentle when she takes the notion."

Matt rose to his feet. "Liang, when you get to
Dodge, bring Festus to Miss Kitty at the Long Branch.
She'll take it from there."

The old man nodded. "It shall be done as you
say."

With Liang's help, Matt got his groaning deputy
into the saddle. He watched the two men ride away
until they were swallowed up by distance before he
stepped into the leather and again headed north.

The ambush had not accomplished what the bushwhackers had intended, but they had achieved one
vital goal—with their own lives they had bought the
McKennas more time.

chapter 26

Fate Takes a Hand

The day was mellowing, the sun dropping lower in the sky, when Matt caught sight of the Mc-Kenna cabin on the Pawnee.

He reined in his horse and studied the place through his field glasses. The corral was empty and no smoke came from the chimney of the cabin, its blank windows staring out across the prairie like hollow, unseeing eyes. The marshal scanned the bunkhouse. That too seemed deserted, the door hanging wide open on its rawhide hinges, banging in the wind.

The same wind tossed the branches of a solitary cottonwood growing beside the dry wash near the corral, and nearby the rear axle of the ancient chuck wagon had collapsed, its tailgate dragging in the grass like a great animal with a broken hip.

The entire place was empty and lifeless, and if the McKennas had been here, they were long gone.

Matt pushed the field glasses back into his saddle-bags and rode closer, his Winchester across the horn of his saddle. He fetched up to the cabin and sat the bay, looking the place over.

There was nothing to be gained by stepping inside, so Matt swung his horse away and scouted around, searching for tracks. Within a couple minutes he found the parallel marks of wheels headed due east.

He was many hours behind the McKennas, and unless something happened to their surrey, he could chase them clear to the Missouri border and never catch up.

A sense of frustration nagging at him, Matt led the bay back to the front of the cabin and let him drink from the trough at the hitching rail. He laid his rifle against the side of the trough, rolled up his sleeves and splashed water on his face.

The surrey might throw a wheel or break an axle on a rock and that would slow them. It was a slender hope, but it was all he had.

With Festus out of action, Matt had to be back in Dodge before the town woke up and came roaring back to life. He untied the bandanna from his neck, dried off his face and glanced at the sky. There were maybe two more hours until nightfall. It was high time he started after the McKennas.

Matt leaned over to pick up his rifle, but stopped his hand in midmotion as a voice said: "I wouldn't do that, if I was you."

Straightening, the marshal saw Roman Pollock standing at the corner of the building, the Colt in his hand pointed right at his belly. "Afternoon, Roman," he said. "I didn't expect to find you here."

"I know who you expected, but they're long gone." Pollock waved a hand toward the prairie to the east. "Thataway."

"I'm tracking them, Roman," Matt said, his body tense. "Will you give me the road?"

The gunman shook his head. "Can't do it, Matt. See, I plan to leave you here dead on the ground, then go after them two my ownself."

"Harsh talk, Roman," Matt said, smiling. Pollock had the drop on him and he was desperately clutching at a straw, any straw. "We were friends once."

"Like you said yourself, Matt, a man moves on, changes. Our friendship is over and I'm all through stepping aside for you."

"They're not worth it, Roman," Matt said, trying to keep the man talking. "Why are you protecting them?"

Pollock laughed, the mad black fire glinting in his eyes. "Hell, I don't aim to protect them. I plan to kill that yellowbelly Abe, then take the woman and the money for myself. Abbey wants to go east, but I'll be changing her plans. We'll go to Mexico. I have friends there."

Matt shook his head. "Roman, Abbey will kill you. Maybe in your sleep, maybe by a backshooting, but in the end she'll get you one way or another."

"She's a spirited filly, no doubt about that." Pollock smiled. "But I'll break her like I do my horses—with the whip. Don't worry. After she's tasted the lash a few times, I'll throw my saddle on her and she'll do as she's told."

The gunman took a step closer to the marshal, his eyes hardening. "Matt, once I wanted to give you an even break, see which of us was faster. But I can't take the chance you might shade me. The stakes are too high." The gun muzzle came up an inch, held steady as a rock. "Now I got to be going. No hard feelings?"

"One thing, Roman," Matt asked quickly, playing for more time. "I have to know before you shoot— did you kill Andy Reid?"

"Sure I did." Pollock nodded. "And that cattle buyer feller. And yeah, before you ask it, I led the stage robbery. I did it because Abbey asked me to do it. But she didn't appreciate my efforts. I'd walk around the cabin at night and hear her giggling and cooing in bed with that no-good husband of hers. But she will appreciate me. I'll make damn sure she does."

The gunman tensed, his finger whitening on the trigger. "Sorry, Matt. I'm all through talking. It's time."

Matt Dillon's life was now hanging by the slimmest of threads and the thread was fraying fast. Yet fate often has a way of intervening in the affairs of men, and it did now.

In Matt's case, destiny came in the shape of a dry willow twig, 8.5 inches long and as thick around as a woman's little finger. The twig was being carried in the beak of a blue jay as it headed toward the nest it was constructing in the cottonwood by the dry wash.

The jay, struggling to gain height but dragged down by the weight of the twig, perhaps realized it was too large for nest material anyway and let it go—just as the bird was flying over the head of Roman Pollock.

The twig fell twenty feet and thumped off Pollock's right shoulder. The gunman was surprised, and his eyes flickered to his right, a movement that took only a split second.

But it was enough for Matt.

The marshal's hand blurred as he drew and his gun came level and roared. Matt's bullet crashed dead center into Pollock's chest and the gunman slammed back against the cabin wall. Pollock recovered and fired. Too fast. A miss. Matt fired again, then thumbed off another shot. His first bullet splintered into the wood near Pollock's head, but the second hit the gunman just above the belt buckle.

His face shocked, he realized he was already a dead man. Pollock took a single stumbling step toward Matt. His gun hand hanging loose at his side, the man triggered a shot into the grass, then four more, one after another, until his Colt was empty.

Pollock dropped to his knees and fell facedown on the ground.

Stepping to the gunman's side, Matt turned the man over on his back. Pollock's eyes were open, but the black death shadows were already collecting in the hollows of his cheeks and under his eyes, and his breathing was a struggling, painful thing.

"Never thought it would end this way between us, Matt," he said.

The big marshal nodded. "Me neither, Roman. You and me were friends once."

The gunman managed a smile. "We were something back then, weren't we? All of us."

"Sure were. Lived through some hard times, but mostly what we had was good."

Pollock nodded. "Good times." The life was ebbing out of him, but he struggled to speak and finally managed: "No hard feelings, Matt?"

"No hard feelings," the marshal said. But he was talking to a dead man.

Matt rose to his feet, punched the empty shells from his Colt and thumbed fresh rounds into the cylinder. Looking down at Pollock, he holstered his gun, a vague sense of loss in him. But whether for Pollock or for the remembrance of his own reckless, carefree youth he could not tell.

As the afternoon faded, the plains were bathed in translucent amber light under a red-and-jade sky that burned like fire all the way to the horizon. The wind had risen, tugging at the marshal's shirt, lifting the wide brim of his hat, and the bunkhouse door opened and closed endlessly, banging like a muffled drum, an echoing, lonely requiem for a fallen gunman.

Matt looked out across the far-flung prairie, a land

seemingly empty of life, the only movement the ceaseless ripple of the grass. Somewhere out in all that vastness were Abbey and Abe McKenna. Could he catch up with them? The marshal knew the answer to that question was no, but it was not in his nature to give up so easily. A man who does not move forward goes backward. Matt caught up the reins of his horse, swung into the saddle and, a weariness weighing heavy on him, set out to follow the wagon tracks east. Night must inevitably end his chase, but until then he would keep trying.

The marshal crossed the upper fork of Sand Creek just south of where it ran off the Pawnee River, and picked up the trail again. Ahead of him lay many miles of wide-open country, a landscape of low, rolling hills cut through by shallow streams and dusty, dry washes.

He rode for an hour, the light slowly fading around him just as his hope of hunting down the McKennas was dimming. A far-seeing man, Matt constantly scanned the distance stretching forever in front of him and spotted nothing.

Slowing his horse from a lope, he finally reined up and sat his saddle, once again staring into the desolate, darkening distance.

Then he saw it.

At first it appeared as a dark speck against the endless green of the surrounding grass. Then as it grew bigger, slowly heading toward him, Matt made out the vague shape of a fringe-top surrey drawn by a tired, plodding horse.

The marshal stayed where he was, letting slow minutes tick by as the surrey rolled toward him. Now he could see that two people rode in the fancy rig, one of them with the reins in his hands.

The driver was Abe McKenna and sitting next to him was Abbey.

Matt slid his holstered Colt around on the cartridge belt, settling it just behind his hip where it would be handy. Abe McKenna might be yellow, but it didn't pay to take chances with his kind. And come to that, Abbey was no bargain either.

Kicking his bay forward, the marshal rode toward the surrey at a walk, his eyes wary. It was only when he was fifty yards from the surrey that he realized something was wrong . . . terribly wrong.

He rode closer until he could hear the soft footfalls of the weary horse in the traces. The animal looked up, saw him and stopped, blowing softly through its nose.

Matt reached the surrey, and he suddenly found himself fighting for breath, like a gigantic hand was clutching at his throat. His shocked gaze was unbelieving and horrified, witnessing a scene that made the blood run like ice in his veins.

Abe McKenna, shot several times in the chest, had been scalped. The man's open eyes stared sightlessly through a scarlet curtain of dried blood that began at the top of his head and extended all the way to his chin. Like Abbey beside him, Abe had been lashed to the seat of the surrey, the rope crossing his chest holding him upright. The man's livid face under the torrent of blood was frozen into a look of absolute terror. Abe had lived long enough to feel and understand the appalling nature of his death.

Abbey had not been scalped. But like her husband, she'd been shot many times. Her eyes were closed, as though she was asleep, her face looking young and pretty in repose. But this was a sleep from which she'd never waken. A final bullet to the middle of her forehead had seen to that.

Swinging out of the saddle, Matt stepped to the back of the wagon. The couple had hurriedly packed a pair of carpetbags and between the bags was the strongbox. The box was secured by a brass padlock and the marshal was reluctant to search Abe's bloody clothes for the key. He lifted the heavy box from the surrey, carried it aside a distance, then shot away the padlock, the sound booming loud and harsh in the quiet of the gathering twilight.

It was all there, in paper and gold and silver coin, the money Abbey McKenna had killed and schemed to accumulate.

And she might have gotten away with it, but for Iron Hawk.

Matt returned the strongbox to the surrey and looked again at Abbey and Abe, both sitting bolt upright but unnaturally still and silent amid the darkness that was now descending on the plains.

Iron Hawk had met up with the couple somewhere back along their trail and the Cheyenne had enacted his final act of revenge. Abe McKenna's debt, incurred one drunken night in the saloon, had been paid in full.

The marshal looked around him, staring out at a shadowed land he could no longer see. Iron Hawk was out there somewhere. The man must know that his killing of the McKennas guaranteed that ahead of him lay only a brief, hunted life and then, inevitably, his own death. Sometime very soon, the last Dog Soldier would be chased down. A warrior come to grant favors, not beg them, he would not ask for mercy, staking himself to the ground with his scarlet sash, as had been the custom of his people. He would sell his life dearly, singing his death song, making his fight to the very last. But in the end, one man against many, he would die, and with him would die all the warrior pride and the final hope of the Cheyenne.

It was not in Matt Dillon to condone what Iron Hawk had done, but there was a confused sadness in him. He was an officer of the law, and he knew where his duty lay. Had Iron Hawk been near, he would have arrested him—or killed him if need be.

Nevertheless the words came unbidden to his lips, a token of respect from one warrior to another. "Good luck," Matt whispered. He lifted his face to the uncaring wind and the air smelled clean, of grass and distant wood smoke.

The big marshal stood in silence for a few moments longer, then swung into the saddle. He took the bloodstained reins of the surrey from Abe Mc-Kenna's cold, stiffening hands.

Ahead of him, the prairie was shrouded in darkness, the moon having not yet begun its climb into the night sky.

It was going to be a long ride back to Dodge City.

chapter 27

Of Deputies, Bartenders and Calico Cats

Two weeks after the deaths of Abbey and Abe Mc-
Kenna, Matt Dillon stood on the boardwalk outside his office, watching the nightly promenade of
couples along Front Street.

Kitty had asked him to come by for her at nine,
since she wished to join the parade. "Matt, this will
be the first chance I've had to show off my wedding
finery," she'd said. "And I want you by my side so
people will say—"

"I know what people will say," Matt had interrupted. "They'll say, 'What a handsome couple.'"

Kitty had flashed her dazzling smile and nodded.
"I believe you're finally getting the picture, Marshal
Dillon."

Over to the Long Branch, Festus was still bedrid-
den in one of Kitty's upstairs rooms, and his prestige
had grown enormously among the Chinese. Not only

was the Idle One lying abed and getting paid for it, he was being pampered and petted by Kitty and a bevy of her beautiful ladies.

Nor were the saloon girls the deputy's only female visitors. Demure married matrons and fashionable young belles from across the tracks visited constantly. They listened to their wounded hero's tales of derring-do while they fluttered and fussed over him, spoon-feeding him cake and ice cream, all the while swooning over his gallantry.

Festus' version of the gun battle at Sand Creek had lost little in the retelling. His own part had grown, relating to his enthralled female audience that, though grievously wounded, he had saved the marshal's life by single-handedly fighting off a dozen bloodthirsty bushwhackers.

Even Mayor Kelley, letting bygones be bygones, had been impressed. Yesterday the mayor had elbowed his way through the crowd of adoring ladies and admiring Chinese and declared, to much applause, that he was having a special gold medal struck to commemorate the deputy's valor.

"At city expense, mind you," Kelley had added with a dramatic flourish, drawing many feminine sighs and even more applause.

Only Doc Adams remained unmoved. Earlier in the day he'd told Matt: "Festus said I should consult with his personal physician, Dr. Liang, before I made any diagnosis of his condition." His latent crankiness bubbling to the surface, Doc added: "However my . . . ah . . . colleague and I agree that Festus can

return to light duties in a day or two. It shouldn't
be difficult. Light duties are all he ever performs."

When Matt had passed on the good news, Festus
had demurred. "Matthew, I'm still feelin' so peaked
I'd have to get better to die. Maybe in another two
or three weeks I'll be able to set up an' take a little
nourishment."

At this statement, one pretty Southern belle from
across the tracks had burst into tears and hollered that
Deputy Marshal Festus Haggen was the bravest man
in the world. "Ah do decleah," she added, "that ah
feel mahself quite undone when ah'm in his presence."

Matt took his watch from his vest pocket and
glanced at the time. In another fifteen minutes he
would need to keep his appointment with Kitty.

Couples passed the tall marshal on the boardwalk,
the spurs of the cowboys chiming in tune to the ringing laughter of their female companions.

Then Matt saw a familiar figure walking toward
him. It was tall, lanky Sam Noonan dressed in a fashionable frockcoat, a young girl on his arm. The girl
worked at the Alhambra, a pretty blonde with huge
brown eyes, and she was all got up in a gown of
vivid red satin, a silk shawl around her naked
shoulders.

As the couple drew next to him, Sam stopped and
touched his hat brim. "Evening, Marshal."

Matt nodded. "Sam."

"This here is Lou Anne," the bartender said, grinning from ear to ear. "Isn't she a real little darlin'?"

As Matt touched his hat to the girl, she giggled and

said: "Oh, Sam, you're so silly!" Lou Anne looked at Matt and fluttered the dark arcs of her long lashes. "Marshal, tell him to stop talking those pretties." She pouted. "Maybe I'll think he doesn't really mean it when he says he wants to marry me."

"I mean it every time, Lou Anne," said Sam, an adoring light in his eyes. "You know I'm just crazy about you."

"Silly Sam." The girl giggled again.

The bartender nodded to Matt. "Well, we've got to be on our way, Marshal. I promised Lou Anne I'd take her to see Dora Hand at the Comique."

Matt watched the couple as they made their way along the boardwalk.

Every now and then Sam leaned over and whispered something into the girl's ear, and she giggled and slapped him on the arm with her fan.

The marshal was about to step across to the Long Branch when a shadow emerged from the darkness of an alley. The little calico cat jumped onto the boardwalk and walked toward him. The tiny creature had a dead mouse in its mouth, holding it as delicately as a peach.

As always, the cat stopped and looked up at Matt with glowing eyes, demanding the road. And as he always did, he took one step back and then, more reluctantly, another.

Walking on silent paws, the calico moved along the boardwalk and halted in front of the big marshal. It glanced up at Matt's towering height, then lowered its head and dropped the mouse at his feet.

As Matt watched the little animal pad away before it faded into the night, he smiled and shook his head.

There was, he decided, just no accounting for deputies, bartenders . . . or calico cats.

Read on for a preview of the
next exciting *Gunsmoke* novel

BLIZZARD OF LEAD

Coming from Signet
in September 2005

Winter was cracking down hard on the plains as
two riders loped across the frozen prairie north
of Dodge City, Kansas, following the tracks of three
horsemen.

His face grim and set, Marshal Matt Dillon had
already made up his mind. When he caught up with
the McCarty brothers he'd give them two choices—
surrender or die. They would get no other option.

An upright man doing his best to preserve law and
order in a violent, unforgiving land, he judged men
by the light of his own experience and inclination
because he knew of no other yardstick.

And so he had judged Len, Elam and Jed McCarty
and found them wanting—guilty, according to a
dozen eyewitnesses, of shooting an unarmed man in
the back.

A product of his time and place, Matt Dillon lived

by the gunfighter code that a man met his enemies face-to-face, while they were belted and armed and stood ready. Within the rigid confines of that code, there was little room for cold-blooded murder, and where Western men gathered to talk, no crime was spoken of as lower or more cowardly.

The McCarty boys, tumbleweed trash out of the Neuces Plains country, had killed a gray-haired whiskey drummer for the few dollars in his pockets and the nickel watch, chain and Masonic fob across his belly. Then they had fled Dodge . . . and that was when their options had started to run out.

Now they were running, north across the vast empty plains, perhaps unaware that vengeance rode their back trail and was drawing closer.

"Cold day an' a cold trail, Matthew," Deputy Marshal Festus Haggen said from deep within the upturned collar of his ragged mackinaw. "Neither calc'lated to comfort a man."

Matt turned to his deputy and grinned. "I'm not arguing that the weather's a mite sharp, Festus, but you're wrong about the trail. It isn't cold. Those McCarty boys were less then thirty minutes ahead of us when they hightailed it out of Dodge. They've probably gone a fair piece by now, but not enough." The big marshal's far-seeing eyes scanned the flat, long-riding country ahead of him. "The tracks are headed for Saw Log Creek. I reckon they'll fetch up to the creek, then head east. Plenty of tree cover along the bank to keep them out of sight."

"You figure they know we're after them, Matthew?" Festus asked, his breath smoking like a ten-cent cigar in the frigid air.

The marshal nodded. "They know. And if they don't, they should."

The two riders crossed a small frozen stream running off the bottom reaches of the Saw Log, then headed into a shallow draw between a pair of low, humpbacked rises, their crests shaggy with brown-tipped clumps of buffalo grass. A cold wind was blowing steadily from the north and the sky was cloudy, a few stretches of pale blue showing here and there.

Festus, who had been silent for a few minutes, turned to Matt and said: "They say Elam McCarty, that's the oldest brother, has himself a reputation for bein' mighty slick with the Colt. They say he killed a man over to Cheyenne and another down to Texas somewheres. Now I don't know if'n that's true or not, Matthew, but that's what folks say."

"You worried, Festus?" Matt asked, a smile tugging at his lips. "That McCarty feller's reputation nagging at you some?"

"Hell no," the deputy said, suddenly lowered eyebrows revealing his chagrin. "I was just passin' time by makin' polite conversation is all."

Matt nodded. "Well, if it's any consolation I heard the same thing my ownself. Seems hard to believe that a backshooting tinhorn like Elam McCarty would have the sand to meet armed men face-to-face and earn himself a gun rep."

"Don't seem right to me either, Matthew," Festus

said. "Anyhow, folks have all kinds of queer notions about things and sometimes they say stuff that just ain't true."

"Well, we'll soon find out one way or the other," Matt said.

"That we will," his deputy agreed. Then, more quietly and thoughtfully: "Like you say, one way or t'other."

Around the riders, the vast prairie rolled away flat, featureless and empty in all directions. Even in this year of 1876, settler cabins were still few and far between and only the telegraph poles that marched alongside the tracks of the Santa Fe Railroad broke up the monotony of the landscape. It had snowed an inch or two during the night and a broad white sheet sparkled in the sunlight, reaching into the distance until it met the cloudy bowl of the sky at the horizon.

The land was quiet but for the sighing song of the wind, and it would be months before the crickets once again made their small sounds among the spring grass.

The light was strange, touched with pale amber, and the air was so icy cold, it passed across the tongue like broken glass.

There was an odd tension in Matt Dillon's belly, a coiled spring inside him that had nothing to do with the coming showdown with the McCarty brothers. It came from the land itself. Now and again the wind dropped to a thin whisper, unusual on the plains, as if the silent earth was holding its breath, waiting for something to happen.

Festus felt it too. The deputy gave the sky a wary glance, slowly shook his head, then turned to Matt, his eyes tangled with thought, an unspoken question on his hairy-cheeked face.

"You're feeling it as well, huh?" the marshal asked.

Festus nodded. "Matthew, something jest don't seem right with the day, but I can't seem to set down on a notion about what's wrong."

As his deputy had done earlier, Matt looked up at the sky. "I think there's more snow on the way, Festus. Big snow."

"Sky's clouding over, Matthew, but it don't look like snow clouds to me," Festus said. "Rain maybe?"

"Not rain, I reckon a blizzard is coming," Matt said. "I can feel it, tapping me on the shoulder like a gray ghost."

Festus opened his mouth to speak, but his words died in his throat. He reined in his mule and pointed to the northeast. "Three riders, and it looks like they ain't foggin' it out o' here." The deputy's shocked face revealed his utter disbelief. "Matthew, I reckon it's them McCarty boys—an', hell, they ain't a-runnin'—they're comin' right for us."

Matt's eyes followed his deputy's pointing finger. Moving across the plains from the direction of Saw Log Creek, marked by a straggling line of cottonwoods, men were riding fast toward them, three dark exclamation points of danger against the white backdrop of the snow.

"I thought for sure they'd keep on running," Matt

said. His smile tight and grim, he added: "I guess I was wrong."

The big marshal slipped the rawhide thong off the hammer of his Colt, slid the Winchester from the boot under his leg and cranked a round into the chamber. Festus unlimbered his Greener, thumbed open the shotgun and checked the loads. Satisfied, he snapped the scattergun shut and laid it across the saddle horn.

"How do we play this, Matthew?" he asked without turning, intent eyes fixed on the rapidly approaching horsemen.

"We give them a chance to surrender," Matt said. "After that, if they want to open the ball, then we all choose partners."

Matt and Festus sat their mounts, waiting. Feeling a sudden alertness in his rider, the marshal's big bay got up on his toes, his prancing hooves kicking up brief spurts of snow. Catching the bay's nervousness, Festus' mule tossed her head, her bit jangling, gray Vs of steaming breath jetting from dilated nostrils.

Matt leaned over and patted his horse's neck. "Easy, Buck, easy," he whispered.

The three McCarty brothers came on, spreading out slightly.

"They're ridin' fast," Festus said. "Matthew, you reckon them boys are gonna stop an' palaver like they ought?"

The deputy's question was answered a heartbeat later. The leading rider threw a rifle to his shoulder and fired. Matt saw the orange muzzle flare and heard a bullet split the air above his head with the spiteful whine of an angry hornet.

"Damn them," he gritted between clenched teeth. "Damn them to hell."

Now only fifty yards separated the two lawmen from the galloping horsemen.

Matt raised his rifle to his shoulder and snapped off a fast shot at a rider breaking to his left. A miss. He levered another round, fired again, and this time the man threw up his arms and tumbled off his horse.

Beside him, the marshal heard the loud *Boom, boom* of Festus' Greener. Torn to shreds by two rounds of double-aught buckshot, a rider slumped in the saddle, swung to his right and fired his rifle from waist level, three shots, very fast. Fesus let out a sharp cry and reeled in the saddle, sudden blood splashing scarlet over the front of his mackinaw. "Matthew," he yelled, "I'm hit hard!"

The third rider, the bearded, long-haired man who had fired the first shot, was charging directly at Matt. Both men fired at the same time and the outlaw jerked upright in the stirrups under the impact of the marshal's .44.40 slug, sagged back into the leather and kicked his mount into a fast gallop. Matt rode to cut the man off. The outlaw's big sorrel was running too fast to stop or swerve and it smashed into Buck. Taken by surprise, the bay lost his footing on the icy snow and went down, falling hard on Matt's left leg. The marshal felt a white-hot bolt of agony from knee to ankle as bone shattered.

Buck scrambled to his feet and staggered into an aimless, unsteady trot. Matt's boot was caught in the stirrup and he bit back a agonized yell as Buck dragged him by his injured leg. After a dozen yards of searing pain, the marshal managed to free his boot and let his leg fall to the ground.

Matt lay stunned for a few moments, his head swimming. He tried to rise, fell back again and stayed still, fighting to stem the nausea churning in his belly.

"Damn you, Dillon. You've killed me," a man snarled from close by. "But I don't plan on going to Hell alone. I'm taking you with me."

Matt turned toward the sound of the man's voice and saw the outlaw slowly walking his sorrel toward him, its hooves making a steady *crump, crump* on the hard-frosted snow. Elam McCarty's lips, glistening with blood and saliva, were peeled back from his yellow teeth in a smile and there was the hungry gleam of the killer wolf in his black eyes.

McCarty raised his rifle at the same instant Matt drew. The marshal was on his back, an awkward position from which to pull a gun, yet his motion was smooth and lightning fast. His first shot hit McCarty just under the chin, his next, a split second later, crashed into the outlaw's chest.

McCarty's rifle spat flame, but the man was already dead, and his bullet went wild, kicking up a slender spout of snow three feet from where Matt lay.

The marshal thumbed back the hammer of his revolver, but a third shot wasn't needed. Elam McCarty tumbled off his horse and thudded facedown onto the frozen ground.

From long habit, Matt shucked the empty shells, reloaded from his cartridge belt and holstered his Colt. Only then did he look around him.

The two other killers lay still, sprawled and undignified in death, the snow under them stained red. Festus was sitting, bent over, rocking slightly, his face ashen, trying to keep his pain knotted up inside him. Matt tried to rise, but the spiking hurt in his broken leg was a vicious, living thing that forced him back, groaning, to the ground.

Gritting his teeth, he knew he had to get to his deputy. Festus must be hit hard because he had made no attempt to get to his feet and was still hunched on the ground, small, hissing noises escaping between his white lips.

This time Matt crawled on his belly toward his deputy, inching his way slowly, his useless leg dragging, each yard of ground its own separate ordeal, its own clench-jawed, searing moment of Hell.

After a few yards, he stopped and caught his breath. He looked back at his leg and saw that from below the knee it was sticking out at a strange angle. The pain was intense and it never let up for a second.

It was a bad break, and Matt knew it.

He began to crawl again and after what seemed an eternity he reached Festus' side. "How bad are you hit?'' he asked, his voice, made hoarse by the hammering agony of his leg, a barely audible whisper.

The deputy turned, and Matt saw the answer to his question in Festus' haunted, pain-dulled eyes. ''Right shoulder's broke, Matthew,'' the deputy gasped. ''Here.'' He touched the front of his mackinaw and his fingers came away glistening with blood. ''An' I've got another bullet in my arm. My gun arm too.''

Matt lay in silence for a few moments, thinking things through. He had not rounded up a posse to go after the McCartys because he'd believed the brothers were sure-thing killers who would give up without a fight. Back in Dodge, people would think he and Festus were still chasing after the fugitives and no one would come looking for them. Not today, maybe not tomorrow or the day after that.

Festus was badly wounded and he was losing a lot of blood. Without medical care he would be dead by morning.

There was nothing else for it—they would have to try to make it back to town.

The only question was—how?